ALSO BY SOPHIE LARK

Brutal Birthright
Brutal Prince
Stolen Heir
Savage Lover
Bloody Heart
Broken Vow
Heavy Crown

Sinners Duet
There Are No Saints
There Is No Devil

THERE IS NO DEVIL

SOPHIE LARK

Bloom books

Copyright © 2022, 2023 by Sophie Lark
Cover and internal design © 2023 by Sourcebooks
Cover design by Emily Wittig
Cover images by R-studio/Depositphotos, Croisy/Shutterstock
Internal illustrations © Line Marie Erikson

Sourcebooks and the colophon are registered trademarks of
Sourcebooks. Bloom Books is a trademark of Sourcebooks.

Published by Bloom Books, an imprint of Sourcebooks
P.O. Box 4410, Naperville, Illinois 60567-4410
(630) 961-3900
sourcebooks.com

Originally self-published in 2022 by Sophie Lark.

Cataloging-in-Publication Data is on file with the Library of Congress.

Printed and bound in Canada.
MBP 10 9 8 7 6 5 4 3

Part two is for everyone who has suffered abuse.

I grew up poor and was severely bullied as a teen. I got married at nineteen to someone who hurt me in every possible way, tearing apart my self-esteem until I felt lower than dirt.

Mara's struggles are drawn from my own experience. Her rebirth into a new life likewise parallels my own. It doesn't matter where you started or what you've done. Maybe you're all fucked up, and the world around you looks dark and cruel.

This book is about finding love and acceptance in another person and, more importantly, loving and accepting yourself.

You are worthy of love. You are worthy of a more beautiful future. It can happen for anyone. It happened for me.

Love you all,

Sophie Lark

SOUNDTRACK

1. "Terrible Thing"—AG
2. "Amore"—Bebe Rexha & Rick Ross
3. "6 Underground"—Sneaker Pimps
4. "Psycho"—Mia Rodriguez
5. "Mad World"—Michael Andrews & Gary Jules
6. "Venom"—Little Simz
7. "Black Out Days"—Phantogram
8. "Paranoia"—HAVEN
9. "911"—Ellise
10. "I Don't Want to Set the World on Fire"—The Ink Spots
11. "I Feel Like a God"—DeathbyRomy
12. "How Villains Are Made"—Madalen Duke
13. "This Is Love"—Air Traffic Controller
14. "Heart Shaped Box"—Neovaii
15. "The Devil Is a Gentleman"—Merci Raines
16. "Animal"—Sir Chloe
17. "Demons"—Hayley Kiyoko
18. "On My Knees"—RÜFÜS DU SOL
19. "Survivor"—2WEI
20. "Always Forever"—Cults
21. "Girl With One Eye"—Florence + The Machine
22. "INDUSTRY BABY"—Lil Nas X & Jack Harlow

23. "I Did Something Bad"—Taylor Swift
24. "I am not a woman, I'm a god"—Halsey
25. "Bust Your Knee Caps"—Pomplamoose
26. "Fire Drill"—Melanie Martinez

Music is a big part of my writing process. If you start a song when you see a 🎵 while reading, the song matches the scene like a movie score.

Spotify   Apple Music

1

MARA

I WAKE TO THE SOUND OF WAVES CRASHING AGAINST THE CLIFFS below. Cole keeps all his windows open on the north side of the house. I smell salt and iron, the scent of the bay. Fog drifts into the room, swirling around the posters of the old-fashioned bed.

I slip out from under the heavy coverlet, naked, my nipples stiffening in the cold. The fog condenses on my warm skin, making me slippery as a seal.

Cole left a silk robe for me—the kind a vintage film star would have worn. It swirls around my body, heavy, sumptuous, and ridiculously extravagant.

He left slippers for me as well. I ignore those, preferring to pad across his thick Turkish rugs on my bare feet.

Walking through the halls of Sea Cliff is like walking through Versailles after hours. It seems outrageous that I'm even allowed inside this place, let alone that I live here.

I could never have imagined what real wealth looks like, what it feels like to the touch. Palatial, empty, echoing space. Priceless art hung in distant wings where months or even years could pass without a single person viewing it. The aesthetic perfection of every faucet and doorknob.

Motion sensors are everywhere. He already knows I'm awake.

Cole is the most observant person I've ever met. He uses

technology to enhance what he can see, what he can hear, until he's godlike in his reach.

Inside this house, he could always be listening. He could always be watching.

I want him to be.

I'm safe from the rest of the world when I'm under his eye, under his protection. No one can hurt me; no one can touch me.

Except Cole himself.

I walk down the wide curving staircase to the main level, the long train of the robe trailing behind me like a wedding gown. I haven't belted it. I see the hunger in Cole's dark eyes when he sees my bare breasts slipping in and out of view within the folds of the shimmering silk.

He's already dressed for the day, the soft black waves of his hair still damp from his shower. Freshly shaved, the sensual curves of his mouth and the sharp line of his jaw look impossibly youthful. He's ageless. Eternal. Beautiful in a way that hurts me, that grabs my heart in my chest and squeezes hard.

He holds out a double-walled glass cup, the layers of espresso, milk, and foam seeming to float in space.

"I made you a latte."

He must have started it the moment I opened my eyes. Perfectly timed to the minutes it would take me to stretch, slip out from under the covers, pull on the robe, and pad down the stairs.

His precision terrifies me.

In the same breath, I feel deep admiration for what I could never hope to accomplish.

I could never be this calculated, this patient, this effective. He really is superhuman.

And he's not even trying. It's just a game to him. A game to hand me this perfectly prepared latte, exactly the way I like it. The right temperature, sweetness, extra foam, thick and rich as whipped cream.

I trail my tongue through it, unembarrassed. I lick it off my lips. Because I'm learning, too.

He likes to watch me enjoy things. It gives him more pleasure to watch me lap up this foam, to lick it off my fingers, than it could ever give him to taste it himself.

I saturate my mouth with the delicious flavor, and then I kiss him so he can taste it on my lips.

The coffee makes my mouth warm and sensual.

That's why he made it for me.

This is all calculated so I won't walk over the fridge and start rummaging. He wants to select what I eat, what I drink, what I wear. He wants to choose better than I could choose myself so I won't fight him, so I'll submit to him.

Each time I accept one of his choices, I see the glint of triumph in his eyes. This is how he intends to tame me.

I'm not an easy pet.

I'm wild and feral. What I want is capricious; it changes every moment.

I ask, "Do we have any more of those peaches from last night?"

I see the flame flicker in his eyes, irritation that he failed to anticipate this. "You ate them all before bed."

"You didn't think I'd eat six at once?"

My teasing infuriates and arouses him. He grabs my wrist, pulling me toward him.

His rough growl swipes up my spine like sandpaper: "If we were on a ship stranded in the ocean, and all we had left was one bar of chocolate, you'd eat the whole thing in five minutes and lick your fingers afterward."

I smile up at him, unrepentant. "I wouldn't want to be hungry while I got our ship working again." I gulp down the rest of the meticulously prepared latte. "Rationing is for people who only want to endure."

"I would have thought hard times would have taught you the

value of planning." Cole snakes his other hand around the back of my skull, gripping me tight, his fingers twined through my hair.

I tilt up my mouth to him. "I don't want to survive. I want to thrive."

He kisses me like he does every time, like he's eating me alive. He slips his hand inside my robe, cupping my bare breast. His sensitive fingers explore my body, learning every curve by feel, not sight.

I try to resist the power of those hands, but it's impossible.

I go limp, falling back against the supporting strength of his arm. The robe opens, giving him full access to the naked body beneath. I'm dizzy and swooning as that warm, powerful hand roams my exposed flesh.

The ornate tin tiles on the kitchen ceiling glow silver. Cole's fingertips dance across my collarbone, his hand closing around my throat. His cock stiffens against my hip as he slowly cuts off my air.

"What were you dreaming about last night?" he murmurs in my ear. "You were moaning in your sleep..."

"I don't remember," I lie.

His fingers tighten until black spots bleed over the tin tiles and I can barely feel his arm beneath my body.

"You can't keep secrets from me, Mara." His teeth scrape against the side of my throat. "I will break you down systematically, relentlessly, until you give me what I want."

I turn my head, looking directly into his eyes. "What do you want?"

He licks his lips, our mouths so close together that his tongue slides across my lips as well. "I want all of you, every single part. I want to know all your secrets and every thought that comes into your head. Every desire, no matter how dark or how perverse. I want to occupy your thoughts like you occupy mine. I want you obsessed with me, bound to me, dependent on me. I want you to live *for* me, not just *with* me."

This is more terrifying than when I thought Cole might murder me.

My whole life has been a struggle for independence.

Every person who was supposed to love me tried to control me instead. They tried to bend me and shape me to be what they wanted so they could use me, so they could consume me like fuel.

I pull away from him, standing straight, then closing the robe and belting it. "I put my life in your hands. I never said you could take my identity."

Cole smiles, unabashed. "I'm not trying to change who you are—I'm trying to reveal it. A diamond can't shine until it's cut."

I cross my arms over my chest, already knowing where this is going. "And where do you plan to cut me today?"

He's trying to hold back a laugh—never a good sign. "Always so suspicious, Mara. It's quite unjust, considering I've yet to make a plan for you that you haven't enjoyed."

"That's a generous interpretation. Especially since the journey to 'enjoyment' tends to be nothing less than horrifying."

Now he does laugh, flushing me with heat. When the devil chuckles, someone is making a fatal mistake.

Cole says, "There's nothing horrifying about me taking you shopping."

"No fucking way," I snap. "You promised to get my things from my old house."

"And I have—your 'things' will be delivered this afternoon. Though I ought to have them fumigated first."

"You don't want my thrift store jackets hanging in your immaculate closets? Don't worry—I'm sure there's some wing of this house you've never even seen."

"Oh, I know every inch of this house," Cole assures me. "There's nowhere you can hide from me out in the world, let alone here in my own home."

Locked in his dark gaze, I believe him.

Opposing Cole feels like standing in the path of a freight train.

Yet here I stand, staring down the headlights as the horn blares in warning.

"I like my clothes."

"You don't have your clothes," Cole says. "I do. And I'm not giving them back to you until you come shopping with me. If you don't like what I pick out, then you don't have to wear it. But you will accompany me, or you'll go to the studio in that robe." He grins. "Or naked. I'm happy with either."

I'll wear this damn robe all week long to spite him. That would offend his sensibilities much more than mine. It's only the chill gray fog outside the window that dissuades me—silk isn't warm.

"Fine," I grumble. "But I mean it—I'm not wearing anything I don't like."

"I'd expect nothing less," Cole replies with irritating smugness.

I take my glass to the sink and set it down a little harder than necessary. "Let's get this over with."

Cole raises an eyebrow. "You need to shower first."

My hand itches to snatch the glass again and fling it at him. It's never enough for him to get what he wants—it has to be exactly the way he wants it.

Instead, I slip out of the robe and drop it in a puddle in the middle of his kitchen floor. "As you wish, Master."

The tone is pure sarcasm, but I see the flush of pleasure it gives him all the same. He picks up the robe and follows me like a dark shadow, silent and close.

I walk back up the stairs to the main suite. Cole's bathroom is triple the size of my old bedroom. The sinks are massive slabs of raw gray stone beneath waterfall faucets. A bathtub sits directly in the hardwood floor, right up against the window like an infinity pool. The shower is the size of a car wash, with dozens of nozzles pointing in all directions.

Cole turns them on for me while I send the playlist on my phone to his Bluetooth speakers.

The music echoes off the stone walls, bouncing around the space, melding with the thick steam of the shower.

♫ *"Terrible Thing"—AG*

"Why do you need music for everything?" Cole asks.

"Because it makes everything better." I step into the pounding spray.

Cole stands outside the glass, roaming his eyes over my wet body.

He has no shame in watching me. He does it openly, all the time. Not bothering to hide his pleasure.

It's flattering.

I'm an exotic creature to him. Everything I do is interesting.

Cole's gaze makes me aware of myself. How I tilt my head back under the spray, exposing my throat. How the soap suds slide down between my breasts. How my skin flushes in the heat.

I shower slowly, sensually. Running my palms over my own curves. Rotating in place so he can admire me from every angle.

When Cole watches, his eyes come alive. He leans back against the wall, his arms folded over his chest, the muscle of his arms visible through his shirt.

Each turn of my body sends a twitch down the tight line of his jaw. His gaze crawls up my thighs, my ass, over his own artwork running from my hip to my ribs, even over the ugly scars marking both my arms. He likes it all.

I lift the showerhead down from the wall so I can direct the flow exactly where I want it. I let it rain down on my face, keeping my eyes closed and my mouth open so the droplets pound on my tongue. I run the water across my breasts in slow strokes in time to the music.

Sitting on the shower bench, I spray the water on the soles of my feet, squirming a little at how it tickles. I run the water up my leg.

Cole stands motionless, watching. His endless fascination creates a voyeuristic energy that spurs me to stranger and stranger behaviors.

Leaning back against the cool stone wall, I spread my knees, opening my pussy to his view. Now he steps forward, his eyes darker than an oil spill, his lips pale.

I point the shower spray directly at my pussy. It's almost too hot to bear, so I splash the water lightly against my exposed lips until I'm used to it, until I can direct the pressure right at my clit.

My head falls back against the wall, my eyes closed.

I'm not watching Cole watching me anymore.

I'm just feeling it.

The water caresses me, sliding in and out of my folds, running everywhere. The closer I bring the showerhead, the more intense the sensation becomes.

"That's right…" Cole murmurs. "Good girl. Don't stop."

The flush rises through my body, filling my breasts, crawling up my neck.

The heat is almost too much. I want to turn it down.

Sensing this, Cole steps inside the shower. He drops to his knees in front of me, closing his hand over mine on the shower-head, locking my fingers in place. He points the spray right where he wants it and holds it there as the heat and pressure rises.

His trousers are drenched, as are his expensive Italian loafers. Cole barely notices. For all his perfectionism, Cole is a pleasure-seeker just like me. He wants what he wants, and he's willing to pay for it.

Right now he wants to make me come, and he doesn't give a fuck what clothes he ruins.

"You've done this before," he growls.

"Yes," I gasp.

"Is this how you learned to come? In the bath, spreading your legs under the faucet?"

I press my lips together, hating how he uses sex to dig information out of me. Hating how arousal makes me weak.

Cole brings the showerhead closer until it's only an inch from my pussy, until the pounding spray is almost unbearable. He wraps the rope of my wet hair around his hand and jerks my head back, growling in my ear, "Admit it, you dirty girl. You were taking baths to come, not to get clean."

"Fuck being clean," I snarl. "I'll sleep in a dumpster if I feel like it."

Cole's chuckle is what tips me over—rich and wicked, vibrating down to my bones. "I know you would, you little psychopath."

The orgasm is as hot and pounding as the shower spray. My lungs fill with steam. My skin blushes redder than rose petals.

When I'm panting against the wall, limp and loose, Cole orders, "Stay right there. Don't move a muscle."

I couldn't even if I wanted to.

Cole exits the shower to retrieve something from his drawers. He's not rummaging—his toiletries are so perfectly organized that it only takes him a moment to gather what he needs.

He returns, carrying shaving cream and a straight razor.

"I can shave myself," I inform him.

"Not as well as I can."

It annoys me how true that is. Even though I'm pretty fucking good with my hands, I still can't match Cole in precision. He's a machine, if a machine had a soul. Or part of a soul, at least.

I lean back against the wall, my thighs open, my pussy swollen and flushed from the hot spray. It's deeply thrilling to offer him access to my most vulnerable parts.

My heart races as he flips open the razor, clearing the gleaming steel blade from its bone handle.

"Hold this for me." He presses the handle into my palm.

I close my fingers around it, looking at the cruel edge of the blade, thinner and sharper than any knife.

Cole kneels before me. He squeezes a puff of shaving cream onto his palm before gently massaging it over my bikini line. His cheek is an inch from the razor, his neck exposed as he tilts his head for a better view.

I could cut his throat right now.

Cole spreads the shaving cream across my pussy and upper thighs. It feels thick and cool after the heat of the water.

"Are you wondering what it would feel like?" he says in his smooth low voice.

I grip the handle so hard that it bites into my palm.

"You're wondering if you could do it quickly enough to surprise me. If you got me in the right place, one slash would be enough…"

I shake my head so vigorously that it bumps against the stone wall. "No. I wasn't thinking that."

Cole closes his hand over mine again. This time he's forcing me to grip the razor instead of a showerhead. Forcing me to brandish it between us. He looks up into my face, his dark eyes locked on mine.

"You're never going to be the biggest or the strongest in the fight. You have to be the most ruthless. You may only get one chance."

Who does he imagine I'm going to be fighting?

Shaw…or him?

I twist my wrist away from Cole, dropping the razor on the shower floor. "I told you—I'm not going to hurt anyone."

Cole ignores the razor, only looking at me. "Oh, really? And what do you plan to do about Shaw?"

"I don't know. Find some evidence. Get his ass tossed in jail where he belongs."

Cole makes a contemptuous sound. "You're not going to *find evidence*. You go near Shaw without me right next to you, and all you'll *find* is your head on a beach."

I glare at him. "You want me to think there's only one way this can end."

"No. There are two ways: Shaw dies, or we do."

Cole is trying to drag me down this path I don't want to travel. At the same time, I can't help feeling perversely comforted that he said *we* instead of *you*. Cole thinks we're in this together.

Honestly, nothing terrifies me more than the thought of facing

Shaw alone. I want Cole right next to me. But I can't see how we'll ever agree on what we should do.

Cole plucks up the razor, making a *tsk* sound. "Now I have to sharpen this again."

He returns to the counter for his leather strop. He moves swiftly, aggressively, snapping the leather taut and drawing the blade down the grain with a vicious purr. Steam ebbs out of the shower. A chill runs down my spine instead.

Cole returns, kneeling before me, the blade gleaming brightly in his hand.

He looks up at me, his full lips curved in a smile. "Hold still."

The touch of the blade is colder than ice. It slides over my skin like a whisper, cutting so close that my flesh looks strangely pale, stripped of shaving cream and every trace of hair.

Every place he bares becomes instantly sensitized. I feel the cool air on my pussy lips, and Cole's warm breath.

His fingertips press against my flesh, spreading my lips apart so he can shave the inner rim.

I keep expecting the bite of the blade, some slip of his hand, but he's too careful. It doesn't even scratch me. He shaves my most delicate parts, touching and testing with his fingertips, re-shaving any area that doesn't meet his standard of perfection.

He's intensely focused on the work, his face inches from my pussy, examining every part of me, inside and out.

Maybe I should be embarrassed. Maybe it should feel clinical.

It doesn't.

I'm shivering under his touch. Each press of his fingers is intensely erotic. I can hardly hold still, dying to press my clit against his palm, aching for him to rub the ball of his thumb across it. I want his fingers inside me. Then his tongue. Then his cock.

Cole lifts the showerhead once more, rinsing the last remnants of shaving cream.

My pussy gleams, as smooth and soft as a fresh spring peach.

Cole can't take his eyes off it.

"Feel that." He takes my hand and places it on the silky mound.

My fingers glide over the skin, ten times as sensitive as it's ever been. It feels like I was made this morning. Like nothing bad has ever happened to me. Venus, rising from the sea-foam.

Cole pushes my knees all the way apart.

He leans forward and trails the tip of his tongue across my pussy—tracing the path of the razor back and forth, up and down. Testing his work with the most perceptive part of himself.

I let out a groan, thrusting my hand in his hair, pushing his face into my cunt. I grind that smooth little pussy all over his face, shivering with the sensation of his soft lips, wet tongue, and barest trace of stubble. I feel it all like I've never felt it before, melting into his mouth, starting to come before I even realize what's happening.

I ride his tongue, the softest part of him against the softest part of me. The warmth, the bliss, is intensely intimate. I've never had oral from a man who wants it more than I do. He's tasting me, smelling me, lapping me up. So hungry that I could never satisfy him, even while he's gorging me with pleasure.

When the second climax passes, I almost feel guilty. I reach for him, wanting to return the favor. "Let me suck your cock."

"No." He pushes me back down on the bench, still holding the razor in his left hand. "I don't want a blow job."

"What do you want, then?"

His right hand rests on my thigh, holding me in place. "I want to taste you."

That's what he just did—my wetness is all over his mouth.

Then Cole lifts the razor over my thigh, and I understand.

My heart skips. Every time we cross another line, the edge of what I used to know retreats in the distance.

"Do it," I say.

He makes one thin slash on my inner thigh, so quick and sharp that the pain flares and vanishes before I even register it. Blood wells up, darker than wine. He catches it on his tongue, lapping the shallow wound, closing his mouth over it. His tongue slides across raw nerve, gently sucking as he latches on.

His mouth soothes me.

I lean back against the wall, my eyes closed, slipping my fingers into his thick soft hair once more.

I scratch my nails gently against his scalp while he sucks at the cut. When he pulls back, I'm no longer bleeding.

I look at the mark, thin and clean. I know from experience that this won't scar.

The ones you cut deep and ragged, the ones you make sobbing and crying, cutting over others that haven't even healed…those are the marks that stay forever.

Cole rises, pulling me up with him. He kisses me on the mouth. I taste the sweet musk of my pussy and the metal of my own blood. Neither feels wrong. In fact, it's a combination so perfect, I might have come up with it myself, given enough time to experiment.

The orgasms have made me placid and calm.

"What do you want me to wear?" I ask Cole.

He drives us to Neiman Marcus on Geary Street. The venerable stone building stands on the corner, its layers of glass display windows impossibly chic and imposing.

"Can't we just go to Urban Outfitters or something?"

Already I'm regretting the cooperative spirit that prompted me to climb into Cole's passenger seat. I don't want to go in some stuffy store where the salesladies are sure to give me the kind of side-eye employed on Julia Roberts in *Pretty Woman*. They can tell when you're poor, when you don't belong.

"Or better yet," I say, "I can keep wearing *your* clothes."

Cole let me borrow a pair of his old-money wool trousers and a cashmere sweater. He even punched a new hole halfway down one of his belts to keep the pants up. It's all way too big for me, but I like baggy clothing.

"Absolutely not," Cole says. "That was a desperate measure. One we're about to rectify."

Just walking through the doors makes me uncomfortable. We have to pass under the glare of the security guards entrusted with keeping the homeless people out. I'd feel more relaxed in one of the many tents camped out in Union Square. I'd rather smoke a blunt with one of those dudes than cringe under the aggressive "good morning! What are you two shopping for today?" from a lipsticked blond brandishing a perfume bottle.

"Good morning," Cole replies, coolly ignoring the question as he sweeps past her, keeping his vise grip on my arm while he steers me onto the steep escalator to the upper levels.

Compared to the crowded streets outside, the ladies' department feels oddly empty. I stare around at the pristine racks of clothing organized by designer, bright and rich and appealing but unseen by anyone else. We're alone up here, besides a few scattered sales associates.

"Where is everyone?" I whisper to Cole.

"There is no 'everyone.' You're shopping with the one percent—there aren't that many of us."

The surreal silence unnerves me. I approach a rack of fall coats before gingerly lifting one sleeve. The material is thick and heavy, with elaborate embroidery along the cuff. Real elk-horn buttons are hand sewn along the placket. The fur trim on the collar makes me think of arctic animals that burrow in the snow.

After flipping over the tag, I let out a startled bark of laughter.

"*Eight thousand dollars?*" I squeak to Cole. "For one coat? What's it made of—hair clippings from Ryan Gosling?"

It boggles my mind that someone could stroll around in an outfit that represents a year's earnings for me. I mean, I knew expensive clothing existed, but I hadn't touched any before.

It feels different in here. Smells different. I've stepped into another world—the world of privilege, where numbers become meaningless, where you just swipe a card for whatever you want.

Cole's not even looking at the price tags. He grabs whatever catches his eye, laying the garments over his arm.

A saleswoman materializes, saying with unctuous politeness, "Can I start you a fitting room, sir?"

Cole hands her the clothes, already striding toward the next rack. He surveys the collections with a practiced eye, pulling out a mix of tops and bottoms, dresses and coats.

I don't even try to help him. I'm intimidated and conflicted. I always wanted to make money, but I never really pictured myself using it. I have too much resentment for the rich to ever believe I'd become one of them.

Besides, I'm not rich. I sold a single painting.

Cole is beyond rich and apparently planning to splash out a lot more money on a new wardrobe than I was expecting.

I grab his arm. "This stuff is too expensive."

He takes my hand, pulling me toward the fitting room. "You don't know anything about money. This isn't expensive—it's pocket change."

That only makes me feel worse.

The economic chasm between Cole and me is far wider than any of our other differences. We both lived in hundred-year-old San Francisco houses, but mine was a moldering shack, and his is a legitimate palace. The more I step into his world, the more I see how little of it I understood from a distance. He knows everyone in this city, everyone who matters. They're intimidated by him, or they owe him favors.

He can accomplish things with a snap of his fingers that I couldn't manage in a hundred years. Even people who don't know the Blackwell name, like this woman waiting on us, fall under the spell of Cole's effortless confidence, which tells her he's someone of value, someone who must be obeyed.

I've never been someone of value.

Not to anybody.

Not even to my own goddamned mother, the one person on this planet required to give a fuck about me.

I've had friends, but I was never the most important person in their life, the sun in their solar system.

As fucked up as it sounds, the first person who truly took an interest in me was Cole.

His attention can be coercive and selfish. But I want it all the same.

The man who never cared about anyone is fixated on the girl nobody gave a shit about.

In some twisted way, we're made for each other. And that really fucking scares me. Because I haven't even plumbed the bottom of the dark things Cole has done. If we're drawn together...what does that say about me?

I always suspected I might not be a good person.

I tried to do the right things. I tried to be kind and helpful and honest. It never seemed to get me anywhere. Maybe because people could see that I had to try, that I was never naturally, effortlessly good.

As soon as I went to school, I knew I was odd. It wasn't just the too-small clothing or the fact my lunch was in a plastic grocery bag with the same chips in it day after day. I never ate the chips because then I wouldn't have anything to bring to school in the bag.

Other kids were poor. There was something uglier in me, something that repelled the other children. That made them whisper about me behind their hands and avoid me at recess.

I always thought it was my sadness or the stories kids told, the few times anyone came over to my house and met my mother, saw how we lived.

Now I think...it was just me.

Randall saw it the moment we met. I was only seven. A grown man shouldn't hate a little girl so much.

"What's wrong?" Cole says, zeroing in on my private thoughts with unnerving precision.

"I don't fit in here," I mutter. "This changing room is bigger than my apartment."

"You don't live in that apartment anymore," Cole says. And then, because I'm staring at the carpet, he grabs my face and forces me to look into his eyes. "You deserve to be here as much as anyone. *More* than anyone. You're talented, Mara, really fucking talented. You're already a star. Everyone else doesn't know it yet, but I do. You're going to make art that makes people think and cry and burn with envy."

If anyone else said that, I'd assume they were only trying to cheer me up.

Cole doesn't say things to be nice.

I loved his art before I ever laid eyes on him. It spoke to me long before we met. His opinion matters to me more than anyone's.

My eyes burn; my whole face is hot. I don't allow myself to cry because I won't do anything that would make Cole think less of me.

All I can do is grip his hands and press them harder into my face until the pain brings me back to earth.

Cole says, "Try on these goddamned clothes and enjoy yourself. Feel the fabric. It's gorgeous. You'll appreciate it more than anyone."

♫ *"Amore"—Bebe Rexha & Rick Ross*

Pulling on the first dress, I discover Cole is right. He's always right.

The clothes caress my skin. They fit my body like they were made for me—some heavy and comforting, others light and floating. Rich and soft, the materials cling and stretch and flare, like the garments are alive, like they've fallen in love with me...

Cole has impeccable taste. He seems to intuitively understand what colors and silhouettes suit me best. He's chosen rich jewel tones, a few prints. The embellishments are rustic embroidery or sumptuous draping—nothing that would scratch or irritate me. The clothes are all bohemian with vintage influences; he hasn't picked out anything that would make me feel like I was cosplaying as a socialite. He knows me. He knows what I like.

I'd only intended to let him buy me a few things, but piece after piece piles up in his arms, each so lovely that I can't seem to choose. Minidresses with bell sleeves, satin rompers, peasant blouses, leather skirts, embroidered jeans…

I, too, have to stop looking at the price tags so I don't make myself sick.

As Cole orders the salesclerk to ring it all up, I turn to him, forcing myself to meet his eyes even though I'm deeply embarrassed. I never meant to take charity. I always told myself I was strong and independent, that I could take care of myself.

"Thank you, Cole," I say humbly. "Not just for the clothes…for everything you've done for me."

"Feeling grateful, are you?" His dark eyes glint wickedly.

"I was…" I'm already regretting it.

"Then why don't you do me a small favor in return?"

Of course. "What is it?"

"Don't worry, this will be fun."

Cole's idea of fun terrifies me.

He's leading me back inside the changing room, though I already tried on all the clothes.

I try to keep my heart rate within range of a light jog instead of an all-out sprint. "What are we doing?"

"Calm yourself, little Caravaggio. I just want you to wear something for me."

He holds up what looks like a small piece of rubber—soft, curved, and about the size of my thumb.

"What is that?"

"It goes right in here…" Cole pushes me up against the wall, slipping the piece of rubber down the front of my underwear. It nestles in place between my pussy lips.

I have no idea what the purpose of this is. Cole is so odd that almost nothing surprises me anymore.

Obediently, I follow him out so I can watch him swipe his credit card for a sum that eclipses my entire net worth, including the painting I just sold.

Breathless, I say, "Well, I guess we should head over to the studio…"

"Not even close." Cole laughs.

"What do you mean?"

"We're not done shopping."

"What could you possibly—"

"Come on." He grabs my hand, dragging me along.

So begins the second half of our shopping spree, wherein Cole attempts to clean out Neiman Marcus in a single afternoon. I tire of arguing with him long before he tires of swiping his card. He buys me earrings, necklaces, perfume, cosmetics, shoes, and lingerie so scandalous that it would make Joseph Corré blush.

I can hardly focus on the purchases because Cole is amusing himself in an entirely different way.

It starts as I'm sampling a selection of perfumes laid out by the willowy blond who accosted us on our way in the door. She's wafting a sample of Maison Francis Kurkdjian beneath my nose when I feel a sudden buzzing in my nether regions. I jerk upright, almost slicing off my nose via paper cut.

"What the hell!"

I whirl around, finding Cole with his hands in his pockets and an artfully constructed expression of innocence on his face.

"Mosquito bite?" he says.

My face is burning, my knees going wobbly beneath me. The buzzing has dialed down to a low thrum, steady and insistent.

Cole's hand shifts within his pocket as he manipulates the

controls. The buzzing ramps up again, almost loud enough for the perfume-counter lady to hear. I take several steps away from her, trying to squeeze my legs together, then quickly separate them again because that only makes it worse.

"Are you all right?" she asks, her Botoxed brow unable to wrinkle in concern.

"Could I...have some water?" I squeak.

I'm trying to get rid of her so I can yell at Cole.

Wheeling on him, I bark, "Turn that off!"

Instead, he turns it up.

I have to lean against the glass counter, my cheeks burning and my hands sweating. "Stop," I beg.

He turns it off, giving me a moment of blessed relief to recover myself.

The perfume lady returns with a small bottle of water. "Feeling better?"

"Yes, thank you." I pant. "I think the perfume was making me dizzy."

"Try this." She passes me an open canister of coffee beans. "It can help clear your head."

I lean over to inhale their scent.

Cole activates the vibrator again.

"Oh my god!" I clutch the countertop with both hands.

I'm helpless as the sensation thrums up and down my legs, churning in my lower stomach.

Cole has discovered a fatal weakness, one I didn't even know I possessed. Vibration is my kryptonite, and Cole is employing it with Lex Luthor levels of evil genius.

How the fuck did he even find one this small? He probably made it himself, that crafty bastard.

He's ramping it up again, while I desperately try not to moan in front of the confused blond.

"Do you need a doctor?"

"She'll be fine," Cole assures her. "This happens all the time."

That makes no goddamned sense, but Cole is so convincing that the blond simply smiles. "We have a powder room if you need to sit down."

Cole puts his arm around my shoulders, leading me away from the perfume counter but not shutting off the vibrator.

I turn into his chest, holding him for support, hiding my face against his body as I start to come. My legs shake like an earthquake, my arms wrapped tight around his waist. I make a muffled groaning sound.

When it finally passes, I gasp. "Turn that damn thing off!"

Cole complies, though I can feel him shaking, too—from laughter.

I look up at him.

Cole is illuminated with the purest, brightest amusement I've ever seen. It lights up his whole face, making him beautiful on a whole new level.

I can only stare.

Then I start to giggle as well.

Maybe it's the rush of dopamine, or maybe it's the fact that for the first time, Cole and I are laughing together at a secret only we share.

"Why are you so awful?" I snort.

"I don't know," he says, with real wonder. "I only want what I'm not supposed to have."

Me, too.

Nobody wanted me to be an artist.

Nobody wanted me to achieve anything.

Until I met Cole.

He turns the vibrator on several more times while we're shopping. It becomes a game between us: him trying to do it at the most inopportune times, and me fighting my hardest not to show any sign of it on my face, to keep talking and picking out mascara while my knees tremble and my skin flushes pink as a baby pig.

Soon I'm giddy and overstimulated, hanging off his arm because I can barely stand. Cole carries all the bags for me, laden like a Sherpa.

I've never felt so spoiled.

I've never had so much fun.

2
COLE

When we return from shopping, Mara pounces on me, shoving me on the nearest chaise, saying, "Now it's my turn," in that husky voice of hers.

If I could describe the attraction I feel for her and the way it eclipses what I've ever felt before, I'd have to say Mara is just…gritty. She has an edge of roughness, wildness, neglect.

Even though I should dislike certain aspects of her person—the way she bites her nails ragged, for instance—it all becomes a spice I crave more than any bland and perfect beauty.

The artist in me desires what is truly unique. The slope of Mara's upturned nose, her wild fling of freckles, the fox tilt of her eyes, the lower lip's ratio to the top…these proportions are so exaggerated that they ought to be wrong. Instead, they could never be more right.

She looks up at me, a wild creature, no captive pet…I've lured her here but not yet tamed her to my will.

I lean back against the cushions, my arms spread across the wooden frame, looking down at her. Watching her work.

She unzips my pants, her sleet-gray eyes flirting with mine. She's smiling, licking her lips with anticipation, fumbling with the zipper.

Her excitement ignites mine like a firestorm. The more eager she seems, the more my cock throbs and rages for the touch of her tongue.

The sunset flowing in through the plate-glass windows colors her skin pink, peach, and gold. Her hair illuminates like electrical filaments. She glows with energy and light.

She wore home one of the dresses I bought for her—cloud-light linen, soft and floating.

My cock springs out, almost slapping her in the face. Mara jumps and lets out a peal of delighted laughter. When she's happy, she laughs easily. Each throaty note runs down my spine like a scale.

She floats her fingertips over the head of my cock, teasing me. Her hands look naked—bare and unadorned, with no rings or polish. Stained around the nails by ink and paint.

Her mouth hovers inches away, partly open, the tip of her tongue curled up to playfully dance around her teeth.

Her lips are swollen as a bruise. I'm aching to feel them closed around my cock. I might blow the instant they touch me.

Mara puts out her tongue and runs it softly up the sensitive underside of my cock. It feels like she's stringing a wire all along the path of her tongue, sparking it to life.

She enfolds the head of my cock in her warm, velvety mouth.

I make a sound I've never made before. My brain exits my skull, floating several inches in the air.

She sucks slowly, gently, for what seems like forever. She's not trying to make me come. She's blowing me like she intends to do it all night long.

I look down at her. Her eyes are closed in peaceful satisfaction. Her ear rests against my thigh. She might be asleep, except for the steady warm pressure of her mouth licking, sliding, sucking.

Some mistake has been made: I died, heaven exists, and they let me in.

After a blissful eternity, I start to come. While I drift through this dreamy, endless orgasm, Mara never stops sucking for a moment.

She finally raises her head to look at me.

I ask her, "How do you do that for so long?"

She shrugs. "I like it. It feels good."

"I know it feels good," I say. "For *me*. Doesn't your jaw get sore?"

"Sometimes. But I just switch the angle or depth. The longer I do it, the more sensitive my lips and tongue and throat become. The better it feels, the longer I can do it."

I'm struggling to understand what she means. "You're saying… the better it feels *for you*."

"Yeah." Mara squints at me like this is obvious.

It's not obvious, and I must look confused, because she frowns and says, "Doesn't it feel good for *you* when you touch me?"

"It does…" I pause, trying to articulate something I've never consciously considered. "What I'm enjoying is the effect on you. The way it puts you under my control. If I can make you feel pleasure, I can get you to do anything I want. When I'm getting what I want, I can eat your pussy for hours."

"So when you suck my tits, you're doing it for me because it drives me insane. Not because it makes your tongue feel good," Mara says.

"That's right."

We're looking at each other like we just discovered one of us has been speaking Spanish and the other, Portuguese.

Slowly, Mara climbs onto my lap, straddling me on the chaise. She pulls her linen dress overhead before letting it drop on the floor behind her. Underneath, she wears only a skimpy lace thong, no bra.

Her bare breasts sit directly in front of my face, small, round, soft, and ripe. Her tight little nipples poke out, brown as her freckles, pierced with silver rings.

Cupping the base of my skull in her palm, Mara draws my head toward her breast. "Close your mouth around my nipple."

Flushed from that long orgasm, I don't think or plan. I only obey.

"Suck on my tits," Mara says. "Softly. Slowly. Feel what they feel like in your mouth against your tongue."

I latch on to her breast, taking the whole nipple in my mouth. Its stiff pebbled tip lies firmly against my tongue. The round swell of

her breast presses pleasantly against my lips. Her skin smells of the intoxicating perfume Mara chose at the store, selecting the one that incited me the most without me ever saying a word.

I suckle on her breast, trying to shut off my impulse to look at her face and gauge my effectiveness. I close my eyes, focusing on my own sensations instead. Letting the soft sounds of her moans, and the tightness of her waist between my hands, guide me.

Her nipple swells in my mouth, warming and softening against my tongue. The silver ring remains cool and unchanging, ice that can never melt.

I increase the pressure, not because I can feel that it causes Mara to grind harder on my stiffening cock, but purely for the satisfaction of sucking harder.

Mara pushes herself up, then lowers herself on my cock, her lace thong pulled to the side. Her pussy is drenched; I feel her wetness on my thighs. She's so close to climax that she's already riding me hard, starting at a gallop.

I release her breast and seize the other with my lips, sucking hard, ravaging it, trying to fit as much as possible in my mouth.

The silver ring is like the tines of a fork, serving her nipple to me. Sucking her tits satisfies me like eating, like drinking. I'm devouring her. Gulping her down.

Mara starts to come. She's clutching the back of my head, pushing my mouth harder against her breast, slamming her pussy down on my cock.

I swallow her breasts. When I'm full to the brim, I explode inside her.

Sometime later, we're still sitting on the couch in the same position. Mara's head rests on my shoulder. I trail my fingertips lightly up and down her spine.

I can tell she likes it—her body is heavy and sleepy, her soft sighs tickling my ear.

I'm not thinking about that. I'm focusing on the feeling of her skin beneath my fingertips. Her warmth and her softness.

When Mara finally lifts her head and sits back on my thighs, the silver rings on her chest glint in the moonlight. We've yet to turn on any lamps. Stars reflect on the glassy ocean below us, like half have fallen into the water.

I say, "Those rings are the only useful thing Shaw has ever done."

Mara's mouth falls open, letting out an outraged laugh. "That's so fucked up!"

"Oh, shut up," I say. "You like them, too."

Mara smacks me hard on the shoulder, unable to hide that I'm right.

"Why is that?" I ask her.

She considers. "They suit me. I like the way they feel. And in a strange way, as awful as that night was, it brought me to you. The value in horrible things is what you make of them. As long as you're alive, you can still turn shit into gold."

"You're glad you're here?" I fix my eyes on her face. Wanting to know the truth, whatever she might say.

"Yes," Mara says softly, without hesitation.

"Why?"

I'm thinking it's what I bring her: the money, the clothes, the connections, the orgasms.

Mara grins. "I told you—you're interesting. And I hate being bored."

"Me, too." I'm just as passionate on this topic as Mara. "I really fucking hate it."

3

MARA

WHEN I FIRST CAME TO COLE'S HOUSE, I THOUGHT OUR CONFRONtation with Shaw was imminent.

Instead, Cole sucked me into a cycle: long bouts of labor on our respective work, hedonistic meals to recover, and wild, experimental sex.

Cole means what he said, that he will always be with me, always by my side. He even breaks his own routine of working in his private studio, joining the rest of us plebs in the shared building.

With his designs and materials transported to the largest studio at the end of the hall, we're never farther than a few doors down from each other.

This is to protect me from Shaw but also to satisfy Cole's obsessive need to know where I am and what I'm doing every moment.

It should feel suffocating, but it doesn't. Probably because Cole is not trying to interfere with what I want to do. Quite the opposite. He wants to help me so he can increase my reliance on him.

Sometimes I wonder if he's going to pull the rug out from under me. Will he suddenly become violent and cruel when he thinks he has me trapped?

It's hard to believe he could still be tricking me, that he has some secret plan. I've seen him in too many unguarded moments.

But I may be only fooling myself.

Many people have believed they knew Cole, that he was their friend.

I don't know if it's ever been true.

He does seem to have some real affection for Sonia. He certainly respects how good she is at her job. She accomplishes her tasks creatively and effectively, without instruction from Cole. As kind as she's always been to me, she's ruthlessness at getting things done. I've heard her cut the Artists Guild panel down to size when they dare oppose what Cole orders.

I don't believe Sonia's warmness to me is only because Cole expects it. She regularly comes to see my work, seeming to feel real pleasure when I'm invited to participate in another show or when another painting sells.

On a late-November day, she comes to my doorway, carrying two mugs of tea.

Sonia doesn't ferry tea for anyone, not even herself—that's Janice's job. So I know she's here for a reason.

"Cream and sweetener, right?" She presses a mug into my hand.

"Thank you," I say gratefully.

As much as I love all the bare glass in my studio, it's difficult to keep the space warm. Even with an oversize cardigan and fingerless gloves, I'm still chilly. The air lies heavy and wet outside my window, opaque as milk. Trails of condensation run down the glass like tears.

"Cole told me he's been working on a design for Corona Heights Park," Sonia says.

"He has a few ideas. I don't think he knows which he wants to submit."

I sip the tea, which is deeply steeped and just the right temperature. If Cole and Sonia ever opened a coffee shop, it would put Starbucks out of business.

Sonia mirrors me, taking a sip, watching over the rim of her mug. "Cole's been asked to do monumental sculptures before. He always refused."

I shrug. "I guess he's ready for it now."

Sonia lets that sit between us for a moment, taking another slow sip of her tea.

She remarks, "He's different since he met you. He smiles occasionally. And he hasn't made Janice cry in weeks."

I squeeze my mug, trying to draw warmth through the smooth ceramic. "I don't know that I have any great effect on him. No tree can stop a landslide."

Sonia quirks her mouth up, enjoying that analogy. "I'd call him a volcano. You can survive a landslide…not a lava flow."

I can't tell if that's a warning.

If it is, Sonia's giving it from inside the volcano's umbra. She's not safe from Cole either.

She's worked for him for the better part of a decade. As brilliant and observant as Sonia is, I have no doubt that she's learned some of his secrets. Whether Cole intended to share them or not.

Yet she remains unusually loyal.

I set my tea down before picking up my brush once more, loading it with paint.

My new canvas perches on the easel, the shapes blocked out, the work just beginning.

Swiping my brush gently across the virgin space, I ask Sonia, "You have a son, don't you?"

Her manicured nails tap against her mug. "Did Cole tell you that?"

"I saw you carrying a backpack out the other day. From the *Cuphead* patches and the skateboarding stickers, I guessed he's about twelve."

"Thirteen." I can hear Sonia's smile, the affection in her voice. "His name is Will. He goes to the STEM school in Laurel Heights."

"Oh, so he's a genius, then." I grin.

"Yes." Sonia laughs. "And like all geniuses, absent-minded—he forgets that damn backpack in my car at least once a week."

I dip my brush onto the palette, adding a little more navy into the silvery gray. "Will lives with you full-time?"

Sonia wears no rings. I've never heard her mention a boyfriend, let alone a husband.

"That's right." She takes another leisurely sip of tea. Today she's dressed in a tailored pantsuit, no blouse beneath. The streaks of shocking white around her face look stark and bold, like she was struck by lightning in just that spot. "His father was an aerospace engineer, designing drones for the military. That's where Will gets his math skills. God knows it's not from me."

My respect for Sonia battles my curiosity. As someone who hates personal questions, I don't want to pry. On the other hand, I'm sure Sonia will have no problem shutting me down if she doesn't want to talk about it.

"Where's his father now?"

Sonia perches on the edge of my table, her long legs stretched in front of her. She looks down into her tea, swirling the mug slowly in both hands.

"It was an ugly divorce. Will was eight, just starting third grade. His father wouldn't agree on split custody. He worked long hours, weekends, too, but he couldn't stand the thought of me having Will even half the time. He hired a men's rights attorney, a fucking snake. They threw everything they could at me. Month after month, drowning me in paperwork and court hearings. Trying to intimidate me. Trying to drain my bank account to the point where I'd hand over my son just to make it stop."

I stop painting, turning to look at her.

Her face falls into deep lines of exhaustion as she remembers the ordeal.

"It was relentless. Vindictive. Irrational. He'd pretend to be willing to reach an agreement if I'd meet him for mediation, but then he'd yank the football away again. I started to worry that even if I could force him to come to terms, he'd never abide by them.

He was already flouting the temporary custody agreement, refusing to bring Will back to my house, shutting off Will's cell phone so I couldn't call or text. He had family in Saudi Arabia and plenty of job opportunities overseas… I lived in terror that one day he'd take my son and never return."

"I'm so sorry," I say. "That's awful."

Sonia nods, anger still burning in her eyes. "It was."

"Did the judge sort it out?"

Sonia snorts. "Not fucking likely. The system is a stick in the hand of the biggest bully. The lawyers get rich, and everyone else gets fucked."

"What happened, then?"

"A miracle," Sonia says. "I had Will at home for the weekend. For once his father wasn't calling and texting, trying to interrupt us, blowing up my phone. I remember thinking he must be slammed at work. I certainly didn't believe he was turning over a new leaf—I wasn't that stupid."

Sonia's voice goes low and dreamy as she gazes into her tea. "Monday morning, I drove Will back to my ex's house. He was renting a place in Oakland, a little modern bungalow with an attached garage. I parked out front, noticing that all the lights were off in the house, even though I was right on time and he should have been expecting us. I told Will, 'Wait in the car.' I must have known something was off. I walked up to the front door, rang the bell, knocked. No answer."

I swallow, my throat tight with anticipation, even though this all happened years ago.

"I heard this sound. Sort of a low rumble coming from the garage. I couldn't have told you what it was, and yet, deep down, I think I already knew. I felt myself walking over, wrenching up the door. Standing still while exhaust billowed out all around me."

"He was…in the car?"

"He'd driven home late from some bar. Fell asleep in the garage. Never turned off the engine."

I let out a long sigh.

"It was a '67 Camaro—his baby. I told him that car would be the death of him if he ever got in an accident on the freeway. I guess I was half right."

"And that was the end of the custody battle."

Sonia nods. "Will came to live with me full-time. Cole even gave me a raise to pay off what I owed my lawyer."

"He's generous like that." My voice comes out faint and slightly strained.

"Oh yes," Sonia says quietly, her pale blue eyes fixed on mine. "He can be very generous when it suits him."

Sonia stands, still holding the tea gone cold in her mug. She only drank half of it. "I'll always be grateful to Cole for everything he did for me during that time," she says. "It was the darkest point in my life."

She's walking toward the door, leaving so I can get back to work.

"That's interesting," I say.

Sonia pauses in the doorway, looking back at me. "What's interesting?"

I swirl my brush through the silvery gray, loading the horsehair with pigment. "I also met Cole on my darkest day."

Sonia's lips curl, her smile enigmatic. "That's his gift. He knows how to choose his moment."

I start to paint again, thick clouds of gray, the color of car exhaust.

"By the way," Sonia says as she departs, "I love the new composition."

I finished my Sinners and Saints series. Six paintings in all, each selling for more than the last.

Actually, seven sales occurred because my painting of the beautiful devil has already resold for twice its original price to Betsy Voss herself.

"That's a very good sign," Cole told me. "Betsy has an eye, and she doesn't make purchases just to inflate value. She believes it's an investment."

The giddy trajectory of my bank account is terrifying. I try not to look at it. The numbers seem impossible.

I hardly need to access it anyway, living at Cole's house. I don't need more clothes. And I'd prefer not to spend the money in case it evaporates as quickly as it came.

I do withdraw a thousand dollars each for Frank and Joanna, who lent me money in my most desperate moments.

Cole drives me back to the old Victorian, then waits at the curb while I climb the uneven steps to the front door.

The house already looks smaller and infinitely shabbier. I feel ashamed, not of its ugliness, but that I'm now perceiving it. Judging it. I loved this house—I felt at home here.

I knock at the door like a stranger. The flutter in my stomach when Joanna answers tells me that I was hoping it would be Frank instead or even Melody.

Her dark eyes are unsmiling. She doesn't say hello—just waits for me to speak.

"I brought you some money," I say awkwardly, trying to put both envelopes in her hand. "You and Frank. For the times you gave me slack..."

Joanna looks at the envelopes, unmoving. "You always paid me back," she says.

I don't know how to make her take them.

Her eyes flick down to the Tesla pulled up to the curb, Cole sitting behind the wheel. "He gave you that money?"

"No. I sold some paintings."

"Congratulations."

There's no warmth to the word. We might have only met this morning.

I helped her clean out her grandfather's house after he died, stopping regularly to hug her while she cried. Joanna sublet her studio to me, over all our other roommates who would have jumped at the chance.

Friendship feels so real until it pops like a soap bubble.

Her coldness doesn't stem from jealousy or the belief Cole is giving me an unfair advantage.

This is about Erin.

Joanna doesn't know what happened, but she knows it's my fault.

I'm the one who drew the evil eye upon us. I was attacked first. And I didn't finish the fight—instead, I began to change.

I didn't want to be the old Mara—the loser, the unlucky one, the victim.

Cole appeared in my life like a dark genie, offering me everything I ever wanted: money, fame, success.

I took his offer before I even knew the terms of the contract. Before I knew the price.

I shed my old life like a molted skin. And I left Erin to die in my place, in my bed.

For that, I feel as guilty as Joanna could wish.

I just don't know what to do about it.

I have no evidence against Shaw. No way of fighting back against him, of getting justice for Erin.

Cole wants to kill him. That would break my vow to keep swimming to the surface, never sinking to the bottom, never becoming more vicious than the monsters trying to devour me.

My worst fear is to become like my mother. When I catch myself doing anything her way, I want to slap my own face. I won't do it. I refuse.

"If you don't want the money, will you give it to Frank?"

Now Joanna does consent to take the envelopes. I have no doubt she'll give them both to Frank. Joanna's principles are as ironhard as her posture. I always respected that about her.

"Thank you again," I say. "If you ever need anything—"

"I won't."

She closes the door, not slamming it in my face but certainly not waiting for my response.

Making the long descent back to the car, I can tell Cole followed the conversation from a distance.

"She's still upset about Erin," he guesses.

"So am I. What are we going to do about Shaw? Why has he been so quiet?"

"He usually goes dark after three kills. This time it was four—but the third was a prop, to trap me. He meant the real climax to be you."

Cole's intimate understanding of Shaw's process unnerves me.

Stomach clenching, I ask him, "How do you know that? How did you find out what Shaw does? And how did he find out about you? Were you friends?"

Cole sits tall in the driver's seat, seeming to fill the whole space of the car. Seeming to loom over me.

Asking him questions is terrifying.

"You want me to tell you information that could put me in prison, while you refuse to share any of your secrets with me."

I flush. "It's not the same."

"No. What you're asking is more dangerous…for both of us."

I take several shallow breaths, finding no oxygen in the car. My brain races faster than my heart.

I don't talk about my past with anyone.

And Cole is no therapist—he'll use whatever I tell him to manipulate me. To gain even greater control.

On the other hand, we're equally curious. I want to know his history as badly as he wants to know mine.

Tit for tat. Pay to play. That's how the world works.

Sighing, I say, "I'll tell you what you want to know. But you have to tell me something first."

Cole's fingertips give one restless tap on the woolen thigh of his trousers. He weighs the offer.

"You can ask one question. Not about Shaw."

The devil always counters.

"Fine," I say, so quickly that he narrows his eyes at me.

The silence stretches between us as I consider what he might answer fully and truthfully. And what I most want to know.

Finally, I ask, "Who was the first person you killed?"

4
COLE

I START THE CAR, TURNING THE WHEEL IN THE DIRECTION OF SEA Cliff.

"Aren't you going to answer me?" Mara asks from the passenger seat.

"I'm not going to tell you...I'm going to show you."

She falls silent beside me, watching the narrow roadways widen as we leave her run-down neighborhood, venturing into the broad, tree-lined streets leading up to China Beach.

Tension builds in her body with each passing minute. Mara can't help her curiosity, even when she's afraid of what she might learn.

I rest my hand on her thigh to calm her.

It works—the tight muscle relaxes under my palm. She leans against my arm, her head resting on my shoulder.

Mara told me she doesn't even have a driver's license. In some ways she's remarkably independent, but she has these holes in her education. Things she couldn't teach herself.

Abruptly, I pull the Tesla against the curb.

Mara sits up. "What are you doing?"

"You're going to drive us home."

She sputters, holding up her hands. "I don't even have a learner's permit."

"Oh, well in that case, we better not. I don't want to break any laws."

Mara snorts but remains stubbornly seated on the passenger side. "What if I scratch it? What if I run into a tree? This car probably costs a hundred grand!"

"A hundred and sixty, actually. It's the performance model."

She blanches. "No fucking way!"

I reach across her to open the door before unbuckling her seat belt and shoving her out. "We're not negotiating. You need to learn to drive."

"What if I crash it?"

"Then I'll buy another one. It's a hunk of metal—I really don't give a shit."

I'm climbing out myself, trading positions with her. We cross paths in front of the headlights, Mara warily eyeing the car as if it's an animal crouched and ready to swallow her whole.

"Doesn't it drive itself?" she asks, slipping behind the wheel.

"You're gonna do it. Sit down and buckle up."

Once we're both seated, I walk her through the controls, showing her the paddle shifters, the turn signal, the accelerator, and the brake.

Understanding that I'm not going to drop it, there's no getting out, Mara pays attention. She remembers everything I tell her and asks questions when she doesn't understand.

"The regenerative brakes will kick in automatically once you lift your foot off the accelerator," I tell her. "So you won't even need the brake pedal most of the time."

Mara sighs. "Let's get this over with."

She puts the car in drive, then slowly presses down on the accelerator. The Tesla leaps forward. Mara shrieks, slamming on the brake. We're thrown against our seat belts, our faces inches from the dash.

Keeping my voice low and calm so I don't stress her out worse than she already is, I say, "Take it easy. Light on the accelerator and ease off if you want to stop or slow down."

"I barely touched it! This thing's a fucking rocket-powered go-kart."

"Yeah"—I laugh—"that's why it's fun. Now try it again."

This time she presses her foot down gingerly. The car surges forward, still jerky at first but smoothing out as Mara gets the feel of it.

"You don't need to hug the line like that," I tell her. "Stay in the middle of your lane."

"I'm scared I'm gonna hit something on your side."

"You won't."

I tell her where to go, pointing out stop signs she might miss, reminding her to use her turn signal. Mara's awkward and jumpy, but she's getting the hang of it.

I enjoy telling her what to do, correcting her, encouraging her. She has to obey me or risk running someone over.

When I think she can handle it, I turn on the music.

♫ *"6 Underground"—Sneaker Pimps*

As soon as the first notes fill the car, Mara relaxes. Her shoulders lower, and her turns smooth out.

"There you go," I growl. "Now you're getting it."

Mara shivers with pleasure.

She loves to be praised; she can't get enough of it. She'd probably take a compliment over a body-shaking orgasm.

I return my hand to her thigh, massaging gently. "Turn left here. We'll go down to Skyline Boulevard and then up along the beach. It's a prettier drive."

We pass through Lake Merced Park, water on both sides, the zoo up ahead.

Mara is no longer driving ten under the speed limit, drawing honks and forcing annoyed commuters to speed around us. Now she's cruising along, sitting up straighter, loosening her death grip on the wheel. Watching the birds soar low over the lake and the golfers shank their shots into the hazards. Actually smiling.

"This feels good," she says. "It's almost fun."

She's doing great until it's time to exit onto Point Lobos Avenue and a teenager in a Jeep tries to switch lanes right on top of her. Mara jerks the wheel hard to the right, way overcompensating, almost sending us spinning into the median.

I grab the wheel, wrenching it back to center again.

Mara is shaking so hard, her teeth are chattering. "Help me pull over. I don't want to drive anymore."

I refuse. "You're doing great and we're almost home."

She's pale and sweating, frightened to an irrational degree.

She knows I see it.

"My mother's had four DUIs," she says. "I was in the car for three of them."

Hot, roiling anger surges inside me. I'm really starting to despise this woman I've never met.

"She'd pick me up, and at first I wouldn't know. It was hard to tell with her—she was always some level of buzzed. She'd start driving faster and faster, missing turns, swerving across lanes. And I'd realize she was not at a normal level; she was fucking blitzed. By then it was too late. I was trapped in the passenger seat. All I could do was make sure my seat belt was clicked and cling to the little plastic handle inside the door, hoping she'd take us home and not drive around for hours like she sometimes did when she was pissed at Randall or when she just fucking felt like it."

Mara grips the wheel tight in both hands, staring at the street in front of her but probably seeing a different road, one where the painted lines swoop back and forth under the tires of a weaving car piloted by no one.

"Anyway," she says quietly, "cars scare me."

"Everyone should be more careful when they're in a three-thousand-pound death machine."

Mara glances at me quickly, her lashes going up and down like the flick of a butterfly's wing. "You're very...understanding."

"It's not difficult to understand you. Of course, you're scared of driving if your mother used to careen around like the fucking teacups ride. People drive their cars with one hand, scrolling on their phones like nothing can happen to them. Meanwhile, they're terrified of some statistically improbable event like a shark attack on their vacation to Hawaii. The real dangers are all around you all the time."

"Maybe even in the car with you right now." Mara throws me a look with a hint of mischief in it.

"Are you talking about me or about yourself? You've gotten *me* in more trouble than I've caused for you."

"You think I'm a threat?" Mara's fingertips caress the wheel as she turns, well familiar with the route to my house.

"You threaten everything I thought I knew and everything I believed."

We've left the other cars behind us, now alone on the long, winding drive up to Sea Cliff. She's speeding up, taking the curves with confidence. She looks sexy behind the wheel of my car, wearing the suede moto jacket I bought for her. Her skin glows with health. Even her nails look less ragged—she hasn't been biting them as much.

Mara is flourishing under my care. Becoming more beautiful, more powerful by the day.

I'm doing this. I'm changing her.

"You like it," Mara says. "You can't get enough of it."

I seize her face and force her to kiss me, pulling her eyes away while the car flies along the road.

She gasps as I let go of her, gripping the wheel tight once more.

I say, "At first it was against my will. But now I'm all in. I have to have you. Even if it blows up my life."

Mara pulls into my driveway, the towering facade of Sea Cliff looming over us. The weathered dark stone is cave-like, as if the house is just more of the cliff, jutting up against the sky.

"Do you like this house?" I ask Mara.

She tilts her head, examining it anew.

"It suits you," she says. "On the outside: stark and intimidating. On the inside…surprisingly beautiful."

"You haven't even seen it all yet."

"I know," she says, looking at me, not the house.

I take her hand. "Come on."

I lead her around the side of the house, down the stone path that winds through thick hedges of wisteria long past their bloom. The private entrance is sheltered from all sides, so no one but my father could see who was coming and going.

I open his office door.

Mara steps inside first, looking all around her.

I follow her in.

The office has been destroyed: Books torn down from the shelves, their pages ripped out and scattered all around. The desk hacked to pieces with a hatchet. The artwork smashed where it hung on the wall. Even the sofa and chairs slashed open, stuffing hanging out like entrails.

Mara stares, her mouth open.

Hesitantly, she approaches the desk, drawing her fingertip across its scarred and broken top, leaving a trail in the dust. "Did you do this?"

"Yes. The night my father died."

"Did you…were you the one who killed him?"

"No. That's why I was angry. He was gone, with too many things left unsaid."

"What happened to him?"

"Degenerative kidney disease. I knew it was coming, but it happened sooner than I expected. There's no closure from the dead."

Mara gazes at the photographs hung on the wall, the images distorted by the shattered glass in each frame.

Unerringly, she finds one of my father. He's standing on a

windswept hilltop in New Zealand, wearing his hunting jacket, his rifle over his shoulder. His black hair and beard are immaculately groomed despite the rustic setting.

Mara is drawn to the figure next to him. A man with hair and eyes as dark as my father's but a much more youthful face.

"Is that...?" Mara squints through the spiderweb of glass. "Do you have a brother?"

"That's my uncle. He was twelve years younger than my father. Almost as close to me in age."

Mara turns, understanding that this photograph is the reason I brought her in here. "He looks just like you."

"That's not the only thing we had in common."

She crosses the detritus blanketing the floor, her boots crunching on splinters of wood and glass. Sinking onto the slashed sofa, she says, "Tell me everything."

I sit next to her, my weight causing her to slide closer until her thigh rests against mine. "My uncle, Ruben, was the only person my father ever loved. My grandparents had him late in life. He was unruly; they didn't know what to do with him. My father was the only person he'd listen to, occasionally."

Mara sits up straight, her hands clasped in front of her, her eyes fixed on my face like she's a child enthralled by a fairy tale.

"My family's money came from hotels and breweries, but by the time Ruben came along, most of it had been parceled out or frittered away, so the Blackwells were no longer truly rich. Meaning my grandparents still lived well, but there was only a modest trust fund waiting for their sons. My father used his to start his venture capital firm. He offered Ruben a job, but Ruben didn't want it. He waited till he turned twenty-one, got his money, then fucked off to LA to spend it. Around that same time, my father married my mother."

Mara interrupts. "How did they meet?"

"Have you ever read *The Great Gatsby*?"

Mara nods.

"It was like that. She was from a level of wealth that made the Blackwells look poor. My father wanted her from the moment he laid eyes on her. She was very beautiful but innocent and sheltered. Her parents had full control over her. My father had to impress them first to get access to her. When his company went public, he donated six million to her mother's foundation. That's how he got an invitation to one of their dinner parties so he could start the process of seducing their daughter."

"Do you have a picture of her?" Mara asks.

"Upstairs. There are none in here."

I can't hide the bitterness in my voice. Mara presses her lips together, understanding.

"My father wanted anything he couldn't have." I pause, laughing softly. "I guess that's something we had in common. He wanted to prove himself to anyone who'd ever looked down on him. But he was petty and vindictive. He didn't just want acceptance—he wanted to rub their noses in it. That extended to my mother. He had to have her, but once they were married, he treated her like she'd been the enemy all along. Like she was the one keeping him out of the Pacific-Union Club."

"She told you this?" Mara asks, her brows drawn together in sympathy.

"I read it in her journal. She was confused how the man who worshipped her could turn into a completely different person the moment they were alone in his house."

I close my eyes, quoting from memory the words she wrote in her delicate script, "It's like he hates me, and I don't know why. I don't know what I've done. He used to kiss my fingertips and tell me I was the most exquisite thing in the world. Now he snarls if I even touch him..."

"Why did he change?" Mara asks.

"He never liked anything once he actually had it. It took him years to get this house—he had to bully and threaten the old woman who owned it. Had to fight with the zoning commissioner and the society that was trying to get it named a historic landmark. Once he moved in, he never stopped complaining that it was cold and drafty and the wiring was ancient."

"You're not like that," Mara says.

"No. To me, something has value if it's rare."

"I value things if they make me happy," Mara says.

"But why do they make you happy?"

Mara considers. "Because they're beautiful or interesting. Because they remind me of something I love."

I put my hand on the nape of her neck, rubbing gently. Making her purr. "That's because you're a pleasure kitten. You like anything that feels good."

Mara cuddles against me, comfortable even in this destroyed space. "That's true."

I continue the story. "He was cold to her. Cruel, even. She wrote in her journal that she wanted to leave, but by that point, she knew him well enough to fear what he might do. And then she found out she was pregnant.

"At the same time, my uncle, Ruben, came back to San Francisco. He'd burned through his money and was beginning to see the value of a place in my father's firm. My father gave him a job immediately.

"My uncle was clever and could work hard when he wanted to. In fact, he was doing so well that my father promoted him again and again until he was acting VP, second only to my father.

"That wouldn't have been a problem, except that my father now had an heir. At one point, Ruben might have believed he would inherit the company or receive equal shares. I was a complicating factor. Very much in his way. Especially after my mother died."

Mara stirs against my side. I know what she wants to ask, but she hesitates, knowing instinctively that this is a wound inside me, never healing, always raw.

I promised to answer her question. This is a part of it.

"It's all right," I tell her. "You can ask."

"What happened to your mother?"

Why is it still so hard to say the words out loud?

I hate that it hurts me. I hate that I care.

"She hung herself."

Mara winces. She takes my hand, squeezing it tight.

I look down at her hand, wondering why that feels so good. Why it comforts me.

Maybe because no one knows better than Mara what it feels like to be young, frightened, and deeply alone.

"I felt like an orphan. I had no warmth or connection from my father. Ruben terrified me. He was already showing his aggression, as much as he could get away with. He tripped me on the stairs. I broke my arm. He said it was an accident, and I was too young for my father to believe anything else. Later, he tried to drown me on the beach below the house. He kept pushing me under the waves, over and over, laughing like it was a joke. All I could see were his teeth and the wild look in his eyes. He'd shove me under again before I could get any air.

"That time my father saw it. He hauled me out. It was the first time I saw him truly angry at Ruben. Ruben was more careful after that. But I knew he hated me. He was jealous when my father gave me attention. He sabotaged me any chance he got."

Mara rises from the couch to inspect the photograph once more. She brushes the glass out of the frame, frowning at Ruben's handsome face, clear and uncovered.

"It was around that time that I started to draw. I'd always liked tinkering with machinery, working with my hands. My father encouraged it because he could see the use of it. He didn't like me sketching. He didn't care for the arts. He only donated to them because he knew philanthropy was part of empire building."

"What made you start drawing?" Mara asks.

"At first I was sketching designs of machinery I wanted to build. The designs became more experimental, more aesthetic. Sculptures instead of machines." I pause because this makes me curious in turn. "What was the first thing you drew?"

Mara blushes. "The girls at school had coloring books. I didn't have one, but I could get my hands on paper and pencils. I made my own coloring pages—mostly princesses in dresses because that's what they had. I realized I could draw any dress I could think of. Then I drew other things I wanted. Roller skates, unicorns, a bed with a canopy, ice cream sundaes..."

She trails off as if realizing that, to her, roller skates seemed as unobtainable as unicorns.

"Anyway." She shakes her head. "Keep going..."

I lost the thread, distracted by thoughts of Mara as a child. I want to know all her secrets. She keeps them buried deep. If a shovel won't work, I might need dynamite.

After taking a breath, I continue. "I was having conflict with my father. I wanted to go to art school. He expected me to take over his company. He knew by then that he was sick."

"What about Ruben?"

"Well, that was the contrarian in my father. If I wanted the business and Ruben didn't, then he probably would've given it to Ruben. Ruben was acting up, pissing him off. I was playing hard to get—or at least that's how he saw it. The more I pulled away from him, the more determined he became to mold me in his image. I'd already decided he was a fucking hypocrite."

"Why?"

"Because he thought he was this ruthless titan of industry. He taught me to avoid emotional entanglements—only family deserved loyalty. But he never gave a damn about my mother, and *she* was the one who should have been his family. He loved Ruben, while Ruben would have cut the heart out of my father's chest and eaten it raw if it suited him."

"Ruben didn't care about anyone," Mara says.

"That's right. And that's what we truly had in common. I looked like Ruben, more than my own father. Sounded like him, even. Most of all, I understood him. I knew he was stone-cold inside because I was, too. He didn't only hate me because he was jealous—he hated me because I saw what he really was."

"Was he still trying to hurt you?"

"Worse. He convinced my father to make him my guardian. I was sixteen. My father was getting sicker all the time. If he died, the money, the house, the company, all of it would fall under Ruben's control. I'd be fucked."

Mara looks down at the framed photograph clutched in her hands, lifted off the wall. She glances between Ruben's face and mine, equally handsome, equally cruel. She understands the havoc he could have wreaked in the two years before my eighteenth birthday. "What did you do?"

"I organized a hunting trip for the three of us, knowing my father would be too ill to come. Ruben knew it, too. I think he anticipated what I planned—or at least he thought he did."

Mara returns to the sofa. She's stiff with apprehension, unable to sit back against the ruined cushions. "Why did he go?"

"He thought he'd turn the tables on me. I let him think it. We went out into the woods in northern Montana, just the two of us. It was the coldest week of January. I'd been there before, and so had Ruben, but not together. You have to leave before sunrise to hunt mountain lions, tramping through snow up to your knees."

Mara rubs her palms against her upper arms as if she can feel the chill.

"I was a teenager, skinny, half-grown. He was twenty-eight, bigger than me, stronger. He thought he was smarter, too. I let him load my gun with blanks, pretending not to notice. I let him walk behind me in the woods. I could hear his breath slowing, his steps pausing. I felt him lift his rifle, point it at my back…"

Mara presses her fingers against her mouth. I know she desperately wants to bite her nails but refrains for my sake.

"I heard the rifle blast, and I thought I'd timed it wrong—I was dead. Then I turned around and saw the hole in the ground. He'd walked across the deadfall just as I hoped. The rifle shot went up in the sky. He plunged twenty feet into the pit."

Mara lets out the breath she's been holding, her sigh rolling over my forearm. "Was he dead?"

"It took six more hours for him to actually die. I sat and waited. That was the hardest part. He begged and pleaded. Then he cursed and screamed. Then he pleaded again."

"Did you want to let him out?"

"If I did, I might as well have cut my own throat. It was him or me long before the pit."

"What were you waiting for?"

"I was making sure no one else came along."

Mara's throat jumps as she swallows. Even with everything she knows about me, my callousness shocks her. "What about your father?"

"I told him it was an accident. That I tried to run for help, but I got lost in the woods."

"Did he believe you?"

"He knew I'd never get lost."

"What did he say?"

"He said, 'That was the only family you had left. When I die, you'll be completely alone.'"

Mara takes my hand again. Not squeezing it this time, just holding it in her lap, her fingers linked with mine.

"And you were," she says softly.

"I thought it was better to be alone. Safer. More pleasant, even."

"But you still did this." Mara looks around at my father's office, smashed to pieces with a rage that still screams from every corner of the room, all these years later.

"It affected me more than I expected," I admit.

Mara lifts my hand to her mouth, brushing my knuckles against her lips. "I can't blame you. Your uncle sounds terrifying."

I set her hand gently on her lap, facing her and looking her in the eyes. "That was the first time I killed. But there were more. It's like losing your virginity…the first time seems so significant. Each one after is less and less important. Until you barely remember their names."

Her tongue darts out to moisten her lips. "Who was the second person?" she murmurs.

"I was drunk at a club in Paris. Three men followed me out, planning to mug me. I fought one off. The second ran away. The third…I slammed his head against the alley wall until his skull cracked."

Mara's hand floats up to her mouth. This time she bites down hard on the edge of her nail.

"That was the only time I killed on impulse, without a plan. The others were more strategic."

"How many?" she whispers.

"Fourteen."

Mara makes a faint choking sound. Her cheeks have gone grayish, her knuckles white.

"None were women," I say, as if that will comfort her.

"Why not women?" she asks faintly.

I shrug. "Men deserve it more."

Mara sits forward, her elbows on her knees, her hands covering her face. I give her time to process, knowing she suspected some of this but could never have guessed the full truth.

After a moment, her shoulders stiffen, and her head snaps up. She regards me with sudden animation. "You killed Sonia's ex-husband," she blurts.

I frown at her. "How do you know that?"

"Sonia told me how he died. I thought it was…convenient."

"It was very *inconvenient* when he was dragging her to court for months on end. It affected her work."

Mara squints at me. "You could have just fired her."

"Hiring someone new is even worse."

"You wanted to help her."

"I helped myself. It just happened to benefit Sonia as well."

Mara shakes her head at me, already recovering her amusement. "You have a soft spot for women."

"The fuck I do. Don't forget how we met."

"I remember."

The office is growing dark. I never switched on the lights because I shattered the overhead fixture along with everything else in the room. We've been sitting in the little light that filters through the wisteria and the dusty windows. Now it's all fading.

"You know, that wasn't the first time I actually saw you."

Mara blinks, her lips forming a small circle of confusion. "What do you mean?"

"I saw you at the Oasis show. Shaw did, too. He saw me watching you. Jack Brisk spilled wine on your dress. I thought you'd leave the party—instead you used more wine to dye the dress. It surprised me that you were so innovative. Surprised me more how beautifully you did it. I was impressed. Shaw couldn't understand that, of course. He thought I wanted to fuck you."

Mara stares at me, open-mouthed. "Is that why he took me?"

"Yes," I admit. "I insulted him. I said he was undisciplined, out of control. He wanted to prove I'd act the same…under the right temptation."

Mara blinks slowly. "*You* chose me."

"I didn't know it then, but I already had. I tried to leave you on that mountain…you survived anyway. From that moment, I was obsessed. I had to know how you did it. I had to understand."

Mara's eyes are liquid in the failing light. "And do you? Do you understand now?"

I rest my palm against the edge of her jaw, stroking my thumb across her lips. "I know you can't be broken. I'm still testing if you can be tamed…"

Mara catches my thumb in her teeth, biting down. "You're not tame yourself."

I like how hard she bites, the little savage. It makes me want to bite her back.

"No, I'm not," I agree. "And I never will be."

"Neither will I," Mara hisses, equally fierce.

She's not afraid of me. She never has been.

I remember how she confronted me in my own studio, her eyes blazing, her fists clenched at her sides. Demanding to know how I dared leave her to die. Scoffing in the face of my lies.

I seize her by the throat and kiss her, pinning her against the slashed sofa.

She's out of her fucking mind, and so am I.

Our madness aligns in all the right ways.

When we've pulled on our clothes again, I remind Mara, "A question for a question. I haven't forgotten."

Mara sighs. "You kept your word. I'll keep mine."

I take her hand, pulling her up from the sofa. Mara doesn't flinch away from me—she loves when I touch her, even knowing of all the blood on these hands.

Her Normal meter is broken. She's been around too many horrible people. She doesn't know how brutal I truly am, how unredeemable.

Lucky for me, I suppose.

"Come up to the kitchen," I say. "I can't get you a unicorn, but I can damn sure make you an ice cream sundae."

Mara follows me up to the main level. Despite my telling her exactly what I was going to do, she's still delighted when I set a giant bowl of vanilla ice cream in front of her, covered in chocolate syrup and mounds of whipped cream.

She's always more surprised by kindness than by cruelty.

Mara takes a massive bite, her eyes closed, letting the ice cream melt on her tongue before she swallows.

"I needed that." She sighs. Then, setting down her spoon, she says, "All right. I'm ready. What do you want to know?"

I sit next to her at the counter, our knees touching.

"Tell me about Randall."

5

MARA

♫ *"Mad World"—Michael Andrews & Gary Jules*

I'M WALKING HOME FROM SCHOOL, SLOWLY SO I WON'T CATCH UP TO the group of girls in front of me, but not so slowly that Randall will be angry that I'm late.

Mandy Patterson is at the center of the pack like usual, impossible to miss with her long flow of ash-blond hair, curled and tied with the kind of oversize cheerleader bow that's become such a trend at school.

I don't have any bows.

I asked for one for my birthday. Randall and my mother got me a used violin instead. I have to take lessons with Mrs. Belchick every Tuesday and Thursday. Her house smells like rancid cooking oil, and I'm allergic to her budgies. My eyes swell every time I'm there, and my fingers are so itchy that I can barely grip the bow. I've begged my mother not to make me go anymore, but this is my punishment for not practicing piano enough.

I fucked up badly at the recital.

I hate performing in public, hate everyone staring at me.

I'd never played on that particular piano. When I sat on the bench in the awful silence of the auditorium, the glaring overhead lights reflecting off the glossy black Steinway, I was hit with the horrible realization that I wasn't sure which key was middle C.

It sounds ridiculous after all the years I've played, but I always orient my hands relative to the chipped golden script on our own piano, which reads *Bösendorfer* across the fallboard, only missing the second *o*.

I stared at the keys, the seconds ticking past.

I could see my mother standing just offstage, already starting to pace in agitation, snapping her fingers at me to start.

"I don't know where to put my hands," I whispered at her.

"*Play the song*," she hissed at me.

I was already sweating under the blazing lights, my hands shaking as they hovered above the keys.

Desperately, I repeated, "I don't know where to start."

She marched across the stage, furious and embarrassed, before grabbing my arm and wrenching me off the bench. She dragged me off, not listening as I tried to explain that I could play it, I'd practiced it over and over and knew it all by heart, but I just needed her to show me where to put my hands…

That was six months ago. It could be six years past, and she'd still enjoy punishing me for it.

They're always watching, always waiting for me to make a mistake.

And that's the one way I never disappoint them. They can always count on me to fuck up.

The girls ahead look back over their shoulders, giggling and whispering behind their hands.

I can't hear what they're saying because I'm wearing headphones. This is the one gift Randall gave me that I truly love. He didn't want to hear music leaking out of my room. Wearing the headphones encloses me in my own bubble of song. It protects and comforts me. My own little pod that follows me wherever I go.

I drag my feet, trying to create more distance between me and the girls.

They're slowing in pace, too.

Kinsley Fisher calls back to me, "Mara! Are you coming to Danny's birthday party?"

I can hear this, just barely.

Sighing, I take a bud out of one ear.

Mandy replies for me: "She can't. She wasn't invited."

She makes the statement calmly, factually, her soft-pink lips curved in a satisfied smile.

I thought Danny might invite me. Out of all the boys in our class, he's one of the few who's occasionally nice to me. Once, he gave me a pencil with little black cats all over it. It was a week after Halloween, and he said he didn't want it anymore, but I thought maybe it was because he knew how much I like cats.

"Why didn't Danny invite you?" Kinsley asks with mock concern.

She already knows the answer to that question. In fact, she probably knows better than I do. The three Peachy Queens—Kinsley, Angelica, and Her Royal Highness Mandy Patterson—surely were party to the conversations where it was publicly discussed who would be invited and who wouldn't, how our classmates ranked as potential guests, and all the reasons why.

"Danny said his mother wouldn't like it," Mandy explains in the same matter-of-fact tone.

Mandy isn't above lying, but this has the uncomfortable ring of truth.

The parents at Windsor Academy are much more involved than at my old school. They seem as highly interested in the social lives of their middle schoolers as the children themselves.

It's only too likely that Mrs. Phillips has seen and judged me on some scale I can't even begin to imagine. All I know is that I came up short.

"Maybe she knows Mara's a little whore like her mother,"

Angelica says sweetly. Angelica has the round, cherubic face you'd expect from her name, but she's the meanest cunt in their group. Worse even than Mandy. "Everyone knows she married your stepdad for his money."

This is something so fundamentally acknowledged, even between Randall and my mother, that I can't possibly deny it.

The problem is Randall doesn't have that much money anymore. From the shouted arguments I've overhead, even with my pillow pressed over my ears, I've gathered that Randall's sons are running his business into the ground, and my mother is trying to spend whatever is left before it all runs out.

"I guess those short skirts don't work on Danny," Mandy says, smiling enough to show her pearly white teeth.

We all wear the same uniform at Windsor Academy—the same white blouse, plaid skirt, maroon knee socks, and loafers. That's why accessories like cheerleader bows and smart watches are so important—they're the only way to show who's in and who's out.

I'm out.

I was never even close to in.

The short skirts are a different problem entirely. Randall refused to buy me new uniforms this year, even though I shot up two inches. My homeroom teacher keeps making me come to the front of the class and kneel in front of everyone to prove that my skirt doesn't come down to my fingertips. She's given me detention six times.

Randall punishes me every time I'm late coming home, but he won't buy me new clothes.

I'm going to be late now if I don't run the rest of the way home.

I don't have time to continue this conversation with the Peachy Queens. It wouldn't matter either way. I've tried being nice to them. I've tried fighting back. They despise me, and nothing will change that. Even the kids who used to be nice to me, the ones I would have called friends, have learned better than to say a word to me where these girls can see.

"Tell me what does work on Danny," I say to Mandy. "If he ever starts to give a shit about you."

I'm already sprinting away as the calls of "*Freak! Slut! Bitch!*" ring out behind me.

I run until my chest burns and the backpack full of books slams against my ass with every stride.

Once I reach the redbrick colonial, I stop and stand on the sidewalk, dreading opening the front door and stepping inside.

It's hard to believe I was excited when I first saw this house.

I'd never lived in a house before. I'd never had my own bedroom or even a bed with a frame.

Back then, I still believed I could win Randall's approval if I was very, very careful and very, very quiet.

I knew I annoyed him. He wanted my mother, not another kid. His own sons were already grown. I met them at the wedding, where they barely consented to shake my mother's hand. She laughed and said they were worried about their inheritance.

My mother never looked more beautiful than on her wedding day, her dark hair pulled up in a magnificent shining mass topped by a sparkling tiara, her mermaid gown encrusted with even more gems to complement the rock on her hand.

I was so proud of my flower girl dress that I couldn't stop looking at myself in every window I passed. I'd never had a dress like that, as puffy and ethereal as Sarah's in *The Labyrinth*.

I got too excited, though. I vomited, and a little splashed on the skirt of the dress. My mother was so furious that she slapped me across the face. I had to walk down the aisle trying to hold back tears, with my basket of petals and a livid handprint on my cheek.

The day ended sadly for her, too. She drank too much wine at the reception. When it came time to cut the cake, she smashed a handful of it in Randall's face. She laughed wildly, swaying on her stilettos, her head thrown back. Randall couldn't say or do anything in front of all those people, but even I could tell he was shaking with rage.

That was the first night we spent in the redbrick house. From down the hall in my new bed, I heard the familiar sounds of my mother fucking. I was used to her theatrical shrieks of pleasure and even the banging of the bed against the wall. That night there were other sounds: slaps and screams.

In the morning the left side of her face was more swollen than mine. She sat at the kitchen table, drinking her coffee and glaring at Randall, who ordered her to make him some eggs, then calmly sat down to read the paper.

She got up and made the eggs, scrambling them in a fry pan. Then she walked over to Randall and dumped them in his lap. He hit her so hard that she slammed into the wall and fell behind the table, sobbing pitifully.

Randall might have been older, but he was tall and heavily built, with palms harder than iron.

I threw myself on top of her, blubbering and begging Randall to stop.

That was one of the last times I had pity for my mother. She wore mine out not long after Randall's. Seeing how she treated him with open contempt, deliberately angering him, and then how she would crawl back to him whenever she needed something, sitting on his lap and talking in a baby voice, feeding him sips of her drink, destroyed my last shreds of respect for her.

Randall hates her, but he's also obsessed with her. He says he'll kill her before he ever lets her leave him.

I don't know whether it's worse when they're fighting or when they gang up on me.

They're both home all the time. Randall retired right before he met my mother, and she's never held down a job unless she absolutely had to. Her only piano students were those who would put up with our succession of shitty apartments and her constant canceling of lessons.

Her real work has always been leeching off men. Randall has

lasted the longest because he was the first one stupid enough to marry her.

Even my father didn't marry her. Whoever he might be.

When I can't stay outside any longer, I slip my key in the lock and open the door as silently as possible.

I hate the smell of Randall's house. It stinks of dirt from his back garden—in which he's always laboring without ever managing to make it actually pretty—and of the brand of cheap boxed wine my mother likes to drink.

The only part of the house I like at all is my own room. My goal is to get there as quickly as possible without being seen.

I creep down the hall, forced to cross the open doorway leading into the living room. I can see the back of Randall's head as he sits in his favorite recliner. I hate the blocky shape of his skull, the buzzed gray hair, and the fold of fat between his hairline and his plaid button-down.

I'm tiptoeing across that opening when Randall says, "Get in here."

My stomach sinks to my loafers.

I creep into the living room, my hands already clammy.

He expects me to come stand in front of his recliner. I take a quick glance at his face, trying to gauge how bad his mood is today.

Three empty beer bottles sit on the side table next to him. Three isn't too bad.

However, the ruddy flush on his face makes me think those aren't the first three of the day.

"You're late," he grumbles.

Randall's voice sounds even older than he is. It sounds like a bag of rocks tumbling around in the back of a truck.

"I didn't have detention," I say swiftly. "I was walking home with some girls. Mandy Patterson and some others."

I'm hoping this will appease him. Mandy's father is a real estate agent so successful that his handsome grin is plastered across every billboard and bus bench in our town.

"I don't give a fuck if you're walking home with the pope. You get here on time," Randall snarls.

There's no actual reason I need to be home by 3:50 p.m. Other than Tuesdays and Thursdays at Mrs. Belchick's house, I have no appointments. But Randall decreed it, and that means I have to obey or suffer the consequences.

Of course, I'm not going to bring up that rational and reasonable point. That would be suicide. Instead, I swallow my sense of injustice, humbly saying, "I'm sorry. It won't happen again."

It *will* happen again because something always happens to make me late. The universe wants Randall angry at me just as badly as Randall wants it himself.

I'm hoping this is the end of it and I can go hide in my room until it's time to set the table for dinner.

Instead, Randall says, "Change your clothes and come down here to do your homework."

Shit.

I don't bother asking him if I can do it in my room. I simply set my book bag down by the edge of the fireplace before trudging upstairs to change out of my uniform.

Changing clothes is my mother's requirement. She says it's so I don't wear out my uniforms so fast, but I suspect it's really because she noticed how much Randall prefers the plaid skirts. In fact, I'm starting to suspect that's the whole reason he insisted I switch schools.

In response, my mother has been forcing me to wear more and more modest clothing. First, it was no tank tops, then no shorts. Last week she screamed at me over a scoop-neck T-shirt. I'll be wearing turtlenecks in July by the time she's satisfied.

I loathe the way everyone fixates on my clothing—the teachers at school, my classmates, Randall, and my mother. The taller I grow and the more my tits come in, the worse it gets.

I don't get it. It's not like I have some massive rack like Ella Fitz, who started growing them even before we left elementary school. Even the smallest sign of puberty seems to inflame my mother. She was furious when I got my period last year and refused to buy me tampons, even though we have swim class as part of PE and even though every other girl uses them. Mandy Patterson was delighted to tell the whole class the moment she spotted a pad in my bag.

I pull on my baggiest hoodie and jeans so my mother won't pitch a fit when she gets back from wherever she's gone.

When I return to the living room, Randall has turned up the volume on the television. Either he turned it down so he could catch me sneaking in the door, or he's blaring it now to irritate me.

I take my book bag to the dining room table, which is right in his line of sight. I hate how he watches me.

I angle my chair away from him before spreading out my textbooks and notes. Windsor Academy makes us do a lot more homework than I'm used to. The other kids have been there since kindergarten. I've been struggling so bad that my mother hauled me to the doctor for some stupid medication that's supposed to help me focus.

It doesn't help. Actually, it makes me jittery and makes my hands shake. Worse, it amplifies the problems I already had with lights being too bright and noises being too loud. Even normal sounds from the other students—snapping gum or tapping a pencil against a desk—sound like popcorn exploding inside my ears. It makes me jolt and twitch. Marcus Green calls me *Spaz*, and some of the other kids are picking it up, too.

Randall's blaring baseball game is driving me nuts. Every crack of the bat, each abrupt roar of the crowd, sets my teeth on edge. Even though I'm not supposed to wear headphones around him, I sneak one of the buds out of my pocket and slip it into my right ear, under my hair.

That helps a little.

I labor away on my chemistry assignment. We're supposed to draw a diagram of photosynthesis, something I'm actually enjoying. I spend much longer than necessary sketching out the details of the plant cell, filling in the sun, the leaves, and the chloroplast with colored pencils.

Randall hauls himself out of the recliner to get another beer from the fridge. He comes back with two.

"Where's Mom?" I ask him nervously.

"With Leslie." He grunts, sinking back into the chair.

That's not good. Randall detests Leslie. Every time my mother goes over to Leslie's house, she comes home tipsy, making raunchy jokes. Last time she ran her car into the corner of our garage.

Leslie is my mother's oldest friend. They used to work together at the French Maid. My mother told Randall she was a cocktail waitress, but from the pictures in Leslie's old Facebook albums, I'm pretty sure they were both strippers. This was before I was born.

The longer my mother stays at Leslie's house, the angrier Randall will become. While I'm trapped here with him.

Once I switch over to math homework, the baseball game gets even harder to ignore. Knowing it's a risk, I slip in my other earbud, turning my music up loud to drown out the game.

I'm just starting to grasp the properties of parallelism when my earbuds are wrenched out of my ears.

I leap out of my chair, almost tripping over my feet trying to get away from Randall. He's holding my headphones by their cord, his eyes so bloodshot and his face so congested, I realize in an instant that he's quietly been growing drunk while I was working over here, deaf and oblivious.

"I'm trying to talk to you," he snarls.

"I'm sorry," I gasp, holding up my hands in front of me, helplessly, desperately.

Randall balls his fists at his sides. I have no idea how inebriated he is or how angry. He doesn't drink as much as my mother, but when he does, it can get just as ugly.

Luckily, he's not yet swaying on his feet.

"You know the rules!"

He takes my iPod and locks it in the living room cabinet.

I want to cry.

Who knows how long he'll keep it in there. I'll have no music, none at all, until he deigns to give it back to me.

I don't bother to beg—I already know that doesn't work.

Now Randall's out of his chair. Now he's focused on me.

"Your mother's obviously not coming home for dinner." He grunts. "You're going to have to make it."

I don't know how to cook. No one cooks with regularity in this house. Sometimes my mother does it, grudgingly. More often Randall orders in, or we scrounge leftovers out of the fridge.

Rummaging frantically into the cabinets, I decide on spaghetti.

Before I've even filled the pot with water, Randall is already barking criticism at me from the kitchen doorway:

"That's not enough water."

"Why isn't it boiling yet?"

"No salt? Perfect—assuming you want your spaghetti bland as plaster."

"Don't break the noodles, are you fucking stupid?"

He doesn't tell me what I *should* be doing. How am I supposed to make the noodles fit into the pot when they're too long and apparently can't be broken? Desperately, I poke them with a spoon, trying to get them to sink beneath the bubbling water.

The noodles bend, and I'm able to close the lid of the pot. Moments later, it boils over, dousing the stove top in foaming pasta water.

"You fucking idiot!" Randall roars.

He yanks the lid off the pot, turning the heat down.

I want to scream at him to do it himself if he's such a culinary genius. Because I want to keep my head on my shoulders, I bite my lip until it's bleeding, hiding my face in the fridge as I search for the shaker of Parmesan cheese.

Randall has lapsed into sullen silence, furiously wrenching the lid off the jar of sauce and dumping it into the pot so hard that it splashes out on the kitchen tiles.

"Clean that up," he orders.

I have to get on my knees to mop up the sauce with a damp paper towel. I can feel him watching me crawl around, wiping up every last spatter.

I have a horrible feeling that he's angry enough to tip that pot of boiling noodles onto my back. As quickly as I can, I finish cleaning and throw away the wad of paper towel.

I set the table for three, hoping, praying, that my mother is on her way home.

My throat is too tight to eat. Randall takes one bite and then spits the noodles out and shoves away his plate.

"Tastes like fucking Play-Doh," he snarls. "How much salt did you put in there?"

"I don't know." I sob miserably.

He glowers at me, his pale piggy eyes almost disappearing beneath the heavy shelf of his brow. "You're as useless as your mother. The only thing on this earth she's good at is sucking cock. Did you know that, Mara? Did you know your mother is a world-class cocksucker?"

There's no answer to this that won't enrage him. All I can do is stare at my plate, my guts churning, my hands shaking in my lap.

"How do you think a woman gets good at that?" he demands.

When I remain silent, he slams his fists against the tabletop, making me jump. "ANSWER ME!"

"I don't know."

"Practice, Mara. So much practice. I should have known the first time she put my cock in her mouth, looking up at me, smiling like a professional. I should have known then she was nothing but a whore."

The thought of Randall's wrinkly old cock brings me to the edge of vomiting. I swallow the bile, my eyes fixed firmly on my plate. This is the only form of resistance now: Staying quiet. Ignoring him. Not giving him anything that will justify what he actually wants to do.

He knows this, too.

Now we're at the part of the night when he'll do whatever it takes to break me.

He stands before stalking over to me, looming over me. Invading my space, breathing on the top of my head.

"Is that your plan?" He grunts, each breath coming out in a hot puff that stirs my hair, that makes my stomach churn. He's heavy, and his breathing is even heavier. I can hear it all over the house, anywhere he goes. "I've seen your grades. You're not gonna be a doctor or a lawyer. I doubt you could bag groceries right."

He's leaning over me now. Trying to force me to move or make a sound. Trying to get me to crack.

"No, there's only one career path for you." His chuckle is cruel. Spit flecks my cheek as he bends even closer. "You'll be sucking cock, morning, afternoon, and evening. Just like your mother."

He puts his finger in his mouth and wets it with a loud pop. Then he jams it in my ear.

That's what makes me snap.

I leap out of my chair, already screaming, "DON'T YOU FUCKING TOUCH ME! I HATE YOU! I HATE YOUUUUUUUUU!"

My scream is cut off by Randall's hand hitting my ear in a slap that sends me flying into the wall just my mother at their wedding breakfast.

He hits me so hard that I black out. When I sit up, shaking my head, all I can hear is muffled thunder with a high whine on top of it.

I must have been out for a minute because Randall is staring at me with vague alarm, like he was wondering how deep he'd have to bury my body in his garden.

"Stop hamming it up." He grunts as I grip the edge of the table and attempt to stand.

My head throbs. There's a sharp pain on the left side of my neck. Wetness, too. I touch my ear. My fingertips come away bright with blood.

Oh my god. If he made me deaf, I'll fucking kill him.

No, I'll kill myself. I can't live without music. It's all I have.

My mother's key scratches in the lock. Scratches and scrabbles so long that Randall and I both know how drunk she'll be before she stumbles through the door.

My mother is no longer as beautiful as she once was. She used to brag how well she held her liquor, how she could party all night long and get up as early as she liked with hardly a headache.

Time is catching up with her at last. A tube of fat runs around her once-slim waist, stretching the tight dress. Dark circles shadow her eyes. Her hair is no longer long and shining, but frazzled from constant changes in color and length.

She stares at us blearily, the strap of her dress slipping down one shoulder. "You ate without me?" Her voice is mushy and loose.

Either she doesn't notice the blood on my hand, or she's choosing to ignore it.

Randall's piggy eyes flit between me and her, as if trying to decide whether to transfer his rage to a new subject.

My mother must intuit the same thing—she sidles up to him, laying a hand on his bicep, looking up into his face and batting her long false eyelashes.

"Should we go upstairs?" she slurs.

I see the struggle on Randall's face—the offer of sex battling with his undrained rage.

"In a minute," he says. Then, turning to me, he says, "Get my belt."

This is so outrageous that I gape at him. He already took my iPod and slammed me into the wall. There's no way I deserve a whipping on top of that.

Through stiff lips, I say, "You can't do that anymore. The gym teacher said."

"The gym teacher said," Randall mimics me in a baby voice. He points one sausage-like finger in my face. *"Fuck* your teachers."

My mother makes a small sound from behind closed lips.

This wouldn't be her first visit from CPS. Or even her fifth. They've been called to our various apartments many times over the years. The result was a couple of weeks where I had lunch packed for school and somewhat cleaner clothes. Only once was she subjected to drug tests—that made her angrier than anything. We moved again, and our harried social worker never reappeared.

"We don't want trouble," she murmurs to Randall.

It's so rare for my mother to stand up for me that for a moment I feel a slight flush of warmth, the last vestige of an affection that once dominated my entire life. She was everything to me, my only family and my only friend.

Then she says, "Punish her some other way."

And I remember that I fucking loathe her.

They both stand still, thinking.

Randall says, "Go get the teddy bear."

The effect is electric. My last shreds of dignity ignite.

"NOOOOO!" I howl. "No, I'll get the belt! Don't touch him! DON'T YOU FUCKING TOUCH HIM! Please! PLEEEEEEASE!"

Buttons is the only thing I have from my father. I've kept him with me through every move, everywhere we went. I've never lost him and always kept him safe.

He's missing one glass eye, and I've sewn his rips with mismatched thread. But his nubbly texture and warmth is still the most comforting thing in the world when I press him against my cheek.

Randall pins my arms behind me while I thrash and scream. I can already hear my mother's stumbling steps ascending the staircase. I hear her bumping around in my room and the thud of her knocking something over.

I'm praying she won't be able to find him. If I can get up the stairs before Randall, I'll hide him somewhere. And I won't tell them where, no matter what they do to me.

She descends a few minutes later. When I see the old bear in her arms, I let out a scream that tears my throat.

Randall holds me fast, saying to my mother, "Put him in the grate."

She opens the fire grate as I scream and beg. I don't know what I'm saying, only that I've never been more pathetic, more sniveling, weaker. I've never hated them as I do in this moment. White-hot rage burns me alive from the inside.

My mother douses my teddy bear in lighter fluid. She seems strangely sober as she does it, her eyes fixed intently on the bear.

I'm still hoping in some desperate part of my brain that this is all theater. The punishment is scaring me, making me cry.

But I know better than that.

She lights the match, the flame flaring into life with the bitter smell of sulfur. Only then does she hesitate, just for a moment. Probably because of how loud I'm screaming, like I'm being tortured, like I'll die.

"NOOOOOO! PLEASE PLEASE NOOOOOO!"

"Do it," Randall says.

She drops the match.

Buttons ignites.

I watch him burn, and I burn, too, howling with pain that feels physical, like I've truly been lit on fire right next to him.

His fur singes away. His cotton ignites. His glass eye cracks.

I've never known agony like this. I never knew how much I loved him till this moment.

Randall holds my arms, knowing I would still lunge away from him and snatch Buttons out of the fire with my bare hands.

He holds me in place until the bear is nothing but a smoking, melted ruin.

Then Randall says, "You're too old for stuffed animals."

All the love I had inside me is turned to hatred. I'd light this whole house on fire if I could. I'd burn them in their beds like they burned my bear.

I turn to my mother.

She's pretending to be drunk again, her eyes half-closed as she sways in place. Refusing to look at me.

Randall lets me return to my room.

I collapse on the bed, crying so hard that I'm sick, that I'd puke all over this bed if I'd eaten any of that spaghetti.

After twenty minutes or so, I hear them having sex. My mother sounds like an excited chihuahua, and Randall grunts like a buffalo.

I hold my pillow over my head, sobbing.

Hours later, long after dark, my mother brings me a glass of milk.

I'm shaking so hard, the bed frame rattles. "I need medicine," I croak.

I hate it, but when I don't have it, the withdrawals are even worse.

"It ran out," she says.

She keeps the bottle in her room. We both know there were thirty pills in it when we refilled the prescription earlier this week. She might have sold them to Leslie, but more likely she's been taking them herself. She thinks they help her lose weight. Randall has been pinching her belly, telling her she's getting fat.

"Call the doctor," I beg. "I can't wait two weeks."

"I already called," she says, the edge of frustration in her voice giving her away. "They won't refill it early."

I turn my face toward the wall, shivering and shaking.

I feel her sitting behind me, sullen and quiet. My mother knows what Buttons meant to me. But at the same time, she can't ever be at fault. So it's impossible that burning him was wrong.

"Randall was pretty mad," she says at last.

That's her version of an apology. Shifting the blame squarely onto someone else's shoulders.

"You could have hid him," I hiss.

That's not allowed. No one can be a victim except her.

"You know what he would have done to me!" she snaps. "But you don't care about that, do you? You don't care about anyone but yourself. You're selfish. So fucking selfish. You're the one who made him angry! You think I like coming home to that?"

She goes on in that vein for some time. I stay facing the wall, ignoring her.

She hates being ignored. When she can't get a response out of me any other way, she falls silent to regroup.

Then, her voice low and soft and entirely sober, she says, "It was just an old bear."

I turn and face her. She's wearing a *Sailor Moon* nightshirt that belongs to me. Her bare legs are tucked below the short hem. In the dim light, she looks young again, like my earliest memories of her: more beautiful than the prettiest princess in a fairy tale.

Her beauty has no effect on me anymore.

"That was all I had from my father."

Her snort jolts me. "That bear wasn't from your father."

I stare at her, too numb to understand.

She nods slowly, the edge of her mouth quirking up. "It's true. I told you that so you'd shut up about him. He didn't leave you any bear—why would he? He didn't give a fuck about you."

I thought I was at my lowest point. Turns out, there's a level even lower. A level where you stop caring about anything at all.

I turn back to the wall, waiting for her to leave.

Late in the night, when I know they're both sleeping, I creep out of bed and rescue the ruins of Buttons from the fireplace. I want to bury him, but not in Randall's garden. Instead, I walk the six blocks to Percy Park and dig a hole under the rosebushes with my hands.

I trudge back home, feeling a level of misery so heavy that I might be standing on the bottom of the ocean with nine thousand pounds of cold black water on every inch of my skin.

I don't know what hurts me more—the destruction of my bear or the loss of the one tiny connection I had to my other parent.

I used to imagine my dad might be thinking about me. Looking for me, even. I hoped he'd take me to a lovely house in some other state. Maybe he'd let me have a kitten. I'd go to school where nobody knew me, where no one knew my mom.

My mother won't tell me anything about him. She relishes the secret that only she knows, that I can never discover unless she tells me.

Enough time has passed that I no longer think he'll come find me.

Still, the bear meant something. He meant my father had loved me once, if only for a moment.

I don't even have that anymore.

When I lie down in bed without Buttons, I'm lonelier than I've ever been.

I think to myself, *There are 1,794 days until my eighteenth birthday.*

That's when I can leave. When I can run far, far away from here.

In school, we learned fish brought up from the deep pressure of the ocean will explode when they come up into lighter water. They can only stand what they're used to.

I'm leaving either way. Whether I swim or burst.

Assuming I can survive 1,794 more days.

6

COLE

THE NEXT MORNING, I WAKE EARLIER THAN USUAL, LONG BEFORE the sun is up.

Mara sleeps heavily beside me, exhausted from relating just one of the countless ugly stories from her childhood. I'm sure she could tell me one like that every day for a year and never run out.

I'm filled with an anger that sickens me, that makes my muscles shake.

I've never been furious for someone else before. Never felt this need to right the scales. To wreak vengeance on their behalf.

The fact Mara's mother and stepfather have never been punished for their rampant child abuse is an injustice that rankles like a spike jammed in my side.

The only time I've killed for someone else was when I spiked Michael Bridger's drink, drove him home, and left his car running in the garage. Even then, I was telling Mara the truth: it was mostly for myself. I was tired of Sonia showing up to work puffy-eyed and exhausted, distracted by streams of calls and text messages from her fuckwit ex and his rapacious lawyer.

Maybe an infinitesimal portion of pity influenced my decision. If so, it was unconscious.

I'm a selfish person. I always have been. I've always been alone. No one to look out for my interests but me.

Even now, the things I do for Mara are really for me. I like the way she looks dressed in gorgeous clothes. I like watching her eat ice cream. I like the way she melts under my touch. I like that I have the power to further her career. It feels just and right when she gets the attention she deserves because she's fucking talented and her art is far more interesting than the shit churned out by commercial-minded egoists like Shaw.

Everything I do for her binds her closer to me. I want her dependent on me so she can never leave. So she never even wants to.

Mara is distracted by everything beautiful, everything interesting. I have to be *more* interesting, *more* useful to keep her attention.

When I have her focus, her energy surges into me. She fills me with life.

I can't lose her. I can't go back to numbness and boredom.

Which puts me in a dilemma.

I want her parents punished. But Mara is vehemently opposed to revenge. She doesn't even want to kill Shaw, which has locked us in a bizarre three-way stalemate.

I hate how she binds my hands. And yet I know Mara's stubbornness. Her boundaries are not where they should be, but they do exist. If I cross a hard line with her, I risk severing the fragile ties between us. She'll bolt, and I may never capture her again.

I slip out from under the covers, careful not to jolt her. Mara lets out a sleepy sigh. I tuck the blankets around her so she stays warm and cocooned.

Her laptop sits on the dining room table. It's a piece-of-shit Lenovo—yet another thing I should replace for her. I hate when Mara touches anything shitty or cheap.

I open the lid, then let out an irritated tsk when I see she has no password protection. It only takes me a moment to open her email.

She told me she has her mother blocked on every social media platform, and Mara hasn't shared her phone number in years. But

Tori Eldritch still emails her, the messages piling up in a folder Mara never reads.

I knew the messages were here. The volume surprises me.

There are hundreds of emails. Thousands, even. The blue dots show that Mara hasn't opened a single one.

I read through them.

Thousands of messages, each basically the same: threats, insults, and above all, guilt trips.

How could you? I'm your mother. What kind of daughter abandons her family? After everything I did for you. You're ungrateful. You're selfish. You're so dramatic. You think you had it hard? It's your own fault. Who do you think you are? You think you're an artist? Don't make me laugh. Everything you do is for attention. You have no talent, no brains. You're lazy. You're the reason I'm divorced. You're the reason your father left. You were a mistake. Everything bad that ever happened in my life is because of you. I should have aborted you. I was driving to the clinic to do it, do you know that? God I wish I could go back to that day. I'd be doing the world a favor. I'm so ashamed of you. You should be ashamed of yourself. The way you dress, the way you behave. You're a slut, a whore. No wonder men use you and throw you away. No one will ever love you. No one will ever want you. You're immature. Worthless. You don't deserve happiness, and you'll never get it. You're disgusting. You repulse me. This is why you've never had friends. This is why everyone hates you. You think you're pretty? With that face and that body? You're a scarecrow. A fucking mutant. You'll never be beautiful like me. You take after your father and he was hideous. You're disgusting just like him. I'll never understand how you came out of me. I carried you for nine months. You destroyed my figure, my tits have never been the same. You were a massive baby, they had to tear you out of me. You almost killed me. You owe me. You fucking owe me.

On and on, page after page. Sometimes they're rambling and misspelled, (particularly the emails sent late at night), and sometimes they're long eloquent paragraphs recounting mistakes Mara made, times she embarrassed herself. The piano recital is mentioned several times, how she humiliated her mother in front of everyone, how she did it on purpose.

This woman's pettiness could fuel a dictatorship. She's Castro and Stalin and Mussolini all rolled into one. Nothing is her fault. Mara is the architect of all evil in the world.

Her hatred for her own daughter baffles me.

I assume some of it is jealousy. Like Snow White and the Wicked Queen, Mara grew in beauty and vitality while Tori was fading by the day.

And some of it is pure rage that Mara refused to be crushed, refused to be destroyed. Mara was the insect Tori stomped on over and over and over, only for Mara to turn into a butterfly and fly far away.

I'm so distracted by the emails that I fail to see the motion alert on my phone. Mara rises and dresses, padding down the stairs while I'm still deeply absorbed in reading.

"What are you doing?"

I look up from the laptop. I must have an awful expression on my face because Mara takes a step back, her eyes widening.

It's hard for me to speak.

"I was reading your mother's emails."

"Oh," Mara says.

She isn't angry.

We each have our own brand of relentless curiosity. She knows me too well to expect privacy or reasonable behavior.

"They're all the same," Mara says. "She can't stop insulting me even when she's trying to get me to come visit."

"She wants you to visit?" I scoff.

"When she found out where I lived, she showed up at my apartment. I wouldn't let her in, so she broke in the next day when I was at work. Went through all my things. Read my journal."

"You have a journal?"

I'm just as nosy as her mother. Worse, probably.

Mara snorts. "Not anymore. I moved the next week. She can't stand not knowing where I am. Not having control over me. Not having the power to fuck up my life. She used to show up at my job, trying to get me fired…" She laughs softly to herself. "Actually, you two have a lot in common. You might really get along."

"Oh, fuck off. First of all, I'm way better at finding people than she is. She *wishes* she had my skills. And second, I don't fuck up your life—I fix it."

"I know," Mara says, her expression serious. "I'm grateful, Cole."

"You better be. I'm taking you to Betsy's party tonight."

"Are you really?" she squeaks. Then, her excitement fading, she says, "What about Shaw?"

"He'll probably be there."

"What does that mean? What will we do?"

"Nothing in the middle of a gallery. And neither will he. It's safe."

"I don't want to see him, though." Mara shudders.

"We can't avoid him in the city. Besides, I want him to see that you're living with me, if he doesn't already know. I want him to see you under my protection. If we talk to him, I'll make him believe there's a truce. That I'll leave him alone as long as he stays away from you."

"Will you?" Mara asks, her fog-gray eyes fixed on my face.

"Never."

Shaw is a threat. There's no fucking way I'll ever relax enough for him to put a knife in my back or Mara's.

It's then that I realize Mara is wearing her old clothes—jeans and her favorite battered boots. "Where do you think you're going?"

"Sweet Maple."

"The fuck you are."

"I'm working this morning, and you're not stopping me," she says, her jaw set. "You can come along if you like, but I'm doing the full brunch shift."

"What the hell are you talking about? You don't need a side job anymore."

"I'm not doing it for the money. I owe it to Arthur."

"He can find another waitress," I say dismissively.

Mara crosses her arms over her chest, refusing to back down. "My last year of high school, I applied to the Academy of Art. I spent that entire year working on my portfolio. The week I was supposed to submit it, my mother threw it in the tub and soaked it in bleach. Then she cleaned out the twelve hundred dollars I had hidden inside a book in my room. She thought I couldn't leave if I had no money and no scholarship.

"I left anyway, the day I turned eighteen. I bounced around a few couches, halfway to homeless. When I showed up at Sweet Maple, I had a backpack of clothes and six dollars to my name. No résumé. Hadn't taken a shower in a week. My sneakers had holes big enough for my toes to poke through. Arthur hired me anyway. He gave me two hundred dollars up front so I could buy some better shoes. I bought these boots." Mara sticks out one foot, showing the boots that look like they've been through a war.

"He didn't know me. Didn't know if I'd take the money and never show up for a shift. He helped me anyway. So I'm not ever quitting that job, until Arthur doesn't need me anymore."

"All right, all right." I hold up my hands. "I'll drive you over."

Flushed with victory, Mara grins at me. "Can I drive?"

7

MARA

It feels good to be back at Sweet Maple. This place has been my anchor through some of the most chaotic times in my life.

So has Arthur. He may be the only man who's ever done something kind for me without trying to put his hand on my ass afterward.

"There she is." Arthur chucks my apron directly into my face. "You know you're in the paper this morning?"

"I am?"

He tosses that at me, too, already helpfully folded to the right page.

It's an article in the arts section of the *Chronicle*. Just two columns on the bottom of a page, but it includes a large color photograph of *The Mercy of Men* and a smaller picture of me, lifted off my Instagram.

This is Cole's doing, I'm sure.

He's constantly working behind the scenes, pushing me into the spotlight. He seems to get more pleasure out of grabbing attention for me than for himself.

I try to catch his eye, where he's seated himself at the farthest corner table, but true to his word, he's not distracting me and is only quietly taking out his laptop like any normal business bruncher. Assuming that person just so happened to look like an off-duty supermodel in a cashmere button-down.

Arthur raises a grizzled eyebrow. "Isn't that your other boss over there?"

"Yes."

"I could be wrong, but…didn't you drive into work together? Quite early in the morning?"

I can feel my face flaming while I try to maintain a dignified expression. "I've been staying with him."

"What?" Arthur cries with mock surprise. "How did that happen? When you weren't even trying to date him…"

I take back everything nice I said before. Arthur is the fucking worst. "We're not dating. It's…complicated."

"It always is." Arthur nods wisely.

I throw myself into the business of waiting tables so I can avoid further interrogation.

Arthur is not going to be repressed that easily. He's in a shockingly chipper mood, whipped into something approximating actual happiness at the prospect of teasing me all shift long.

This is catnip to Cole.

He immediately shoves his laptop to the side so he can gang up with Arthur against me.

I'm actually quite fucking busy, as Sweet Maple hasn't stopped being delicious. The sidewalk tables are crowded with people clamoring for bacon.

Meanwhile, Arthur has completely abandoned his duties and is sitting with Cole, laughing and chatting like old friends. One thousand percent for sure discussing every intimate detail of my life that I'm heartily regretting sharing with either of them.

As I carry a backbreaking load of mimosas past them, I hear Cole saying, "I'm setting up a show for Mara in December. You should come. I'll put your name on the list…"

The thought of Arthur coming to see my new series is too much to bear.

The more intimate and personal my work, the more it frightens me for other people to see it. Especially people who know me.

I'd rather strangers view it. They won't recognize how I've opened myself, guts and all, laying myself bare across the canvas.

It feels good to work for money again, in a direct exchange where a tray of food equals a five-dollar tip. I'm puffing and sweating, but in a nice way. The way of good, honest labor.

Cole has never had to work a menial job. That's why money's only an abstract concept to him. He knows its power and wields it like a weapon, but he has no attachment to it. Money comes easily, and he can always get more.

I don't know if his way is better than mine.

Cole will never feel the thrill of opening a billfold and seeing a twenty-dollar tip on a fifty-dollar bill.

One thing I know for sure about myself: wherever I go in life, however rich I become, I'm always going to tip big. I know what it means to the server, how it can change their whole day or even their week.

Another useful thing about waitressing: you're too busy to worry about anything else for long. I can't stress over what Cole might be telling Arthur when I have ten tables shouting requests.

The six-hour shift flies by in a moment.

Soon the tables are clearing out once more, Cole has eaten the meal I ordered for him, and Arthur has drunk way too many cups of coffee. He interrupts me as I start my closing duties. "You don't need to bother with that."

I keep rolling clean cutlery into napkins. "What the fuck are you talking about? You used to chew a strip off me if I didn't roll up every last fork in this place."

Arthur taps a heavy finger on the newspaper article still resting on the table next to me. "I'm sure you've got better things to do with your time."

My stomach squirms. I don't want to hear whatever he's trying to say. I keep rolling cutlery, stubbornly refusing to look at him or the newspaper article.

Arthur rests his hand on my shoulder.

I don't know if he's ever touched me before. His hand is heavy, calloused, warm. It lies on my shoulder like a blessing. "I'm proud of you, Mara."

I look up into his wrinkled face, at his faded brown eyes behind their thick smudged lenses.

I want to say something back to him, but my throat is too tight.

Arthur murmurs, "You're really doing it, Mara. And look, whether you want to date this guy or not, take his help. Take as much as you can get. Don't be proud—be successful. You deserve it."

I put my hand over his on my shoulder, holding it in place so he can't let go.

My eyes burn, his wrinkled face swimming before my view. "Why do I feel like you're firing me?"

"You'll always have a home here," he says. "But I don't want to hold you back. Not even for a Saturday morning. You don't need this place anymore."

I've worked at Sweet Maple for six years. Other jobs, I quit or lost, but this one was always here. Arthur was always here.

"Come back to eat breakfast with everyone else who's rich and famous and doesn't have to carry a tray."

"The best people carry trays," I say ferociously. "You carry a tray."

"I will if you come eat," he says, squeezing my shoulder once more before letting go.

I leave quickly so Arthur won't see me cry. Tears run down my face, hot and fluid, like there won't be any end to them.

Cole chases after me, still stuffing his laptop back in his bag. "Mara!" he cries. "What's wrong?"

I wheel on him, furious. "What did you say to him? *What did you say to Arthur?*"

Cole grabs me by the shoulders, forcing me to stop. I was running away from him down the tree-lined street, and I'm still torn between the impulse to shout at him or flee.

My life is hurtling down this new path, and I don't know if I want it. It looks like a dream, but it's mixed up with a nightmare.

Cole's beautiful face is set in an expression of concern, but I know what he is. I know what he's done. Am I insane to think he cares about me?

Arthur cares. But now Arthur is pushing me away because there's no place for my old life in my new one. I can't be the Mara I always was, poor and desperate, *and* this new Mara, replete with money and success.

Cole forces me to look at him. Into those dark eyes that have always been the real window inside him. "Why do you hate when I talk to Arthur? Why are you worried about what I'll say to him? Or him to me?"

My face crumples. I cover it with my hands, ashamed. "I don't know." I sob. "I'm not used to people saying nice things about me."

Cole wraps his arms around me, pulling me close against his chest. He's warm and strong, his heart a metronome that never falters.

He tilts my chin up so I'll look at him. So I'll know he's telling the truth.

"Mara, I'll never tear you down to other people. I'll never degrade you. I want to build you up. Do you understand that?"

I never knew until this moment that I believed every conversation about me had to be negative. It had to be an airing of all my mistakes, all my flaws. What else could they talk about?

"I thought you told him to fire me," I admit.

"Why would I do that? We made an agreement. You can work here as long as you want, if you don't mind me camping out in the corner. It's not just to protect you. I have to be around you. You fuel me. You light me up inside. Just knowing you're in the house enlivens me. I can't go back to the way I was before. I'm afraid of it."

I've never heard Cole talk this way before. I've never seen his face so naked, so exposed. Not blank and emotionless—raw and confused. I look in his eyes and see he's telling me the truth: he's afraid of losing me.

No one's ever been afraid of losing me.

No one wanted me in the first place.

I turn my face into Cole's chest, letting his arms envelop me. Letting him hold me tight.

"I don't want to go back either," I say.

That night, Cole takes me to Betsy's party at her Jackson Street gallery.

I squirm nervously in the passenger seat of the car, worried we're going to see Shaw tonight.

"Maybe he won't come," Cole says. "That cop's still poking around. He came to the studio this morning. Did I tell you that?"

I shake my head.

"Janice didn't let him upstairs, but he made himself such a nuisance that Sonia had to come talk to him. He's insisting on meeting with me later this week."

"Meeting with *you*?" I frown. "What for?"

"He pretended like it was all ticking boxes. But I'm pretty sure he's running his own investigation, separate from what the SFPD thinks they're doing."

I know Cole has been keeping tabs on it all through a casual acquaintance in the vice department.

I remember Officer Hawks. I remember his perfectly polished shoes, his neat haircut and black-framed glasses. This is a man who ticks boxes. A man who notices small details and doesn't leave a job half-done.

"He's perceptive," I tell Cole. "Not like that first idiot who interviewed me. Don't underestimate him."

"I don't underestimate anyone. I'm not as arrogant as you think."

"But you don't think Shaw will be there tonight."

Cole shrugs. "If he's smart, he's lying low. And besides, he killed four girls, one more than usual. He should be satiated."

I don't like Erin being grouped in as one of the four, like she's just another grape on the stem shoveled into Shaw's mouth. Erin had talent—she made watercolors so beautiful, you could weep. She was funny and blunt. She loved to tease me and Frank, but never to the point of actually hurting our feelings.

She loved her life. Shaw had no fucking right to take it from her.

All those other girls could have been just as unique, just as wonderful, if I'd had the chance to know them.

"I want that cop to catch him," I say. "I want him to rot in a cell for a hundred years."

Cole doesn't bother to reply. We both know his opinion on the subject.

We're pulling up to the gallery. The line stretches all the way down the street. People crane toward the windows, several girls trying to take pictures through the glass.

"Why's it so busy?" I ask Cole.

It was supposed to be a cocktail party, nothing out of the ordinary.

Cole marches right up to the doors. He's probably never waited in a line in his life.

Betsy Voss waves us inside. She's bouncing with excitement, her body as buoyant as her lacquered bouffant hair. "Come in, come in! You've got to see this, Cole. You're going to love it!"

♫ *"Venom"—Little Simz*

The entire gallery space is filled from top to bottom, wall to wall, with a brilliant Technicolor spiderweb. The thick strands are woven up and down, all around, with large enough gaps that the guests can walk through, clambering in and under the installation. You're forced to interact with it, to grip and touch the thick ropes. The puffy, loose-woven wool manages to look sticky and dripping but also soft and enticing. The eye-searing shades of magenta, lemon, and teal are so vivid and wet that the strands might have been spray-painted via some sort of pressure cannon.

The aggressive color envelops you, making your eyes burn and your head spin. You're trapped inside a rainbow prism that seems to go on and on forever, disorienting and intoxicating.

Cole stares around at the installation, not touching anything.

We both know the architect of this piece. The signature colors give it away. But it's nothing I could have imagined from him.

"Guess he's not lying low," I murmur to Cole.

Cole is silent. I think I know why.

Cole's disdain for Shaw has been apparent since before I met either of them. He's never spoken of Shaw's work with any level of respect.

But for the first time, Shaw has created something truly impressive. Something even Cole can't deny.

It's slapping us right in the face.

Marcus York comes bustling up to Cole, his frizzy orange hair puffing out on both sides like a clown wig, an impression not helped by York's short legs and too-tight waistcoat stretched across his belly.

"Oh, ho, Cole, someone's putting you on notice!"

"What?" Cole snaps irritably.

"This is Shaw's bid for the sculpture in Corona Heights Park! If chosen, he'll do a larger version of this. I haven't received your design yet. The deadline is this week…"

"I know the deadline," Cole hisses.

"Well, better hurry." York's eyes glint wickedly. "You'll have to come up with something good to beat this…"

York hurries away again, probably spurred by the murderous look on Cole's face.

My own feelings of repulsion are so strong that I find it hard to speak. I feel exactly as Shaw intended: enveloped in this web, trapped by it, screamed at from all sides.

Cole says, "He would never have had the confidence to do something like this before."

"What do you mean?"

"Everything Shaw has ever made is commercial." Cole gestures around at the brilliant dripping ropes. "You can't sell this. It's an experience."

I nod slowly. "He's leveling up."

As if summoned by those words, Alastor Shaw strides toward us.

He navigates the web with confidence, easily maneuvering his bulk through the fluorescent strands.

Shaw glows with health and happiness. His golden hair, rich tan, and shining white teeth beam at us. His shoulders seem a mile wide as he stretches his arms open, greeting us in his booming voice. "Mara! Cole! So glad to see you!"

He's so loud that a dozen people turn to observe our meeting. Camera flashes wink at us. Everyone loves a tête-à-tête between their two favorite rivals.

We're frozen in place. Trapped in his web. Watching the spider approach, grinning at us both.

"Cole." Shaw slaps Cole on both shoulders, with a loud sound that feels like a detonation. "My oldest friend. Look at you. You know the thing I love about you? You're unchanging. Your principles, unwavering. That must be what Mara loves about you, too."

While I still don't know everything about the dynamic between these two, I understand the barb all too well.

Shaw abducted me as a provocation. To tempt Cole into breaking his own rules.

And it worked. God how it worked. Cole is breaking every rule for me, and I, for him.

We've ensnared each other, more deeply than Shaw could ever have dreamed.

Cole *is* changing. And Shaw is mocking Cole's pretensions of discipline and stability. I see how his words dig under Cole's skin.

Cole stands silent—it's too true to refute.

Now Shaw turns toward me. It's my turn for a blast of his smug sarcasm.

"Mara." His face twists in an expression of mock sorrow. "I heard about your friend. Erin, wasn't it? You know she and I had a fling once. She was quite the wildcat." He winks at me. "You know what I mean."

His pretend pout turns into a lascivious grin.

I'm boiling with anger. Shaking with it.

How fucking *dare* he talk about Erin to me. How dare he stand here, flushed with happiness and triumph. Gloating right to my face, in front of everyone.

I look at Cole, expecting him to say something. Expecting him to cut Shaw down to size with some devastating retort.

He's silent, the garish colors of Shaw's web reflecting on his pale face, in his dark eyes. For the first time, Cole has no response. Because for the first time, Shaw truly has the upper hand.

Raising his voice a little louder so everyone can hear, Shaw says to me, "And don't worry, Mara. I forgive you for pointing the finger at me. You must have been in a terrible mental state after how brutally your friend died, in agony. What you must have felt, finding her there in your bed... No hard feelings from me. It's all water under the bridge."

All his shots fired, and every one landing right on target, Shaw gives us one last aggressive "good to see you both," and strolls away.

His departure feels like a vise around my skull finally releasing. I can breathe again, but I'm shaking harder than ever.

I'm sick. Furious. Choking on everything I wanted to shout at Shaw that I had to stuff down inside instead.

Everything about him enrages me, from his taunts to his gloating grin. Even now I'm surrounded by the excited babble of guests interacting with Shaw's triumphant vast installation.

Why should Shaw get to experience a night like this when he's taken so many lives and caused so much pain for everyone else? He doesn't deserve this.

Cole looks at me. "Are you ready to kill him yet?"

My fingers itch with violent impulses. My mind runs wild, too far and too fast for me to rein it in. "I'm damn sure getting closer. Right now, I might be angry enough to do it. But you told me what it does to you. How it changes you. Breaks you away from humanity."

"Good," Cole hisses, jerking his head toward the throngs of people fawning around Shaw. "Why do you want to be like them? A blind fucking sheep?"

I can't take my eyes off Shaw surrounded by admirers, bathed in his own private golden glow.

This motherfucker killed my friend, and don't forget, he abducted me, too, cut my wrists, pierced my fucking nipples. He's living flagrantly, joyfully, rubbing it right in our faces. He can kill anyone he wants, do anything he wants.

"I want revenge," I mutter. "But I don't want to take it. I always said I'd rise above. I swore it."

For the longest time after I left my mother's house, I was tormented by anger. I'd run away from her and Randall, but the memories of everything they'd ever said to me, done to me, came along with me, jammed in my head. I couldn't get them out.

The longer I was away from her, the more I realized how wrong it all was. How monumentally fucked up.

I wanted them to pay.

My mother's always gotten away with everything. CPS came to our house, summoned by teachers who reported the bruises on my body and the lack of food in my lunch. My mother cleaned the house and bought groceries for a week until they went away again. She was pulled over multiple times for DUIs, but she got the fines reduced or charges dropped on technicalities, on overcrowded dockets, by begging and pleading and deploying her best sob stories.

She brought men into my life and me into theirs. Not just Randall—a succession of assholes of every flavor: drug dealers, ex-convicts, and even a fucking neo-Nazi who pushed hand-printed copies of *American Renaissance* and the Daily Stormer into my hands.

While Randall wasn't the first one who put his hands on my mother (or on me), the devastation she wreaked on their lives was always greater than anything they did to her.

She's sailed through life unpunished, unrepentant.

The worst people are free to maim and defame however they like. There's no justice. No fairness.

Cole and I intended to stay at the party for several hours, to network with the dozens of Cole's acquaintances all around us, but neither of us can stand Shaw's malevolent glee or the omnipresent discussion of his work. To say nothing of the Technicolor spiderweb wrapped all around us.

We leave a few minutes later.

We're both silent on the drive back to the house, Cole gripping the wheel with a rigid expression, and me replaying every taunt Shaw threw at me.

You know we had a fling once…

Don't worry, Mara. I forgive you…

You must have been in a terrible mental state…

The moment we step inside, into the dark, cool interior of the house, the tension between us snaps. Cole jumps on me, and I, on him.

♫ *"Black Out Days"—Phantogram*

He tears off the deep-plum gown I was wearing, ripping the straps so the expensive beading scatters across the hardwood floor.

I attack him back just as hard, yanking open his shirt, ripping the material, losing the buttons.

We're kissing each other with more than passion. We're exorcising our anger, our resentment, our fear, and our rage.

It's not directed at Cole, and it's not directed at me. It's a swirling dark energy between us. A bitterness that has to burn out before it consumes us both.

Cole hasn't even gotten my dress all the way off when he throws me over the arm of the couch and takes me from behind. He wraps his hand in the long rope of my hair, jerking my head back, using it as reins while he mounts me and rides me hard.

He's fucking me ruthlessly, roughly, the slap of his hips against my ass punctuated by actual slaps from his hand.

"More," I moan. "Harder."

I deserve this.

My guilt over Erin can only be assuaged by punishment. I want to be spanked harder, faster, meaner. I need the sadist in Cole. I need the psychopath.

Cole obliges.

He forces me onto my knees, the back of my head against the arm of the couch. He shoves his cock into my mouth, my head pinned, with no way to escape.

He holds my head between both his hands, fucking my mouth. His cock is ironhard and relentless, tunneling into my throat. I'm choking on it, drooling around it, trying to steal gasps of breath before he drills into me again.

There's something so satisfying in this. Something I deeply need but have never been able to ask for before.

The more I come to trust Cole, to believe he won't actually hurt me, the more I want him to push the line.

This is the broken, fucked-up part of myself, the part that's furious over every time I was hurt or used but still craves the freedom to seek out roughness and even violence when I want it, on my terms.

I'm a tree that grew in cruel wind, twisted and bent by it. Sex and violence, passion and intensity, are inextricably entwined for me. I can't have one without the other. Right or wrong doesn't come into it—I am the way life made me.

This is the only thing that satisfies: biting, clawing, scratching, struggling. Cole and I fuck on the couch, on the floor. He slams me against the wall, bodily lifting me off the ground.

I need to experience his strength, his power, his ruthlessness, because that's what I need in a man. It's the only way I feel safe. He has to terrify me so I know he'll terrify everyone else. I've never met a real hero; I don't think they exist. Only a monster can protect me.

We're fucking in the dark so we can unleash the demons inside us.

Anguished sounds come out of me: sometimes sobbing and sometimes begging for more.

Our clothes are all gone now, torn to ribbons on the floor. Cole's back is a mass of scratches, his skin under my nails. His teeth marks print my shoulders and breasts.

Still, I moan in his ear, "Don't stop. I need more…"

"You fucking lunatic—I'll kill you," Cole snarls. "You don't know what I have in me…"

"Show me. You promised to show me."

He throws me on the floor so hard that the air slams out of me and stars speckle his ceiling.

He climbs on top of me, our bodies slick with sweat. It drips from the inky tips of his hair, from the sharp planes of his jaw. It splashes on my face and my breasts. I open my mouth to taste the salt on my tongue, and then I lick it off his throat. I want his sweat and his come all over me. I want to be filthy.

He rams his cock inside me. The harder he fucks me, the harder he gets. His cock is on fire; I feel it burning all the way up inside. My wetness could be pussy or blood; I don't fucking care anymore.

I look up into his face and see the naked Cole, that real, true creature: Eyes as black as pits, always burning. Face as beautiful as sin. Mouth forever hungry, swallowing me whole.

This is Cole unleashed. Full of fury and passion and hunger. His control was always an illusion. The real Cole takes what he wants.

He's taking me here and now. Pounding me into this floor. Fucking me mercilessly.

And still he wants more; I can see it in those eyes. He wants something from me that I still haven't given.

His hands close around my throat.

At first I think he'll only squeeze for a moment, the way he's done before: cutting off blood flow so my head spins and my pussy throbs. Turning sex into delirium.

This time he doesn't stop. He only squeezes harder.

"Stop," I gasp. Then, more frantic: "*Stop!*"

The word comes out in a croak. My throat is too constricted for speech. No air, no blood can get through.

Still, he chokes me.

He's looking down into my face, his eyes dark and pitiless.

I try to knock his arms away, but they might as well be iron bars welded in place. His hands compress relentlessly, applying real pressure now, real weight.

Black moths flutter into view: first one, then dozens, blocking my sight.

I'm hitting at his arms, scratching, clawing. Trying to tear his fingers off my throat.

I'm too weak and he's too strong. I'm helpless in his grasp, floating, slamming back into my body, floating again.

Cole speaks, and I can't see his lips moving, but I hear that insistent low voice burying into my brain:

"This is what it will feel like if you wait for Shaw to finish the job. This is what it will feel like when he's on top of you. This is what it will feel like to die as a victim."

"*Stop it! Stop fucking around!*" The words are a rasp, a whisper.

It doesn't matter if he hears them or not: Cole isn't fucking around. He's never been more serious.

He chokes me harder. Fucks me harder. Holds me there while he beats the lesson into me.

"This is your way, isn't it? Hoping for mercy? Never fighting back? Trying to do the right thing? You want to be a good person…good people die every day, Mara. Goodness never saves them."

I'm clawing at his arms, desperate and dying. Black moths carry me away…

He's looking down into my face, as cruel as Shaw while he taunts me.

"Do you want to be a victim, or you want to be a fighter? I thought you were a fighter, Mara."

I *am* fighting—I'm hitting him with all my strength—but it's not enough. I'm only a girl, a skinny girl; it'll never be enough against a man…

I hate that I'm small. I hate that I'm weak.

The anger, the hurt, the goddamned fucking unfairness wells inside me. I'm the volcano now; I'm the fucking lava.

It bursts out of me in a howl so raw, so animalistic that I don't even realize Cole has let go of my throat. I'm screaming right in his face:

"I HATE HIM! I HATE HIM! I HATE THEM ALL! I WANT THEM ALL FUCKING DEAD!"

I'm sitting up now. I don't know when that happened.

My throat is raw, my shrieks still echoing through the house.

Cole watches me, calm and satisfied.

He got what he wanted.

I wait for the guilt and shame to wash over me, but I feel nothing. Only the hot throbbing of my throat.

Cole lays his hand on my head, gently stroking my hair. "It's all right, Mara. It's always better to tell the truth. Lie to the world but not to yourself."

8

COLE

I FINALLY GOT MARA to crack and admit what I'd known all along.

After that, I back off for a while.

We don't talk about what she said or what we're going to do about it. I don't want to risk her retreating into familiarity, back into what feels safe.

What *feels* safe and what will actually keep you safe are quite different.

It's not difficult to distract ourselves from the problem of Shaw.

Both Mara and I are continually pulled into our work so deeply that the rest of the world disappears around us.

Mara is painting a new series for the private show I'm throwing her in December.

I'm finalizing my design for Corona Heights Park.

I sketch it out first, and then I build a scale model that I'll deliver to Marcus York.

I visit Mara in her studio to see how her latest painting is coming along.

She's got her hair piled on her head with several paintbrushes jammed into the bun to fix it in place. Her face and arms are liberally streaked with color, her overalls so battered and stained that I can't tell if they were originally black or dark denim. She's got the legs rolled up to mid-shin, her feet bare beneath, paint on her toes.

She smells of linen and flaxseed oil with an edge of turpentine. For this series and the last one, Mara has used oil paints, not acrylic. The paint dries slowly over several days, so the pigment is malleable. She stacks transparent layers to create deep shadows or the impression of light glowing from within. She blends shades for seamless transitions.

Her technique improves by the day.

Her previous series was mostly photorealistic. This new series blends high-detail figures with scenery that melts and fades like the edges of a memory. It gives a soft, rotting effect, as if the whole painting is beset by decay soaking through the canvas.

This particular piece shows a young girl in a nightgown walking down a placid suburban street. The roses on the hedges are past their bloom, brown at the edges. A charred teddy bear trails from one of the girl's hands. Behind her, a half dozen birds have fallen dead from the sky. Beneath her slippered feet, the grass withers.

"What are you going to call this one?"

"I'm not sure." Mara rubs the back of her hand across her cheek. This leaves a fresh smear of pale pink along her jaw—the pink of the roses, which Mara is touching up in the lower right corner of the canvas.

"What about…*The Burial?*"

Mara nods slowly. "I like that."

I'm looking at one of the fallen birds pitifully lying on its back with its wings splayed.

"What?" Mara says.

"I don't like that orange on the robin's breast. It's too bright. Clashes with the roses."

Mara squints at the robin, then at the roses, comparing the shades.

"You might be right," she grudgingly admits. "Here, tone it down. Make it a little dustier."

She holds out a paintbrush to me.

"You're going to let me touch your robin? You almost bit my head off last time I came near your painting."

"Well, you did pick my favorite design for Corona Heights."

It was my favorite, too. Mara inspired the design, in a sense. Her enthusiasm spurred me to build the model so I can bring it to York this afternoon, right before the deadline.

I'd been debating whether I even wanted to enter. I still don't like the idea of having to outsource the construction.

I add a little brown to the robin's breast, dulling the orange until it almost matches the edges of the rose petals.

Mara examines my work. "That's better."

Our heads are close together.

Unconsciously, Mara's hand slips into mine. I turn my mouth into the side of her neck, kissing her at the junction of her shoulder. Her scent, laced with turpentine, makes my head spin.

"Do you want to come see the model?" I ask her.

"Of course!"

She drops her brushes in a pot of solvent to soak before wiping her hands on a rag. My own hand is paint smeared where she touched me. Instead of washing it, I let the streak of dusty pink dry on my skin.

Mara follows me down the hall to the studio I've been using on this same floor. I don't like it as much as my private space, but sometimes it's good to make a change. There's something energizing about the constant bustle of people in this building—the whistle of Sonia's kettle, Janice's snorting laugh, the chatter of other artists meeting by the stairs, and the thud of Mara's music leaking from under her door.

Mara asks, "Isn't Officer Hawks coming to talk to you today?"

"Oh, fuck, I forgot about that."

I'm debating whether I should tell Sonia to cancel it. I don't want to waste even ten minutes talking to him. On the other hand, it would be stupid to miss the opportunity to observe the detective while he's interrogating me.

I push open the door to my own studio, which takes up half the floor on the opposite end of the building to Mara.

Our studios are equally bright and sunlit, but in truth, Mara has the better view. Hers looks out over the park, while I'm facing the busy intersection of Clay and Steiner. It doesn't matter—I'm here for the view down the hall.

Mara strides directly over to the model, not waiting for me to close the door.

"It's going to be incredible," she breathes.

She looks down over the black glass labyrinth. The smooth, sheer walls will be glossy and reflective. The maze includes a dozen routes, but only one will take you all the way through. The correct pathway is hidden within the walls. The openings can only be found by standing at just the right angle or running your hands along the dark glass to feel where it breaks.

"I hope they choose your design. I want to see this built."

"So do I," I admit.

Mara looks up into my face, her eyes bright with excitement. "They will. They'll choose you."

I could probably strong-arm York into doing it, but I won't. My art is the one area where I don't manipulate. My work will live or die on its own merit.

My phone buzzes in my pocket with a text from Sonia:

The cop is here.

He's early—even more annoying than being late.

I stuff the phone back in my pocket. "I've got to go talk to Hawks."

"Should I come?" Mara's expression is strained.

"No need. I'll handle it. Keep working."

Officer Hawks waits downstairs next to Janice's desk. He's not the lead detective on the case—that's an older officer named Potts. But according to my sources, the SFPD has egg on their face from all the young female bodies stacking up on their beaches. There's a good chance Potts is about to get the boot and Hawks will be promoted. A fact of which he's probably well aware.

That's why he's here at my studio, digging into every possible lead.

I pause at the base of the stairs, examining him before I step into view.

When he interviewed Mara, he wore the standard navy uniform with his gold badge pinned upon his breast.

Today he's dressed in plain clothes: button-up shirt, slacks, and a sport coat. That could mean he's off duty. Or only trying to put me at ease—trying to make me think this meeting is a formality, not an interview.

In the plain tan jacket and Buddy Holly glasses, he looks a bit like a professor. Only the haircut gives him away—too fresh, too short, and too presidential. Our boy Hawks is ambitious. That's the haircut of someone who wants a promotion badly.

He was polite to Mara when he interviewed her. Which means I don't have to hunt him down off-hours. At least not yet.

I step out into the lobby, striding toward him. "Officer Hawks."

"Mr. Blackwell." He holds out his hand to shake mine.

Sometimes I don't shake hands; sometimes I do. It depends on which response I want to elicit.

In this case, I take the proffered hand. Hawks's shake is firm, right on the edge of aggressive. He gives me a sharp look through the clear lenses of his glasses.

I keep my expression calm and relaxed. I already showed Hawks my teeth when he had Mara locked in an interrogation room. Today I'm all politeness.

"We can speak in here." I lead him into a conference room on the ground floor. I have no intention of allowing Hawks any deeper into the building.

"Is Mara here, too?" Hawks inquires pleasantly.

"She has a studio on the fourth floor."

That's not exactly an answer, something Hawks notes as well, his eyes flicking fractionally toward the ceiling before settling on my face. "I heard she's living with you now."

"That's right."

"How long have you two been dating?"

"It's hard to put a time frame on these things. You know how intangible a relationship can be. The art world is small. We've been in the same circle for some time, orbiting each other."

I'm evasive on purpose. I say nothing that can be contradicted or disproven. Hawks will notice this, too, but I don't care. I want to annoy him. I want to push him to tip his cards.

I gesture to the conference table, with its assortment of mid-century modern chairs, deliberately mismatched. Hawks takes a seat directly across from me.

He's not taking notes, but I have no doubt he'll remember everything I say, and probably write it down afterward.

"Did you ever meet Erin Wahlstrom?" Hawks asks.

"Once or twice. Like I said, it's an insular industry. I'm sure we attended the same parties and events."

"Did you ever see Erin with Alastor Shaw?"

"Yes. I saw them talking the night of Oasis."

"Shaw said he and Erin had sex in the stairwell."

I shrug. "I wasn't present for that."

"Did you see them leave the show together?"

"No."

"Did you see Shaw leave at all?"

"No."

"What was the last time you saw him?"

"I have no idea. There's more wine than art at those things."

"Did you see Mara there?"

I hesitate a fraction of a second, distracted by the vivid image of the first time I laid eyes on her. I see the wine splashing across her dress, soaking into the cotton, dark as blood.

"Well?" Hawks prompts me, leaning forward, his blue eyes keen behind his glasses.

"Yes, I saw her. Only for a moment, early in the night."

"But you didn't see her leave."

"No."

Hawks lets the silence stretch between us. This is an age-old technique, to encourage me to add on to my statement. To get me babbling.

I keep my mouth firmly shut. Smiling at Hawks. Waiting with equal patience.

Hawks switches tactics.

"How long have you known Alastor Shaw?"

"We went to art school together."

"Really."

He didn't know that. *Sloppy, sloppy, Officer.*

I can tell he's annoyed at the omission—color rises from the collar of his shirt.

"The *Siren* called you rivals."

"The *Siren* likes to stir up drama."

"You're not rivals?"

"I don't believe in rivalry—I'm only in competition with myself."

"Would you consider yourselves friends?"

"Not particularly."

"Just another acquaintance."

"That's right."

Hawks is tiring of these bland answers. He sucks a little air through his teeth. "I'm surprised you agreed to meet with me without your lawyer present. You were adamant that any communication with Mara go through your attorney."

"I still am. She was treated disrespectfully by the police after she was attacked."

"That wasn't my department."

"I don't care who it was—it won't happen again."

"But *you're* not concerned about being…disrespected."

"I'm sure you know better than that." I smile at Officer Hawks. He doesn't smile back.

Abruptly, he asks, "Where were you the night of November second?"

"I have no idea. Do you remember where you were on random evenings weeks past?"

"Do you keep a calendar?"

"No."

"Does your secretary?"

"No."

This is true. I don't allow Janice to keep any record of my appointments. Sonia memorizes my schedule—but she certainly wouldn't recite it for Hawks.

"Do you know a woman named Maddie Walker?"

"No."

Hawks takes a photograph out of his sport coat's inside breast pocket and slides it across the table toward me.

I look at the picture without touching it. It shows a dark-haired girl lying on a steel table, her eyes closed, clearly dead. Her skin is bluish gray, mottled with bruises around the jaw. Shaw was rough when he wrenched her mouth open and stuffed a snake in it.

I recognize her from the top floor of the tenements, where Shaw had her strung up in his spiderweb.

I want to rip his fucking throat out, remembering how he lured me up there and trapped me, calling in a fleet of cops to catch me with the body.

It was a stupid mistake, one that still humiliates me. But I can't let any hint of that emotion show on my face.

Hawks watches closely for a reaction. That's why he gave me a photo of the corpse and not a picture of the girl taken when she was still alive. He's looking for clues in my expression.

Do I recognize her? Am I shocked by the image?

Or, most damning of all:

Am I a man surveying my own work?

Am I satisfied?

Am I aroused…?

Blandly, I say to Hawks, "I've never met her."

"She was killed in the Mission District. Police saw a man fleeing the scene. He was tall and dark-haired."

"That only applies to half the men in San Francisco."

"It applies to you."

"And thousands of others."

Hawks takes the photograph back before tucking it into his pocket once more, right against his heart.

He takes this personally. It's not only ambition for him.

And he *is* losing patience with my stonewalling. Slowly and surely.

"Have you injured yourself lately?" he demands.

I never visited a doctor when I sprained my ankle jumping from that roof. It's possible someone saw me limping in the week afterward when I wrapped my ankle in a Tensor bandage and swallowed handfuls of painkillers until the swelling went down.

"Nothing comes to mind."

"Don't have much of a memory, do you?" Hawks sneers.

"I like to keep my mind occupied with more interesting things than the minutiae of my schedule and the time people leave parties."

"What's interesting to you?" Hawks's jaw is rigid, his hand still resting against the breast pocket of his jacket.

"I'm curious why you're talking to me and not to Shaw."

"You think he attacked Mara? And killed her roommate?"

"That's what Mara says."

"You believe her."

"She's very perceptive."

So is this cop. She was right about that.

Hawks knows something is fucked up here. He can sense the links between our strange trio but can't quite conceptualize what they mean.

He has no evidence—I didn't leave so much as a fingerprint at the tenements. I'm sure Shaw was even more careful.

How infuriating, to have to work inside the bounds of the law. Your hands always tied by rules and regulations. Only one side playing fair.

I see the strain on Hawks's face. His impotent anger.

He's been around enough criminals to know I'm no law-abiding citizen. But that's true for most of the wealthy elite in this city. We all flout the rules for our benefit. He can't decide if I'm just another rich prick or the killer he seeks.

I've already satisfied myself that Hawks has nothing. No evidence against me—nothing but suspicion.

Hawks takes a breath, steadying himself. Getting ready for one last push.

He leans forward, his voice low and steady. "Was Erin perceptive? Would she have warned Mara about you?"

I snort. "Nobody needs warning about me. It's well known that I'm an asshole."

"You've made enemies."

"Only boring people are universally beloved."

"Take Carl Danvers, for instance."

Now a chill falls between us, which I pretend to ignore with every fiber of my being.

"Who?"

"He was a critic for the *Siren*."

"Oh, right," I say dismissively.

"He disappeared thirteen weeks ago. All his belongings are still in his apartment. No message to anyone."

"Your point?"

"He was no fan of yours. Wrote a scathing article about you the week he disappeared."

"People write about me every day."

"Did you speak to him at Oasis?"

This is a trick. Danvers was already dead the night of the show. His bones resided inside my sculpture, on display for all to see.

Hawks is testing to see if I'll correct him, to judge how closely I followed the disappearance and how well I know my own timeline.

"Jesus, who knows. I probably talked to fifty people that night."

"But you don't *remember*." Hawks's disdainful expression shows exactly what he thinks of that.

Enough obfuscating. It's time for Hawks to take a punch in return.

"This is pathetic," I sneer. "If this is all you have…missing art critics, conversations nobody heard, and timelines no one can pin down…the SFPD is grasping at straws. Mara will be disappointed. Sounds like you've got no fucking clue what happened to her roommate."

Hawks snaps back, "Our profiler says the person who arranged that body fancies themself an artist and a genius. Sound familiar?"

"Oh, wow." I roll my eyes. "Did they also guess it was a white male? Hope Captain Obvious isn't getting a Christmas bonus."

"You think this is funny?"

"Well, you sure as fuck can't be serious"—I push back my chair and stand from the table—"because this interview was a joke."

After striding over the conference room door, I wrench it open and call to Janice, "See Officer Hawks out, will you, Janice? Sounds like he's got a lot of work to do."

I leave Hawks stewing in my disdain.

I'm a good enough actor that I don't think I showed any nerves.

In truth, it rankled me that he connected the dots to Danvers.

God damn Shaw for shoving us both under the microscope. This is all his fucking fault. I've never had a cop so much as look my way before this—now they have a fucking description of me. They'll be watching everything I do.

Usually, I'd head back up to my office to mull this over alone. I feel angry enough to bite the head off anyone who even looks at me.

But I don't want to be alone—I want Mara. I want to tell her everything that happened. I want to hear what she thinks.

I'm only halfway up the stairs when I collide with her hurrying down.

"Sorry," she gasps. "I couldn't wait any longer. I couldn't stand not knowing what was going on."

"It's fine. Hawks left."

"What did he say?"

I take her hand. "Let's get a drink, and I'll tell you."

We leave the building after a quick glance down the sidewalk to be sure Hawks isn't still lurking around.

I take Mara to a dingy little pub that serves home-brewed cider, her favorite.

We sit across from each other in a dark and quiet corner, the oak tabletop already sticky long before Mara sloshes a little cider on it.

Briefly, I recap the conversation between me and the detective. I tell her everything, even the part about Danvers.

"Is Hawks right?" Mara whispers.

"Yes," I admit. "I killed him."

Mara's breath catches on the inhale, then releases in a shaky waver. "Can he prove it?"

"Probably not."

The only evidence is enclosed inside *Fragile Ego*. It was insane for me to sell it. In that moment, my own ego swelled past all reason.

No one knows about the bones except Shaw.

Yet another reason he needs to die.

"The cop's a crusader," I say to Mara. "He's not going to drop it."

Mara looks up at me from under the fan of her dark lashes. "Will you kill him, too?" she asks quietly.

"I'd prefer not to."

Hawks is doing his job, and he's not that bad at it. Nobody else noticed Danvers.

When the fuck did I make this rule for myself not to murder people I respect? It's inconvenient.

"Please don't," Mara says.

"Understand this," I tell her, my voice low and cold. "I'll do what I have to do. No one is taking you from me…and no one is taking me from you."

She shifts in her seat, deeply uncomfortable.

She doesn't want me in jail, but she also doesn't want to be party to the slaughter of a decent human.

I say, "It probably won't come to that."

Mara sips her drink, her throat clenching convulsively.

She knows better than to ask me to promise.

9

MARA

AFTER OUR DRINK TOGETHER, COLE AND I BRIEFLY PART WAYS SO
he can deliver his submission to the sculpture committee.

This is one of our first moments apart since I moved in with
him. I know he's only allowing it because I'm holed up safely in
the studio, with Janice on guard downstairs and security cameras
everywhere.

I can never tell how much of his possessiveness is because of
Shaw and how much is his own obsession.

Whatever the reason, it's not a one-way street.

I'm also becoming unhealthily attached to Cole.

When he's close by, I feel invincible. I can turn to him for help
or advice. I'm completely safe for the first time in my life. No one
would dare fuck with me, or even shoot a dirty look in my direction,
under Cole's terrifying stare.

Even though we're so different from each other, I'm comfortable
in his company. More than comfortable—peaceful and whole. His
absence feels like a piece of me was torn away. I want it reattached
as soon as possible.

The minutes tick by slowly.

I work on my painting for a while, but I feel dull and listless. I
keep staring at the robin's breast, now just the right shade of dusty
orange.

I like that Cole put his mark on my work in a small, subtle way. It makes me love this painting all the more.

My work was never self-referential. I kept my memories stuffed down inside. I didn't mine them for material—I couldn't look at them at all.

It was Cole who picked the lock, cracking me open.

Like Pandora's box, all the evil and ugliness came pouring out.

I thought it would kill me.

I pulled a splinter from my chest, and a whole goddamned stake came out.

I'm bleeding, but maybe now I'll finally heal.

Painting these scenes doesn't depress me. It feels like catharsis, like therapy. Once I have it down on canvas, the memory lives outside me. I can view it when I want, but it no longer festers, poisoning me from the inside.

The paintings are so much better than anything I made before. They're dark and compelling. They pull you in. You stare and stare, a kaleidoscope of emotions turning before your eyes, each angle a new image.

I'm proud of them.

I'm proud of myself.

I never would have gotten here without Cole. Not to the studio, the shows, or even to the point of putting brush to canvas with this fount of inspiration surging through me.

Cole says that I light him up, that I fill him with energy.

The same is true for me.

His dark power surges through me: strong, persuasive, compelling. You can't deny Cole what he wants. And you can't deny me either. Not anymore.

My phone buzzes in the pocket of my overalls.

I pull it out, feeling a leap of excitement at the sight of Cole's name, even though he's only been gone for an hour.

"What did they say?" I cry, by way of greeting.

"Marcus York seemed to like it." Cole sounds pleased.

"When will you hear back?"

"Soon. York is pushing this thing through as quickly as possible. He's got some finger in the pie. I don't know what exactly—probably a kickback on the construction."

"Do you want to win?" I'm wondering how disappointed he'll be if Shaw takes it instead.

"I always want to win."

"And if you don't?"

Cole laughs. "I don't know how I'll feel—I've never lost before."

I love the sound of his voice over the phone, like he's murmuring right in my ear. It makes the little hairs on my arms stand. I don't want to hang up.

"Are you coming back now?"

"I'm almost there already. I'm driving like it's the Grand Prix. Come stand at the window so I can see you as I pull up."

Impulsively, I unfasten the straps of my overalls and step out of them. I pull off my shirt and my underwear as well.

I step up onto the window frame, completely nude, looking down at the street below.

Cole's black Tesla zooms up to the curb before stopping short with a jerk. He steps out, tall and lean, his hair tossed back by the wind.

He looks up at me.

I press my palm against the glass, the phone to my ear.

"Fucking hell," Cole breathes. "You're a goddess."

We head back to Cole's house, which is beginning to feel like my house. Not because I own it, but because I love it so much. I love the stark, forbidding face, the jumble of pointed dormers and dark gables, and the ornate woodwork and black stone.

Most of all, I love this perch high on the cliffs, the endless cycle of waves crashing below.

The wind blows off the bay, wild and cold. It's the chilliest November on record. People keep making stupid jokes about how we could really use that global warming right now. Janice said it to me this morning.

As Cole opens the door for me, I think I like the smell of his house best of all.

He's lived here alone for more than a decade. The scent is all his: leather and clay, the spice of his cologne, ocean salt, and wet rock after rain. Running through it like a vein is my own scent as well. As perfect a pairing as any I've created with food. More delicious than banana and bacon or avocado and jam.

The textures and colors of his house soothe me. Everything is muted and dark but so lovely. Cole could never bear anything garish or loud.

The deep-chocolate boards creak beneath my feet. The diaphanous curtains blow back from the open windows with a sound like a sigh, letting the sea breeze into the house.

Cole heads up to his room to change clothes. He's fastidious and doesn't like to wear the same shoes and trousers that touched the outside world. He'll come down in a minute, probably wearing some old-fashioned smoking jacket and a pair of velvet slippers.

I'll have to change clothes as well; I'm still covered in paint.

For the moment, my attention is caught by my laptop, still open on the table where Cole left it.

I don't care that he was reading my emails. I'd have been incensed if anyone did that a month ago, but we're well past that now.

I walk over to the laptop, intending to close the screen.

As my fingers make contact, I hear the soft chime of another email arriving.

Usually, my mother's emails are shunted to a folder where I don't have to see them. Because that folder is already open, I'm hit with her name and the heading: *Your Mother's Day Card.*

I stare, confused, forced to parse that sentence.

I obviously do not receive Mother's Day cards myself, and I certainly haven't sent one to her.

My index finger moves without my consent, floating over to the track pad and clicking once.

The email leaps up before my eyes.

For once, there's no rambling diatribe.

Just an image, which appears to be an open card, scanned and copied.

I recognize the childish handwriting:

Happy Mothers Day Mommy

I love you so so so so so so so much. I made you cinnimin tost.

    Im sorry I make so many misstaks. Your the best mom. Im not very good. I will try so hard. I will be beter.

    I love you. I hope you never leeve. Please dont leeve even if Im bad. I wont be bad.

    You are so pritty. I want to be pritty like you.

    I love you Mommy. I love you.

XOXO
Mara

Each word is a slap across my cheek. I can hear my own voice, my own thoughts, immature and desperate, crying in my ear:

I love you, Mommy. I love you.

I'm sorry.

Please don't leave.

I won't be bad.

Even my name signed at the bottom makes my stomach clench, the bile rising in my throat.

Little Mara. Desperate, pathetic, begging.

Every word of it is true—I wrote it. I felt it at the time.

My deepest fear was that she would leave like my father did. She used to threaten me with it when I fucked up. When I forgot a chore or broke something of hers.

Later, I was the one who wanted to leave. Who dreamed of doing it.

She's throwing it in my face, the intense connection I had to her. The love to which I clung no matter what she said to me, no matter what she did. It took years for that love to wither and die. Even now, some perverse remnant endures, lodged deep in my guts.

I still think about her. I still yearn for what I wanted her to be.

I hate that about myself.

I hate my weakness.

I hate that she wields it against me as a weapon: Shaming me because I loved her. Guilting me because I want to stop.

Cole comes into the kitchen, dressed as I expected in a dark brocade jacket. "What is it?"

Without waiting for an answer, he grabs the laptop and turns the screen toward him.

He reads the email in a glance. The look that falls over his face would make a grown man stagger. "When did she send this?"

"Just now."

I'm shaking. I feel like she walked into the room and spat in my face.

She still has so much power over me.

I'll never be free of her. She'll never allow it.

Cole slams the windows shut and strips off his jacket before wrapping it around my shoulders.

"I'm covered in paint," I tell him.

"I don't give a fuck."

I feel him shaking, too, with anger.

"Where does she get the fucking nerve?" he hisses.

"She has no shame."

"The fact she thinks that proves anything except how fucking brainwashed you were—" He sees that talking about it is only making me more upset. "Never mind. Come on—I've got an idea."

Numbly, I follow him.

I thought Cole would take me upstairs to the bedroom or maybe into the main living room. Instead, he leads me down to the lower level, to a parlor we've never visited before.

Like all the rooms, its doors are thrown open. I've only seen one locked room in this house: the one leading to the basement.

As in much of Cole's house, the original purpose of this space has been altered to suit his eccentric preferences. While the far wall is a large stone hearth, and the usual sofas and chaises are present, the bulk of the room is given over to a potter's wheel.

Cole lights a fire in the grate. The pale applewood logs give off a sweet scent reminiscent of their fruit. The flames leap, bringing alive the figures in the many paintings on the walls.

"Relax a minute." Cole pushes me gently down on the sofa closest to the fire.

I sink back against the cushions, soaking in the heat. I'm still shaking, though not as much.

Why in the fuck does she still have this effect on me?

I have her blocked on every platform. I haven't seen her face in years.

She's five-five and fifty years old. Why am I afraid of her?

How does she still have the ability to reduce me to a blubbering child in an instant?

I'm so fucking pathetic.

Cole returns to the room carrying his supplies. He pauses to set a vinyl on an old record player.

I have a deep love for vinyl. It's not just something pretentious hipsters say—it really does sound different. The slight scratchiness, the rhythm of the platter rotating…it gives the perfect flavor to old-school tunes.

Cole knows this. The music that flows out of the speakers is old-fashioned and romantic. Not at all what I expected from him.

♫ *"I Don't Want to Set the World on Fire"*—*The Ink Spots*

The potter's wheel spins clockwise because he's left-handed. After moistening the center of the bat with a sponge, he sets a fresh lump of clay in place. He flattens the edges with his large palm, sealing them with his index finger.

Once the clay is firmly in place, he increases the speed of the wheel and wets his hands until they glisten in the firelight.

I watch it all, mesmerized.

Cole's hands are beautifully shaped and marvelously strong. I could watch them work for hours.

The way he strokes and manipulates the clay reminds me of how his hands move over my flesh. I feel my skin burning—and not from the heat of the fire.

Cole asks, "Do you want to try?"

"I've never made anything on a pottery wheel."

"Come here. I'll show you."

He scoots back on his stool to make room for me. Shucking off his jacket so I don't dirty the sleeves, I sit between his thighs, his arms around me.

Cole wets my hands until they're cool and slippery, his fingers gliding easily over mine. His warm chest presses against my back, his chin on my shoulder.

"Use your right hand to push the clay up," he says. "That's backward from normal, but it won't matter to you because you've never done it either way. Your left hand is the support. That's right—squeeze the clay inward, and let it rise between your hands. That's called 'coning up.'"

Under his instruction, the softened clay does indeed rise between my hands like the cone of a volcano.

Cole's hands cover mine, guiding me. Keeping my motions smooth and strong. Caressing my skin.

The earthy scent of the clay mingles with the sweet apple and the smoke of the fire. The crackle of the record player and the pop of the logs send a pleasant friction down my spine.

"I like how it feels," I murmur to Cole. "It's so cool compared to the fire."

"It's as silky as your skin." Cole runs his fingers up my bare forearm. The wet clay streaks across my flesh.

I link my fingers into Cole's, feeling the clay squish between our hands.

The cone collapses. Neither of us cares.

Cole rubs it between his palms, then runs both hands up my arms, plastering my skin. Painting me with the clay.

I turn to face him, straddling his lap, pulling my shirt over my head, then dropping it to the floor.

Cole smears my bare breasts with the clay. It's slick and cool on my burning flesh, my skin glowing pink in the firelight.

I let him paint me all over. I let him cover my face as if with a mud mask, leaving only my eyes and lips bare. He covers my neck, my chest, my back, and my belly.

The ancient Egyptians thought humans were formed of clay. Their ram-headed god turned them on a potter's wheel with mud from the banks of the Nile.

Cole is shaping me under the clay. Massaging my flesh, reforming my body.

I give myself over to him. I let him work.

I close my eyes, bathed in the heat and light of the fire. I'm lying on the rug now, Cole's hands roaming over me. He's stripped off my clothes. I'm naked as the day I was born.

I used to be Mara the victim. Mara the damaged. Mara the disposable.

The day I met Cole, I was dying.

Maybe I did die.

Through Cole, I was reborn.

Now I'm Mara the artist. Mara the star. Mara the unbreakable.

Cole made it possible.

He wants to be the center of my universe.

I want that, too.

I want to worship him as the Egyptians worshipped their gods. I want to pray to him for help and protection.

Cole strips off his clothes and climbs on top of me. He slides his cock inside me, his arms braced on either side, looking down into my face.

He's made my body so warm and relaxed that each stroke of his cock is pure molten pleasure. He slides in and out of me, watching my eyes roll back in bliss.

"Cole..." I groan. "I...I...I..."

"I know," he says.

He can't hold back his grin. He knows exactly what kind of effect he's having on me.

I gaze up at him.

"I love you," I say.

If I'd thought first, I'd have been too afraid to say it.

Cole looks down at me, his eyes black and flickering, full of reflected flame. "What does it feel like?"

"It feels like I'll do anything for you. Jump off a bridge for you, turn myself inside out for you. It feels like madness, and I never want it to end."

Cole considers this, his dark eyes roaming over my face. "Then I must be in love. Because that's what I feel, too."

A week later, while Cole and I are taking a stroll through Golden Gate Park, his phone rings in his pocket.

He pulls it out and answers the call.

It's still a little disturbing hearing Cole talk with his usual level of animation while his face remains flat and smooth. He doesn't bother to make expressions when he's on the phone and the other person can't see.

"Good to know," he says. And then, after a pause, he adds, "Yes, I agree."

He ends the call before slipping the phone back into the pocket of his peacoat.

My arm is tucked in his. I have to crane my neck to look up into his face. I'm trying to guess who it was and what they said—an exercise much more difficult with Cole than with anyone else. He gives me no hints, only looking down at me with that enigmatic smile playing at the corners of his lips.

I can't tell if he's pleased from the call or only because I'm looking at him so curiously. He loves when my attention is fixed on him.

"Well?" I say when I can't stand it any longer.

"That was York."

Cole's giving me no clue from his tone or expression.

I'm jumping on the balls of my feet, bubbling over with anticipation and mounting fury that he won't break the suspense.

"And? *And?*" I shout.

"And I got it," Cole says simply.

It's my shriek of excitement, my sprinting around him in circles that makes him grin. He doesn't register the triumph of the moment until I leap into his arms, my legs around his waist, my wrists locked about his neck, making him kiss me again and again.

"You got it!" I shout. "*You fucking got it!*"

"I always thought I would."

He doesn't fool me. I know he didn't really expect the win. The art world is all about momentum. While Cole's been distracted, Shaw's been putting out piece after piece, each more impressive than the last. He's working almost entirely in sculpture now, deliberately stepping on Cole's toes, shouting his bid for Corona Heights Park in every way possible.

I think we both know how narrow a victory it probably was, Cole's long-standing supremacy in this space just barely trumping Shaw's rising star.

"They probably didn't want to have to deal with him," Cole says. "I may be an asshole, but Shaw's fucking obnoxious."

There might be truth in that. Shaw's relentless drive for self-promotion would overshadow the sculpture and everyone else involved in the project. Besides, he doesn't have the experience. He can't make something that size out of wool.

"What's the point of this project anyway?" I ask. "Like, what's it supposed to represent?"

"I dunno, unity and peace or some bullshit." Cole shrugs. "I'm just making what I want."

I feel a deep thrill knowing I gave Cole the idea. Or, I should say, David Bowie did.

Cole's labyrinth is as dark and enigmatic as himself. One true path through to the center, obscured by a dozen false trails that only turn back on themselves.

"I'm surprised they're willing to make it," I say to Cole. "Aren't they worried about people getting lost?"

Cole laughs wickedly. "I told them it was like a corn maze. They think people will love it."

"You're a sadist."

He kisses me, biting my lip hard enough to draw blood. "You fucking know it."

10
COLE

November flows into December, each day passing quicker than the last.

I'm already regretting winning the bid for the sculpture.

York is demanding I build it as quickly as possible, before the next round of elections in the spring.

And just as I expected, I'm fucking hating it.

I have to command an entire crew of construction workers, none of whom know the first fucking thing about working with these kinds of materials.

I'm out on the frigid, whistling top of Corona Heights Park, in the goddamned coldest December since 1932, shouting at welders who have already shattered a dozen of the smoked-glass plates that make up the walls of the labyrinth.

This might possibly be tolerable if Mara were with me, but she's not. She's back at the studio, finishing her series in time for the show I'm throwing next week.

Whenever I want to snap an incompetent glazier's neck, I pull out my phone and check the camera in her studio. It calms me to watch her dab away at the canvas, her music blasting, her spare paintbrushes twisted in her hair.

She's much too engrossed in her work to think about me.

Once, she seemed to sense that I was watching. She turned and faced the camera, grinning and giving me a saucy wave. Then she pulled up her shirt, flashing her tits at me, before turning back to her work.

She could only have been guessing, but my cock still raged against my clothing, demanding I abandon this idiotic project and speed back to the studio so I could bury myself inside her.

When Mara's working, I might as well not exist.

She's completely absorbed by the project, forgetting to eat or drink or sleep.

It makes me insane with jealousy. I hate when anything pulls her attention away from me.

That's not how my mind works.

I can think about many things at once, and one of those things is always Mara.

Like a computer that can run several programs simultaneously, I keep tabs on Shaw and Officer Hawks, supervise the construction of the sculpture, and think of every possible way I can wrap another rope around my sweet little Mara and pull it tight.

When I can abandon the sculpture at the end of the workday, I head over to the studio to pull her attention back where it belongs: on me.

I used to hate the holidays. They seemed pathetic and manufactured, designed to give some semblance of structure to the year so people could pretend to celebrate when really they'd rather not see their family at all, drinking as much as possible before passing out in front of the tree.

I'm learning how different the world appears when the things you do are for someone else.

Now, instead of Christmas trees and decorations striking me as tacky, I want to find the most beautiful ones possible so I can surprise Mara when she walks through the door and finds the house bedecked in silvery lights. I want to see them reflected on her skin, echoing the smoky color of her eyes.

It's easy to reduce Mara to childlike wonder. To give her what she never had before.

I pile the presents under the tree, dozens of them, all with her name on the tags. She doesn't care what's inside—the fact she has gifts waiting for her reduces her to tears. She has to go and hide in a distant corner of the house, her headphones on, wrapped in a blanket, until she's ready to come look at them again.

Every stupid thing people do, that I used to watch them do, now I'm in the center of it.

I take her skating on the holiday ice rink at Embarcadero Center. In this strange wintery weather, San Franciscans are giddy with the joy of donning scarves and pom-pom hats, zipping around under the frost-blighted palm trees, and drinking their hot cocoa.

The city is loaded with twice as many twinkling lights, as if trying to drive away the freezing fog that blows in off the bay, each day colder than the one before.

The other skaters float in and out of view like ghostly wraiths.

Mara is an angel in the softly glowing light.

I bought her a snow-white parka with fur all around the face. She wears a pair of fluffy mittens and a new pair of skates, freshly sharpened to a razor's edge. Only the best for Mara, no shitty rentals.

I never knew how good generosity could feel. My ability to make her life comfortable and magical gives me a sense of godlike power. Not a wrathful god anymore, but one overflowing with goodness and light.

I don't know if I have any real kindness inside me.

Mara believes I do. She believed I wouldn't hurt her when I had every intention of killing her. Now she believes I have the capacity to love.

What is loving someone?

From all outward appearances, I'm very much a man in love. I shower her with gifts, praise, attention.

But I'm all too aware that everything I do for Mara benefits me.

I feed off her joy like a vampire. The hot cocoa tastes sweeter when I lick it off her lips. The lights are more beautiful reflected in her eyes. The air in my lungs is fresh and sweet when we fly across the ice together, hand in hand.

For now, all our interests align. What's good for Mara is good for me.

It requires no real sacrifice. I'm only doing what I want.

But perhaps I'm changing in the smallest of ways.

Because for the first time, I wonder if she deserves more than this.

Mara thinks she sees who I am and loves me anyway.

Only I know how cold I truly am at heart.

I told myself I was always honest with her, while letting her believe what she wants to believe: that I always had good reason, that I might be justified.

It's time to tell her the truth. To show her, the only way I know how.

I take Mara down to the lowest level of the house. To the locked door she's never seen beyond.

I see her mounting dread as we descend the stairs. Mara is a curious kitten…but she has an instinctive understanding of danger. She skirts away without ever acknowledging the boundary.

I fit the key in the lock and throw open the door.

Mara flinches as if expecting a slap.

Instead, her eyes widen with wonder. She steps inside the cavernous space.

"What on earth…" she breathes, her bare feet sinking into a thick carpet of moss.

♫ *"How Villains Are Made"—Madalen Duke*

The air is rich with oxygen, the cave-like space stuffed with greenery. Ferns cling to the dripping rocks. It's an underground garden, a riot of life and color, locked away in the heart of the earth.

"It was my mother's," I tell her. "She was trying to create a true terrarium—self-sustaining, self-perpetuating. It runs with very little maintenance."

Mara is speechless, stepping into the surprisingly vast space. She had no idea what was hidden under the house. No one knows but me.

"My god," she whispers. "It's so beautiful…"

"She spent all her time down here. Especially at the end."

Mara turns slowly, a shadow falling over her eyes.

She understands that I brought her down here for a reason. Not just to show her the garden.

"This is where I found her," I tell Mara. "Hanging from that tree."

I nod toward a holly tree, its gnarled bough tough enough to bear my mother's weight when she kicked the stool out from under her feet. I ran to her and clung to her cold feet. Not even close to strong enough to lift her down.

Mara's eyes are already welling with tears, but I need to explain this to her before she gets the wrong idea again. Before she builds the narrative she wants to believe.

"I was four years old. She already knew something was wrong with me. She'd been fooled by my father when they met, but since then she'd learned to know him. To see the blankness on his face, his casual cruelty, his lack of normal human warmth. And of course, in his brother, Ruben, she saw the fullest iteration of what we are. The family curse."

I give a hollow laugh.

Mara shakes her head, wanting to object, but I speak too quickly, determined to tell her everything before she can interrupt.

"She hoped I wasn't like them. She hoped I was kind like her. But I was already cold and arrogant and too young to know better than to tell the truth. I told her how little worth I saw in the people who scrubbed our toilets, cleaned our house. I told her how our gardener disgusted me because he was stupid and could barely read, while I was already finishing entire novels. I could see that I was smarter than other people, richer, better looking. At four years old, I was already a little monster."

"You were a child," Mara says.

"That's what she thought, too. She bought me a rabbit. She named it Shadow because I didn't care to give it a name. I hated that rabbit. I hadn't learned how to use my hands and my voice yet. I was clumsy with it, and it bit and scratched me. I couldn't soothe it like my mother did, and I didn't want to. I hated the time I had to spend feeding it and cleaning out its hutch."

Mara opens her mouth to speak again. I bowl over her, my lungs full of all this fresh, green air, but the words coming out dead and twisted, falling flat between us.

"I took care of that rabbit for three months. I loathed every minute of it. I neglected it when I could, only fed and watered it when she reminded me. The way it loved her and the way it hated me made me furious. I was even angrier when I'd see the disappointment in her eyes. I wanted to please her. But I couldn't change how I felt."

Now I have to pause because my face is hot. I can no longer look at Mara. I don't want to tell her what happened next, but I'm compelled. She needs to understand this.

"One morning, we went down to the hutch, and the rabbit's neck was broken. It was lying there, dead and twisted, flies already settling on its eyes. My mother could see it had been killed. She didn't chastise me... There was no point. She looked in my eyes and saw nothing but darkness." My throat catches. I force the rest of the words out anyway. "She hung herself that afternoon. Years later, I read the last entry in her journal: 'I can't change him. He's just like them.'"

Now I do look at Mara, already knowing what I'll see on her face

because I've seen it before, on the only other person I ever loved—
the look of a woman gazing upon a monster.

Tears fall silently down Mara's cheeks, dropping on the soft
green moss.

"You didn't kill the rabbit," she says.

"But I wanted to. That's what you have to understand. I wanted
to kill that fucking rabbit every time I held it in my hands. I only
didn't because of her."

I'm still waiting for the disgust, the repulsion. The understanding that what my mother believed was true: at four years old, I was
already a killer, heartless and cruel, held back by my affection for her,
but who knows for how long.

"But you didn't do it." Mara's jaw is set, her eyes locked firmly on
mine. "You were a child—you could have been anything. She gave
up on you."

Mara is angry, though not at me.

She's angry at another mother who failed in her eyes. A mother
who looked at her own child and only saw ugliness.

"She was right to give up on me. I didn't kill the rabbit, but I am
a killer."

"I don't give a fuck what you've done!" Mara cries. "I only care
what you do now that someone loves you!"

She flies at me, grabbing my face between her hands and kissing
me as ferociously, as passionately, as she's ever done.

"I love you!" she cries. "I fucking love you. Your life starts here,
today, now that I've told you."

I look at Mara's furious face.

I touch the tears running down on both sides. I kiss her again,
tasting the salt on her lips.

In that moment, I finally realize what Mara knew all along:

She won't die like that rabbit. I *will* keep her safe.

11
MARA

I UNDERSTAND NOW WHY COLE HAS ALWAYS STAYED IN THIS HOUSE.

He destroyed his father's office but not the garden. He kept the garden living and growing for his mother, long after she was gone.

I wonder if that one act kept a spark of humanity burning inside him in all the years that followed.

Cole seems strangely buoyant since he told me this last piece of his history. He's unburdened—finally understanding that I *do* see who he is, without judgment.

I can't judge anyone. I've been a fucking mess for most of my life. A literal crazy person at times.

Everyone is a mix of good and bad. Can the good cancel out the bad? I don't know. I'm not sure I even care. If there's no objective measure, then all that matters is how I feel. Cole is a shade of gray I can accept.

He suits me like no one ever has.

He understands me.

How can I reject the only person I've ever felt connected to?

We were drawn together from the first moment we saw each other, when neither of us wanted it. Like recognized like. We bonded like mercury atoms.

If Cole is wrong and bad and evil, then so am I.

When he pushes me to change, the change feels good.

It's like his corrections to my paintings—once he points out the improvement, I can see its merit just as clearly.

He's been encouraging me to promote myself on social media. I was always hesitant to post anything too personal, too specific, still plagued by that old fear of exposing myself as weird, broken, and disgusting.

"You think the painting is the product, but it isn't," Cole tells me. "*You're* the product: Mara Eldritch, the artist. If *you're* interesting, then the work is interesting. They have to be curious about you. They have to want to hear what you have to say."

"I'm the product?" I tease him. "You know who you sound like…"

Sternly, Cole says, "There's a difference between creating a fake version of yourself for market and simply understanding how to show people who you really are."

Cole encourages me to dig out my old Pentacon and take photographs of my paintings in progress, before they're perfected, before they've even fully taken shape. I photograph myself at work, in moments of frustration, even breaking down in front of the canvas, lying on the floor.

I photograph myself in front of the gloomy plate-glass windows thick with fog, tracing my finger through the steam.

I photograph myself eating lunch, food scattered among the paints, my hands filthy on my sandwich.

When I need a break from painting, I pose naked and streaked in paint, wearing a sunburst crown of paintbrushes, swaddled in a canvas drop sheet like the Madonna.

The pictures are moody and grainy—sometimes melancholy, sometimes charged with ethereal beauty.

I don't worry about my privacy or if I might look unhinged. I post the pictures and tell the truth about my mental state, for better or for worse, as I update my progress on the new series.

At first I'm mostly doing this for myself, a digital diary.

I only have a few followers, mostly friends and old roommates.

Slowly, however, I start to pick up a few more. The first are people I've begun to follow myself: A girl who sews hand-drawn patches onto vintage shirts. A guy with phenomenal spray-painting techniques. A woman documenting her heartbreaking divorce with a series of self-portraits.

I comment on their posts; they comment on mine. My feed becomes more inspiring than before. I stop stalking old acquaintances from high school and begin the process of what Cole considers real networking—intentionally making friends among people I respect and admire, people who inspire me with their creativity.

I wouldn't have had the confidence to message any of these people before; they're legitimate working artists. But so am I now. I'm not a cosplayer anymore. I'm passionate about my current series; I believe in it. I'm not embarrassed to talk about it. Quite the opposite—I want to discuss childhood trauma and self-destructive impulses. My mind is full of ideas.

The more I open up, the more I realize how many other people share these experiences. My past was ugly but not so unique that no one else can understand it. Instead of judgment, I find acceptance.

A few of my posts go viral; most don't. I care more about the growing conversation among our group of like-minded artists.

Revealing my true self to Cole, seeing his calm acceptance of even my strangest statements, is helping me to trust other people. To believe they could meet the real Mara and actually like her, flaws and all.

Some of my new friends live in San Francisco. We meet in person at shows. Some are already known to Cole.

Cole is different when he's introducing me around. He turns on the full measure of his charm, which is not as boisterous and loud as Shaw's but is extraordinarily effective nonetheless because of his sly wit and his intense focus upon the person with whom we're speaking.

At a dinner at Betsy Voss's house, Cole sets the whole table roaring with an anecdote from art school.

Afterward I say to him, "I've never seen you like that. You had the whole room eating out of your hand."

Cole looks at me, pushing back his fall of dark hair with one hand. "I only told that story for you."

"What do you mean?"

"You looked bored. I thought, 'Say something funny. Make her laugh.'"

This touches me in the strangest way.

Cole and I spent the whole day together. We fucked in the car on the way to the party. The fact he still felt compelled to entertain me is incredibly flattering.

The *Siren* prints a photo of us climbing out of Cole's car, Cole holding the door open for me, dark and moody looking with his long black coat swept back by the wind, me with my hair in a maelstrom, my sparkly minidress glinting like a disco ball, my head thrown back in laughter as the gust tries to take me away.

The caption reads, *The Crown Prince and Princess of the Art World.*

Below that, a brief article mentions Cole's half-built sculpture in Corona Heights Park and my upcoming show. The photograph shows one of my paintings, not Cole's work.

It's Cole who shows me the magazine, our glossy image far too glamorous to be anyone I know.

I glance up at his face, wondering if it bothers him that they talked more about my show than his sculpture. "I'm sure they'll write about you again when the maze is finished," I say.

Cole snorts. "I don't give a shit about that."

I find that hard to believe. Cole is competitive, with a well-developed sense of his own merit. I can't imagine he enjoys being overshadowed.

He catches my look.

"Give me a little credit." He scoffs. "Whatever else I may be, I'm not a man who has to tear a woman down to shine bright beside her.

If you're not as good as me, then you're no good at all. And when I saw you, Mara…I thought, 'This girl is really fucking good.' I don't want to hold you down, chop you down, diminish you in any way. I already know I found something special. Now it's time for everyone else to see it."

12
COLE

Shaw has killed again.

He might have done it out of anger at losing his bid for Corona Heights. But the body wasn't found in a state of mutilated rage. She was posed like *Flaming June*, something that was hushed up in the papers, though TruCrime managed to splash full-color photographs across its site.

The cold calculation of the slaying disturbs me far more than Shaw's usual lustful rage.

The girl is dark-haired, slim, beautiful. The close-up photographs show one pale hand with roughly bitten fingernails. Two of those fingers are missing entirely.

It's the only mark of brutality on an otherwise pristine body. There's not a single rip on her flowing orange gown. Her face is lovely and unmarked, her eyes closed with a gentleness that might be sleep.

Even more disquieting, Hawks doesn't come calling in the aftermath of her death. Instead, his unmarked car trails mine while I drive from the studio to Corona Heights. His tall upright figure haunts Clay Street.

He knows I see him. He wants me to know.

He isn't following Shaw.

Shaw is allowed to roam free with a different beautiful blond on his arm every night of the week, the girls never suspecting they're riding the cock of the Beast of the Bay, kissing the mouth that ripped chunks of flesh out of girls very like themselves.

Never guessing Shaw's real preference is, and always has been, brunettes.

Erin was the only redhead, something Hawks's brain-dead profiler hasn't seemed to have noticed.

Sometimes I think I could do any job better than the people employed to do it. The rest of the world is a morass of incompetence, everyone playing dress-up at their jobs. Are there any actual adults or just children who grew tall?

Mara can't escape the news of the latest killing. I'd like to hide it from her, but I can't.

Janice pulls up the TruCrime site on her computer. A dozen artists gather around.

I watch from across the room. Mara lingers at the edge of the pack, desperately wanting to turn away but forced to look at the images, to witness what Shaw has done.

When she turns back to me, I see the horror in her eyes.

She feels responsible.

Shaw continues unchecked because of us. Because of her.

While she's admitted her anger, she has yet to act upon it.

Maybe she hopes I'll do it in secret, without her ever having to raise a finger. She'll wake up one morning, and Shaw will simply be dead.

That's not happening.

There will be no pleasant convenience for Mara.

She's going to learn the difference between thoughts and action.

Everyone knows someone they wish would die. Very few will make it happen.

I stand on one side of a chasm. Mara has to join me.

It's the only way we can truly be together.

13

MARA

AT NIGHT, LYING IN BED IN THE DARKNESS, I CAN TELL COLE ISN'T asleep. No slow heavy breaths, only the stillness that tells me he's thinking about something with all his focus.

I'm also thinking hard.

Probably on the same topic.

We both saw those pictures this morning. And we both know what it means.

Shaw is starting another cycle of killing, with barely any break since the last. That means two more girls will be sacrificed to his hunger. Maybe more.

How many will it take for Officer Hawks to get the evidence he needs?

Cole says Hawks isn't even following Shaw. He's tailing us instead.

I'm dreading Shaw crashing my show. He wasn't invited, but I'm sure he'd love to turn up and gloat in our faces again.

I hate him. I hate that he's roaming around unchecked, more vicious and violent by the day.

I could have saved this girl. She was twenty-four, a year younger than me. A med student, apparently.

If I'd agreed with Cole right away, then Shaw might already be dead. He never could have snatched her from whatever sidewalk or alleyway he found her.

My rejection of violence was a pillar in my sense of self. The evidence that I was a good person.

Now I wonder if I'm just a coward.

The idea of facing Shaw, of taking real action against him, terrifies me. I never stopped having nightmares of the night he grabbed me. I've never felt more afraid than when his bull-like body hurtled toward me, too fast for me to run or even scream before he hit me so hard, it felt like my head exploded.

This time, Cole will be with me.

But even Cole isn't looking forward to the battle with Shaw. He knows better than I do how brutal and cunning Shaw can be. It won't be easy to catch him off guard.

If I do nothing, as surely as the sun rises, I'll see another article about a murdered girl.

"Cole." I break the still silence.

"Yes?"

"We have to kill Shaw."

He lets out a small laugh. "I know that. I've known it all along. You're finally catching up."

"Well, I'm here now. How do we do it?"

"You're not ready yet."

This is so infuriating that I roll over in a huff, leaning on my elbow, trying to make out his expression in the dark. "What are you talking about?"

"If you're agreeing that we need to do this, then you're going to help me. We have the best chance of success working together. But you're not ready."

This is outrageous. I've finally agreed to do what he wants, and now he's fucking with me. "You think you're going to train me? Like fucking Miyagi?"

"I'm going to prepare you."

I don't know what that's supposed to mean. And I'm not sure I want to find out. "We don't have time for that! Shaw's going to kill another girl. Or me!"

I'm hoping that will spur him along.

Cole sighs. "You are thinking in normal-person terms. That is not how Shaw or I think. Our time horizon is infinite. Now that the element of surprise is gone, he doesn't care if it takes a week, a month, or twenty years to destroy me. In fact, he'd prefer to prolong it. He enjoys the game. That's the entire point…"

It chills me, realizing that while Cole and I are coming to understand each other, it's still Shaw with whom he shares the most similarity of mind.

"I don't want to watch the bodies stack up. We have to do something."

"We will," Cole assures me. "Very soon."

My show takes place two weeks before Christmas.

It's the first time my art will be displayed on its own, unable to hide among other paintings.

I'm sick with dread as Cole and I drive to the gallery in Laurel Heights, wondering what will happen if no one attends.

I once saw an author sitting alone at a table in Costco with a towering stack of books, not a single person interested in having one signed. Her look of hopeful anticipation as I approached, followed by crushing disappointment as I walked past, is still one of the saddest things I've ever seen.

I don't want to be that author.

"Don't worry," Cole says, squeezing my thigh as he turns the wheel with his other hand. "These things are always packed. Especially when I hired better caterers than Betsy, with enough champagne to drown a horse."

"That actually comforts me." I laugh. "If the paintings are shit, at least the food will be good."

"I'd never let you down with food," Cole promises solemnly. "I know it's your priority."

"I better quit making it my priority. I think I've gained eight pounds since I moved into your house."

"I like it," Cole says. "It's making your tits bigger."

I slap his shoulder. "Shut the fuck up!"

Cole grabs a handful of the breast in question, sneaking his hand down the front of my top faster than I can smack him away. "I'm gonna feed you so much fucking cheese."

I can't stop laughing. "Please, no. I'll be four hundred pounds."

"I want to drown in your breasts. What a way to die…"

We pull up to the curb before I can spend any more time worrying.

I'm relieved to see the gallery is already packed with people. Sonia (wo)mans the door in a gorgeous shimmering cocktail dress. Frank and Heinrich lurk behind her.

Heinrich pops out to pull me into an embrace. Frank does the same, after giving Cole a stare that's half attraction, half lingering nervousness.

"Thanks for coming!" I hug them both hard.

"Joss and Brinley are here, too," Frank tells me.

I assume that means Joanna isn't. I didn't expect anything different, but it still stings.

The gallery throbs with the playlist I spent all week picking out.

Cole encouraged me to choose the music myself, even though I wasn't sure anybody else would like it.

"Who gives a shit? It's what you were playing when you painted the pieces, so the songs will match the work. They already go together, whether you meant them to or not."

He's right.

♫ *"Heart Shaped Box"—Neovaii*

As a cover of "Heart-Shaped Box" pours out of the speakers, the creepy music box backing track perfectly suits my oversize painting of a charred teddy bear, its glass eyes melted, its fur still smoking in places.

I hadn't realized till this moment how the painting's title echoes the lyrics of the song:

> *Meat-eating orchids forgive no one just yet*
> *Cut myself on angel hair and baby's breath*

That one hurt me the most to paint. It's just a fucking bear, but I was overwhelmed with guilt that something I had loved had met such a bitter end.

I almost didn't finish, putting the painting aside, then changing my mind, turning it around again, and setting it back on the easel. I tilted it *I Remember and I Don't Forget.*

This series includes eight paintings in all, each larger than the last. I want the viewer to feel dwarfed by the canvases, overwhelmed by them. Like they themselves have shrunk to child size.

I painted at a speed I never could have managed when I had to squeeze in my art between endless work shifts, already exhausted by the time I lifted brush to canvas.

Some of the paintings are realistic; others include surreal elements.

One is called *The Two Maras,* a reference to Frida Kahlo's famous portrait.

In mine, the first version of Mara stands before a large mirror. The "real" Mara is battered and bruised, with a wide-eyed expression of fear. Her reflection in the mirror looks ten years older: glossy-haired and dressed in a diaphanous black gown, her eyes dark and ferocious, her aura crackling with the terrible power of a sorceress.

I called the painting of the girl in the nightgown *The Burial,* as Cole suggested.

The next one along is the same girl in the same nightgown, sitting barefoot on a bus, her feet filthy and scratched, her head leaning exhaustedly against the window.

All the adults gaze blindly in her direction, their blank faces nothing but a smear of paint. *Mind Your Business*, the title card reads.

Seeing all my paintings together, properly hung and lighted, is the most thrilling thing I've ever experienced.

I'm looking into the window of my own future—a dream I'd hoped for desperately but only ever half believed.

Now it's happening all around me, and I still can't believe it.

"How do you feel?" Cole asks.

"Drunk—and I haven't had a sip of champagne."

As Cole and I make the rounds, I'm starting to remember people's names and faces, and they're starting to remember me. I'm almost comfortable chatting with Jack Brisk, who's forgotten that he ever dumped a drink on my dress and is asking if I'd be interested in showing at his exhibition in the spring.

"It's an all-female show," Brisk says pompously. "Supporting women's voices. Nobody loves women more than me."

Cole says, "That's why you've been married four times."

"Five, actually." Brisk roars with laughter. "I could fund the UN with all the alimony payments I've made."

The pretty young thing on Brisk's arm, sporting an engagement ring that looks quite new, does not seem as amused by this conversation. She flounces off with Jack Brisk in pursuit.

Sonia sidles up to me and whispers, "She's just mad 'cause she's the first one he made sign a prenup."

As Cole gets pulled into a conversation with Betsy Voss, Sonia amuses me by whispering other bits of gossip about everyone else who passes.

"That's Owen Gross over there—he tried to throw a pop-up show this summer. Displaying paintings in posh houses all over the city. Mixing art with architectural porn."

"Not a bad idea," I say.

"It was a fucking disaster. July was broiling, so everybody with money flew to Malibu or Aspen or the Hamptons. Those of us stupid enough to attend were stuck in traffic for six hours trying to drive between houses. Turns out he never got the right permits to sell paintings out of houses. The city slapped him with so many fines that I doubt he made a dollar off the show."

Poor Owen still looks frazzled, with unshaven stubble and a haunted look on his face as he gulps down a glass of champagne, a second glass clutched in his other hand.

"And her over there." Sonia gives a subtle nod toward a slim woman with a long fall of shining dark hair. "That's Gemma Zhang. She's the newest writer for the *Siren*. Now, this I don't know for certain, but I have my suspicions…"

I lean in close so no one but Sonia and I can hear.

"The biggest art mag in Los Angeles is *Artillery*—they ran this gossip column written by a guy called Mitchell Mulholland. Mulholland was a pseudonym; nobody knew who he really was. All they knew was that come Monday morning, this Mulholland seemed to have been everywhere and seen everything. He was writing about shit like he was hiding inside our houses, telling everybody's secrets, stirring up all kinds of drama. Everybody was freaking out. He caused so much trouble that *Artillery* had to stop running the column. Mulholland disappeared. Now Gemma's writing for *Siren*…and a couple of her articles sound pretty damn familiar to me…That biting voice reminds me of a certain someone."

"You think Mulholland was actually Gemma?"

Sonia shrugs. "All I'm saying is to be careful around her…she's a fucking shark."

Gemma takes a sip of her drink, her dark eyes flitting everywhere at once, clever and bright.

Sonia may be right.

Cole escapes Betsy Voss, who was tipsy enough to require the support of his arm, batting her false eyelashes at him until one fell off and landed on Cole's wrist. He flicked it away like a spider, shuddering.

"You owe me for that one," Cole murmurs in my ear. "Betsy has a buyer lined up for *The Burial*. But I had to let her run her hands all over my chest for that entire conversation. I'm practically your gigolo these days."

"Yeah, you want a commission?" I tease. "Or do *you* just want to run your hands over someone's chest…"

Cole lets his eyes roam down the front of my jacket, slipping his arm around my waist and pulling me close.

"That might suffice…" he growls.

I'm wearing a velvet pantsuit in dark plum. I feel like a rock star.

Cole undresses me with his eyes like the velvet can be pulled away with a glance. He's charged up, maybe even more excited than I am. He surveys the packed gallery, not bothering to hide his grin of triumph.

Cole wasn't lying. He really does love to see me succeed.

"Look who's here," Sonia says.

Shaw comes through the double doors, a stunning blond on his arm. The girl looks pleased and excited, clinging to Shaw's bicep.

Shaw's not smiling at all, sullen and abrupt as people try to greet him.

He locks eyes with me across the room.

Cole stiffens, drawing me closer.

"He looks pissed," I mutter.

"I told you he's salty about Corona Heights."

Shaw stares at me, ignoring the girl at his side. Every second that passes, Cole gets more agitated, digging his fingers into my side. He looks like he wants to sprint across the room and put out Shaw's eyes.

When Shaw finally turns away, distracted by Betsy Voss, Cole says, "If he comes within ten feet of you, I'm going to tear out his throat."

"He's not gonna do anything here. You said so yourself."

"I don't want him here at all," Cole hisses. "I don't even want him looking at you."

I can still feel a pair of eyes fixed on me. Not Shaw's—Gemma Zhang. She's been watching the silent stare down between Shaw, Cole, and me, smiling slightly.

"I've got to pee," I say to Cole.

I head back to the bathrooms, where I hear the distinctive sniff of a pick-me-up in the adjoining stall and the crackle of a tampon wrapper from the other side.

I take my time, savoring the solitude after the hubbub of the party. It's heady to be the center of attention, but also exhausting.

When I've finished and washed my hands, I almost collide with Gemma Zhang, who was probably waiting outside the bathroom to orchestrate just this sort of meeting.

"Mara Eldritch." She holds out a freshly manicured hand. "The woman of the hour."

"Gemma, right?" I take the hand and shake it.

"Did Sonia warn you about me?" She smiles slyly. "She's quite the guard dog for Cole Blackwell. Can't take a step in his direction with Sonia barking at you."

"She's good at her job."

I'm trying to decide how I feel about Gemma. She's quite lovely, elegantly dressed in her silk gown, but there's a wicked edge to her smile that doesn't put me at ease.

"You must see a lot of Sonia," Gemma muses. "While you're seeing a lot of Cole. Living together already, aren't you?"

There's no point denying what everyone already knows. "That's right."

"That was fast. Love at first sight?"

"Not exactly."

"I don't know if I've ever seen Cole in love. Is this all part of the rivalry?"

"What do you mean?"

"My sources tell me it was Alastor Shaw who took an interest in you first."

"Your sources are wrong. I've barely spoken to Shaw."

"But he did date your roommate..."

"I don't want to talk about Erin," I snap.

"Of course." Gemma offers an expression of sympathy I don't quite believe. "What an awful thing. I'm sure you heard about the girl they found down by Black Point... People are saying she was posed like a painting."

"That's what I heard," I say stiffly.

"Can you imagine if an artist is doing all this?" Gemma pretends to look around us. "They could be here right now."

"Are you writing about the murders?"

"Actually..." Gemma smiles brightly. "I'm writing about you. San Francisco's newest rising star!"

"I don't know about that."

"Oh, it's certain. Look at these paintings! Just stunning. Drawn from personal experience, I assume?"

"Yes."

"Why so many references to childhood?"

"Childhood shapes us all—the events we remember and even those we don't."

"It's shaped you as an artist?"

I shrug. "Remedios Varo learned to draw by copying construction blueprints her father brought home from work. Andy Warhol was a sickly child who spent his days drawing in bed, surrounded by celebrity posters and magazines. Our history always influences our aesthetic."

"These don't look like happy memories."

"That one might be." I nod toward the painting nearest to us, which depicts a girl and a cat curled up asleep on a bed of tulips.

When I was very young, maybe three, I woke from a nap in an

empty apartment. It might have been the silence that woke me. I slipped off my mattress and wandered through the place, which didn't belong to us, but where I'd been staying with my mother for several weeks. I navigated the empty bottles and scattered trash, afraid to call out and break the eerie silence.

The front door was partly open.

I wandered out into the hall, then down the stairs, never seeing another person.

When I came out onto the sidewalk, a calico cat sat on the steps, gazing at me with unblinking eyes. Being three, I was certain the cat was waiting for me. It jumped off the step and strolled around the corner. I followed.

Eventually, it settled on a bed of tulips in the back garden. I lay down in the warm dirt with the cat, my head against its body. We drifted off with the gentle buzz of bees all around us.

Later, an old woman found me. She took me up to her apartment and fed me coconut cake. I'd never eaten coconut before.

That was a memory I returned to in times of stress or pain. I believed the cat was there to take care of me. I believed it for years.

But I don't tell any of that to Gemma.

"It's lonely," Gemma says, tilting her head to the side as she examines *The Nap*. "The dark color palette...the smallness of the child next to the cat..."

It's true. The cat is oversize, a calico tiger, larger than the girl herself, who almost disappears among the jumbled stems of tulips.

"The girl's always alone," Gemma persists. "Where are her parents?"

"I have no idea," I say before I can think better of it. "Excuse me—I've got other people I need to speak to."

My heart twitches uncomfortably against my ribs.

I don't like Gemma's bright eyes trained on me or her line of questioning.

The rest of the show passes pleasantly enough. Shaw only

stays for twenty minutes, slapping a few backs and shaking a few hands, keeping his distance from Cole and me. It makes me deeply uncomfortable when he stands before each of my paintings in turn, examining them closely before moving on to the next.

I don't like that he's looking inside my head.

That's the nature of art. You open yourself for everyone to see, to judge. You can't make art at all unless you're willing to lay yourself bare and risk what follows.

Shaw's date lingers by the buffet, shifting her weight on her towering high heels, bored and probably a little lonely.

I want to sidle up and whisper in her ear to run far, far away.

"You don't have to worry about her," Cole says.

"Why not?"

"He's not going to kill someone he dated publicly."

"He killed Erin."

"Only on impulse. He was there for you."

I imagine Shaw's heavy hand clamping over my mouth while I lay sound asleep on my old mattress.

Going to Cole's house that night saved my life.

It will lose Shaw his.

Three days later, Gemma Zhang publishes her article about me.

She's complimentary to my work and the show in general.

But the final paragraph makes my stomach lurch:

> *I contacted Mara's mother Tori Eldritch to get her comment on the autobiographical show that references themes of neglect and abuse.*
>
> *Tori said, "It's all lies. Mara had a perfect childhood, anything she could ever want. She was pampered. Spoiled, even. She'll do anything for attention. She's*

always been that way. I took her to so many psychiatrists, but they could never fix her. I don't call that art. Fantasy, more like. A filthy, deceptive fantasy to slander the people who took care of her. My lawyer says I should sue her for defamation."

That puts a different spin on the collection of ostensibly personal images.

When I spoke to Mara Aldrich, she told me, "Childhood shapes all of us—the events we remember and even those we don't."

Perhaps Mara is leaning hard on those events we "don't remember."

I shove the laptop away from me, my face burning.

"That fucking *cunt*!"

"Gemma or your mother?" Cole inquires.

"Both!"

"No one's going to believe your mother," Cole says dismissively. "She's nobody. You're the one with the microphone."

I'm still seething, the room spinning around me. "She can't let me have anything. She can't stand what it will mean if I succeed without her, in spite of her."

"You already *are* succeeding," Cole says serenely. "And she can't do a damn thing about it."

14

COLE

Mara's mother's giving interviews.

If Gemma Zhang can find her, so can I.

It's been too long since I put my online stalking skills to use. I spend an afternoon in my office at the studio hunting down Tori Eldritch and Randall Pratt.

This is something I've intended to do for some time now. I want to know exactly where those two are living and what they're up to.

Randall is surprisingly difficult to locate.

I assume somebody other than myself is interested in breaking his kneecaps, because his supposed address is only a rented office space, with no car registered under his name.

I still manage to find a phone number that I'm pretty sure is a working cell.

He answers the second time I call. "What?"

Rough as a bag of rocks rolling around in the back of a truck— just like Mara said.

The voice I plan to use is clear and friendly, with a slight Midwestern twang. The kind of voice designed to disarm Randall without quite mimicking him.

"Hey there, Mr. Pratt. My name's Kyle Warner. I write for the *Chronicle*, and I'm doing a story on an artist named Mara Eldritch. I was wondering if I could ask you a few questions?"

A long pause.

"Not interested," Randall grunts, rustling the phone like he's about to hang up.

"Well, hang on!" I say. "Could ya at least confirm a quote I got from her mother, Tori Eldritch?"

Another pause, even longer.

I hear his heavy breath on the other end of the line.

"You talked to Tori?"

"That's right."

"In person or over the phone?"

"I flew up to speak with her."

"Flew where?"

Now it's my turn to let a brief silence fall between us. Keeping my tone cheerful, I say, "Well, we can discuss that in person. I need another source for this article. Pay's five hundred bucks, and it won't take but a little of your time."

Breath. Breath. Heavy breath. Hot and wet in my ear.

"All right," Randall grunts. "I'm in La Crescenta. You can meet me at a pub called the Black Dog."

A smile spreads over my face where Randall can't possibly see it. "Perfect."

Mara and I drive out to Burbank together. She's going to be interviewed for the DBS morning show.

"I don't know if I want to be on TV," she tells me, raising her hand to her mouth, then quickly putting it back down on her lap, twisting her fingers together in anguish.

She got a manicure and doesn't want to fuck it up.

"You're going to be great," I reply. "I'll be right there with you, watching the whole time."

"What do you think they'll ask me?"

"Nothing challenging—it's a morning show, for fuck's sake. If they weren't talking to you, they'd probably be interviewing the lady who baked the world's biggest doughnut."

"They *should* interview her." Mara laughs. "What an accomplishment."

"You know we have to be at the studio at four fifteen a.m. for hair and makeup."

"Are you serious?" she cries. Mara's not an early riser.

"That's why they call it a morning show—'cause it's at the goddamned crack of dawn."

"I'm so nervous. I'm not gonna sleep a wink."

"Do you want an Ambien? I brought two with me."

She considers, tapping one nicely polished nail against her lower teeth. "What if I can't wake up in time?"

"You'll be fine. I'll set an alarm."

"All right." She sighs with relief. "Otherwise I'll be exhausted."

We settle in at the Chateau Marmont, where I've booked us a suite overlooking Sunset Boulevard. I thought Mara would like its architecture and the Old Hollywood history.

"Howard Hughes lived here," I tell her. "Desi Arnaz would come stay whenever he was fighting with Lucille Ball. Bette Davis almost burned it down—twice. And Sharon Tate moved out of the hotel six months before she was killed. John Belushi and Helmut Newton both died here."

I looked all this up beforehand, knowing it would interest her. Mara likes anything historical, tragic, or glamorous.

"The hotel's in lots of movies, too," I continue. "*La La Land...A Star Is Born...*"

"Really?" Mara gasps. "*La La Land*'s one of my favorites."

"I know." I laugh. "You play that one song from it all the time."

"That's right." Mara's pleased that I remembered.

Our room isn't as luxurious as some of the places I've stayed, but Mara's never picky. She runs around the room, admiring the old-fashioned furniture and striped wallpaper.

She's keyed up about the interview, equal parts giddy and terrified.

"I always think I want attention until I actually get it... I hope I don't say something weird that gets turned into a meme. Like when Brett Kavanaugh told everybody he was a virgin in school and for 'many years after.'" Mara shudders, imagining her face splashed all over templates.

"All publicity is good publicity."

"You don't believe that."

"It is when you're this hot." I seize her and throw her on the bed, which creaks and groans beneath her.

"Wait," she says. "Give me the Ambien first."

"You sure? Those things are strong."

"Yeah. I like that floating feeling in sex. Like I'm half in my body and half out. Like you could do anything to me..."

My heart rate spikes as a gallon of adrenaline dumps into my bloodstream. I have to bite down hard on the inside of my cheek. "You kinky little fuck."

I hand her the small pink pills and a bottle of water stamped with the hotel's logo. Mara tosses down the pills before chugging half the water as well.

"Perfect." She grins.

She's full of rowdy energy, amped up with nerves and excitement. She pushes me back on the bed, saying, "Sit there."

I lean back against the pillows, waiting to see what this wild little thing has in mind.

Mara is the only person on this planet from whom I occasionally take orders, purely out of curiosity. No matter how much time I spend with her, I still can't predict exactly what she'll do next. That's why she's endlessly fascinating to me. She doesn't fall into routine.

She doesn't pick the obvious choice. And she sure as fuck doesn't behave herself.

Mara takes my Bluetooth speaker out of her suitcase, the one that usually resides in the bathroom. She sets it up on the dresser, streaming music from her phone.

♫ *"The Devil Is a Gentleman"*—*Merci Raines*

The beat flows into the room, mysterious and sultry, with a hint of playfulness. As soon as she hears it, she closes her eyes and starts swaying, her shoulders first, then her hips. She knows how to move. In fact, she *has* to move. She can't hear music without it taking over her body.

I liked music well enough, but I never understood its full power until I met Mara. She unerringly selects songs with an irresistible beat and an overpowering mood. She finds the songs that tickle your brain, that fire up the neurons until you can almost see the notes sparking in the air around you.

Mara throws open the heavy drapes covering the windows, letting in the last of the late-afternoon sunshine, revealing the view of the Hollywood Hills.

She stands directly in front of the window, framed by the glass, her body a shadowed silhouette, gold around the edges. She's still dancing, running her hands through her hair and down her curves.

Slowly, she unzips the front of her hoodie. She shimmies out of it, languorously sliding the sleeves down her arms, then flinging it away from her so it sails across the room and lands on the lampshade. Underneath, she wears only a thin undershirt, through which I can see the outline of her nipples, the shape of the silver rings, and the indent of her navel.

Next, her jeans: She unzips, her fingers light and teasing, taking her time. Turning away from me, she slides the jeans down over the round globes of her ass, which is bisected by her thong.

I want to unzip my own pants. My cock is raging against the fly, but I wait, my eyes fixed on Mara, my cheeks throbbing from how hard I'm biting them. She's stoking my fire. The impulse to jump up from this bed and seize her is torturous. It takes everything I have to stay still.

She hops up on the windowsill before lifting her legs and resting her bare feet on the opposite side of the frame so she can slide off the jeans. She tosses her pants aside, getting to her feet, standing in the frame with her back to me.

She makes slow circles with her hips, swaying that peachy little ass, teasing me, tempting me…

Silhouetted against the setting sun, her figure glows like a caryatid, like she's holding up the whole building.

I could never sculpt anything so perfect.

She pulls off her undershirt and tosses it behind her. It lands on my lap. I pick up the crumpled cotton, still warm from her body. I press it to my face, inhaling her intoxicating scent.

The idea that someone else might be standing below that window, that they might look up and see the view I haven't yet seen myself, makes me wild with jealousy.

I like that feeling. I'm in competition for Mara, for her attention and for her body.

I like competing.

I like winning even more.

Mara doesn't give a fuck that we're seven stories up, with only a thin pane of glass between her and a hundred-foot drop. She dances, her body as lithe and sinuous as a snake's, rolling and swaying, hypnotizing me.

She turns and hops down, taking slow, sensual steps toward me, her hands covering her breasts. She caresses her breasts, squeezes them, then reveals their perfection like the opening of the doors into heaven.

I'm salivating.

My cock throbs with every beat of my heart.

The chorus of the song begins to play:

Oh, don't you know, don't you know
'Bout the devil…he's a gentleman

Mara gives me a naughty little glance, letting me know that she selected this song on purpose.

I was already well aware that she modeled her painting of the devil after me. After Shaw, too—when she painted it, she wasn't entirely sure which of us had abducted her off the street.

She thinks I'm tempting her along the path of evil.

I disagree.

I want to help her find her true self, as she's helping me find mine.

I don't know if I'm becoming a better man. All I know for certain is that I'm finding new abilities inside myself. Powers I couldn't tap until Mara showed me the way.

Turning her body to the side, Mara pretends to slide her thong down her hip, then pulls it back up again.

I let out a groan.

Grinning wickedly, she turns the other way and repeats her tease on the other side.

"Get over here before I rip you to pieces," I growl.

Mara lets out a peal of delighted laughter and pulls down her underwear before kicking it away.

The shape of her soft little pussy makes me die to rub my fingers over it, to taste it. I want to push my face into it like I did with her shirt. I want to eat her alive.

Starting at the foot of the bed, she crawls up to me on her hands and knees, her eyes locked on mine, her body moving with sinuous grace.

She reaches my belt buckle and pauses, her slim fingers deftly working to release me from my clothes.

She unfastens the belt and my trousers before pulling them down—my underwear, too. My cock is raging, so congested with blood that the veins bulge, the pale flesh flushed with angry color.

When Mara closes her mouth around it, I groan like an animal, like a starving beast.

"Not that way," I snarl. "Turn around and feed me that pussy."

Mara flips around so her mouth is still encircling my cock, her ass up in my face. The shell-like shape of her pussy and the tight little bud above are so fucking erotic that for a moment I can only stare, clenching the meat of her firm round ass in my hands.

She's wet everywhere, glistening with it.

Dancing for me turned her on as badly as it did me.

I dive in, licking and sucking and thrusting my tongue inside every place I can reach. I'm ravenous, my mouth watering, fucking dying for her, craving the taste of her, lapping it up with my tongue.

Meanwhile, her hot wet mouth slides up and down my cock.

The deeper I push my tongue inside her, the deeper she takes my cock. When I lap her clit with my tongue, she sucks on the head, keeping pace with me, making me feel what I'm making her feel at the same time.

I can feel her mouth getting warmer and wetter, her lips swollen, her throat relaxing around my cock. The Ambien is kicking in.

I lick all the way up her slit, then press my tongue against the tight bud of her ass.

Mara shrieks and tries to squirm away, but I have her locked in place, gripping her hips.

I know this embarrasses her, that she doesn't want to let me do it. That's exactly what makes it so fucking hot. I'm gripping her, pulling her into me, forcing her to take it.

I lick her ass in steady strokes until she relaxes, and then I push my tongue all the way inside.

The area grows warm and swollen, flushed with blood. Soaked from her pussy, her ass tastes just as good.

The more I lick her, the more she relaxes, and the deeper I can push my tongue inside her. She can't help the sounds that come out of her: whimpers at first, then helpless sighs of pleasure, followed by gasps and groans.

There are a thousand nerve endings here, just like the clit. Licking her ass brings the erogenous tissue alive. It awakens an entirely new source of pleasure.

Because it's new and untested, she's helpless before it. She's trapped in place, by pleasure as much as by my hands locked around her.

I eat her ass like a ten-course meal.

This is an act I never considered doing before. It would have disgusted me.

Nothing about Mara disgusts me. The dirtier our sex, the more it arouses me.

With Mara, I see it, I want it, I crave it. I give in to my impulses. I lose myself in the frenzy. I'm a wild animal, utterly unhinged.

This is the closest I get to the feeling of killing, only a thousand times better because I'm not alone in it. Mara is right here with me, equally as wild, equally as feral. She's choking on my cock, trying to swallow it whole, while I fuck her pussy and ass with my tongue, one after the other, back and forth.

She gives in to me completely, and that's the greatest rush of all, that moment of submission, when I know she's so lost in pleasure, she can't think or fight anymore. She can only moan and beg for more.

I go back to her clit, her hips clamped between my hands, using all my strength to force her to ride on my tongue.

She starts to come, moaning around my cock, then screams as the orgasm rips through her, the hardest I've seen her have from oral alone. Her whole body shakes. Her teeth scrape my cock so sharply that I'm worried she might bite it off.

Mara goes limp, rolling over on the bed, flopping her hands overhead, her nipples pointing to the ceiling.

"Holy shiiiiiiit," she groans.

"I told you not to tease me."

I scoop her up in my arms, rearranging her on the pillows so her head is at the top of the bed, her feet down.

Her limbs are warm and heavy, her pupils dilated until I can hardly see the thin ring of silver around the black.

"You feeling that Ambien yet?"

"Yeah, I'm feeling it." Her voice is soft and dreamy. "Eat my pussy, Daddy…send me to outer space…"

She's never called me that before. I don't know if it's because she's high or if it's something she's wanted to say for a while.

I sink between her thighs, gently licking her pussy with my tongue. My movements are slow and languorous, with soft, melting pleasure.

Looking up at her, I say, "Why am I your daddy?"

She sighs, turning her head slowly side to side like the bed is a boat rocking her across the water. "Because…" she says softly. "Because you take care of me. You protect me. You do everything for me…"

"Yes, I do."

"You always know what to do… You always know what's best."

I suck gently on her clit, smiling to myself. "Keep that in mind," I say.

Mara doesn't respond. She's already drifting away.

———————

In the dark hotel room, I make my preparations for the night ahead.

The Ambien was for me, not for her. I need to know she's safely locked away in this room so I can focus on the task at hand.

I close the drapes and hang the DO NOT DISTURB sign over the doorknob, then take the only key with me when I leave.

Exiting through the lobby, I hail a cab to the airport.

The cabbie drops me off at the sky bridge. Instead of walking over to the check-in desks, I turn the other way, heading toward long-term parking. This is the best place to steal a car. Unless I'm very unlucky, no one will notice their 2018 Camry is taking a little adventure tonight.

It only takes me a minute to break into the car and three more to bring the engine to life.

I pay the attendant with cash on the way out of the lot. He doesn't look up, mumbling, "Have a good night," as I drive through.

I could have taken my Tesla, but California has too many toll roads with cameras.

I drive to La Crescenta, to the edge of town bordering the mountains.

The Black Dog pub is situated in the shabbiest neighborhood I've driven through on my journey, with tiny saltbox houses situated on bald patches of grass between chain-link fences. I'm sure these little shacks still sell in the high six figures because this is California, where a one-bed, one-bath home can easily run a million dollars. This winter notwithstanding, it's still the most temperate climate on the globe. People will endure any level of traffic or taxation to live here.

I wait in the parking lot for Randall to arrive. I'm an hour early, wanting to arrive first so I can see which car he drives and so I can ensure he's alone.

Randall must have had the same idea. He pulls in a half hour early himself, driving a beat-up Ford truck with paint so worn, it looks like mange.

Mara told me her mother and Randall eventually divorced, mostly because their fights had turned so violent, the neighbors called the cops every weekend, with Randall spending the night in jail at least twice. He was running out of money, which meant Tori Eldritch was no longer interested.

Looks like he's yet to make his fortune again. I found him

through tax returns for the construction company for which he currently works. The address on record was the empty office space. I still don't know where Randall lives.

Now that he's here, I make my way inside and pick up a beer at the bar. Selecting a booth in the darkest and most distant corner of the pub, I text Randall:

I'm here whenever you are.

I wait, hoping he's not going to back out.

Ten minutes later, Randall shuffles into the pub. He's well past sixty, but you can tell he was once a man with shoulders to rival Shaw. Now those shoulders droop, and a hard round belly causes his jeans to sag. His scarred hands testify to years of labor. The broken blood vessels on his bulbous nose and the yellow tinge to his eyes tell another story.

Randall walks to the bar to get his own beer. I watch his interaction with the bartender, checking to see if they know each other, if they're friends. The interaction is brief and impersonal. The bartender keeps his focus on the football game playing on the TV hung over the opposite corner of the bar. I doubt he'll look our way.

Just in case, I'm wearing a baseball cap, glasses, and the sort of plaid button-up that Randall should perceive as a slightly more stylish version of his own buffalo shirt.

I ordered a Budweiser, the same bottle Randall sets on the table.

He sinks heavily into the booth, knocking the tabletop askew with his belly. "They make these things so fuckin' tight," he grouses.

"Nothing's made for tall men," I agree.

It's Randall's bulk, not his height, causing the problem. But commiseration is the first step to friendship.

"Didn't even know if I was gonna come tonight," Randall grumbles. "Haven't seen that bitch in years."

"Mara?"

"Tori."

I knew Tori Eldritch would be the hook. Once a woman has her claws in a man, he never quite gets free of her. Randall divorced her and moved across the state, but if Tori showed up on his doorstep in a tight dress, he'd make the same mistakes all over again.

"When's the last time you saw her?"

"Nine years ago."

"Mara would have been sixteen?"

"Fifteen."

"She was your stepdaughter?"

Randall makes a dismissive snorting sound. "I guess."

She lived in his house for almost a decade, but he's behaving as if he hardly knows her.

"What made you split up?"

"She's a fuckin' nutcase. And the apple don't fall far from the tree."

"I've had a hard time tracking down sources. I've gotta interview three family members, and it doesn't seem like Mara has many."

"We're not family. We never were."

"All right." I shrug. "They're paying five hundred bucks, though. So if you know anything, it doesn't take much to get paid."

Randall shifts in his seat, considering.

"And you'll give me Tori's address?"

"Sure. When we're done talking."

Randall grunts his assent. "Whaddaya wanna know?"

"What was Mara like when you knew her?"

"Fuckin' annoying. I never wanted another kid in the house. My boys were bad enough. Ungrateful, too—she's eating my food, wearing the clothes I put on her back, and she has the fuckin' gall to skulk around the house glaring at me. Plus she and her mom were at it all the time like cats, fucking' squallin' and causin' a racket."

"Did you see any early evidence of her talent?"

Randall scoffs. "Drawin' pictures is supposed to be a job now? Don't make me laugh. Fuckin' lazy, just like her mother."

I don't expect any actual insight from this man. There's only one piece of information that interests me, and I'll play through this charade until I get it. The rest is all just fuel on the fire. Though I can't let him see any hint of the fury stoked inside me with every word that comes out of his disgusting nicotine-stained mouth.

"You said her relationship with her mother was bad?"

"Fuckin' hated each other. Tori wished she'd never had her. Said it all the time. I told her she should pack her off to some relative, but there wasn't anybody to take her. Besides, Tori had some weird thing about her."

"What do you mean?"

"She talked shit on her nonstop. But she was obsessed with reading her journals, her text messages. She'd wear Mara's clothes and her perfume. Especially around me."

My jaw ticks. "She thought that would attract you?"

"Fuck if I know. She was jealous as hell. Always screaming at me if she thought I looked at Mara."

This is the delicate part, where I have to put out the lure without scaring off the fish.

I give a low chuckle, the kind that tells a man that locker-room talk is on the table. "Well...Tori wasn't getting any younger."

Randall snorts. "That's for damn sure."

"And Mara's pretty enough..."

Randall takes a long pull of his beer before wiping his mouth on the back of his hand and belching softly. He leans forward, fixing me with his bloodshot stare. "That woman would have let me do anything to her daughter. She offered her up when she realized I was really gonna leave her. Flat-out told me I could have her."

I keep the friendly smirk fixed on my face, pitching my voice low and amused. "Why didn't you take her up on it? Or maybe you did..."

"Wasn't worth it by then. That cunt was gonna get me tossed in jail. And the daughter's all fucked up. A fuckin' spaz. There's something wrong with her. She's some kinda retar—"

He breaks off, his eyes flicking to my upper lip, which is curling into a snarl I can't control. I have to turn it into a laugh that comes out harsh and braying.

"You don't say."

"Yeah." Randall takes another swallow of beer, sitting back in his chair again, his face closing.

I tipped him off. Couldn't keep hold of myself. I'm fucking sloppy.

Where's the old Cole when you need him?

I take a long steady breath. Deliberately slowing my heart rate. Shelving all thoughts of Mara sleeping peacefully back at the hotel. Crushing my fury and the sickening sense of disgust that threatens to overwhelm me every time I look at Randall's smug face.

I clear my mind of everything but the goal.

When I do, the old Cole is right there waiting for me.

Hello, old friend.

The room sharpens. The babble around me separates into distinct conversations. I smell the hops in Randall's beer and note the pinesap stain on his left sleeve—evidence that he's been out in the woods sometime recently.

I can practically hear his heart beating.

I lean forward, taking off my cap and running a hand through my hair.

In a conspiratorial tone, I say, "You might be right. I know one fucked-up thing about her… My boss won't let me print it, which is a fuckin' shame."

Randall can't resist. He leans forward on his knees, too, his piggy eyes glittering.

Everybody loves a secret.

"What did she do?"

I look around as if making sure nobody can hear us. I already made damn sure this booth in the corner was out of sight, but it gives the proper effect.

"Guess Mara needed some cash a while back. She filmed a porn."

"She did?" Randall's trying to play it cool, but I hear his breath catch. I see the way his thick hand clenches around his beer bottle.

"Yeah. Some nasty, dirty shit. She bought it back from the studio, doesn't want anybody getting their hands on it, but you know the Internet never forgets."

"You found it?"

I grin, my molars grinding in the back. "You're damn right I did."

Now I sit back, triumphant, sipping my own drink. Waiting for what I know is certain to follow.

Another long silence from Randall. Then the low urgent mutter: "You think you could send that to me?"

"I've got it on a flash drive back at the hotel." I take another drink of my beer, letting him squirm. Watching the flush rise up his neck. Then I put out the real lure: the one he can't possibly resist. "Some crazy shit in some kinda schoolgirl outfit…"

He needs it now. He has to have it.

"You can send me a copy, can't you?"

"It sounds like we're negotiating." I give him a smile with just enough sleaziness to seem genuine. "You got something for me? What about Mara's dad—you know where he lives?"

"I don't even know his name." Randall grunts. "Tori never said shit about him."

Damn it. "Well, I need pictures for the article. Any old photographs, yearbooks, letters…"

"I didn't keep any of that shit." Randal scoffs.

"Too bad." I pretend to give up on the idea.

Randall can't let go of the prize. He's licking his lips, clenching that beer like a grenade. Then he thinks of something. "I got a picture of her mom fuckin' some Nazi."

I grin. "That sounds like a trade. Bring it to my hotel room."

"Nah." Randall shakes his head. "I can't drive that far. I got a cabin fifteen minutes from here. You can follow me up."

"Even better."

15

MARA

COLE WAKES ME UP NICE AND EARLY, ALREADY LOOKING BRIGHT-
eyed and freshly showered. He doesn't seem tired at all but
invigorated.

"Get up, sleepyhead. Time for your TV debut."

He's already got blueberry scones and a latte waiting for me,
both warm and fresh.

"What time did you wake up?" I say, stumbling out of bed. I'm
still a little groggy from the Ambien, though my body feels warm
and relaxed.

"I didn't sleep at all."

"What? Why not?"

"No point when we had to get up this early. I'll catch a nap later
if I feel like it."

I guess that makes sense. Cole rarely goes to sleep before
midnight, so it would only have been a few hours' rest at most.

I wouldn't be that chipper on zero sleep, but good for him.

I climb into the shower, luxuriating in the pounding hot spray,
which feels particularly sensual after my hibernation.

"What do you think I should wear?" I crack the glass door to
call out to Cole.

"What did you bring?"

"The blue dress and the velvet jumpsuit."

"Wear the jumpsuit. It's sexier."

"Do I want to be sexy, though?"

I'm shampooing my hair, my eyes closed, trying to picture both outfits. I do love the jumpsuit, but I don't want to give the wrong impression. The world is so much harder on women than on men when it comes to our looks and our clothing. Especially when you're competing in a male-dominated field.

Cole comes into the bathroom before leaning against the doorframe so he can watch me. "Which one do you like wearing? Which feels the most like you?"

I consider, standing still under the spray. "The jumpsuit."

"There you go."

I'm not used to someone agreeing with me, supporting my decisions. I don't feel like a fuckup with Cole. And I don't agonize over the little choices so much. It feels like it doesn't really matter what I wear—everything will work out just fine.

"I'm kind of looking forward to this," I admit as I step out of the shower, vigorously toweling my hair.

"Of course you are. It's exciting."

Cole's in the most energized mood I've ever seen. His dark eyes roam everywhere at once. He can't hold back his grin as he thrusts a scone into my hand. "Eat it while it's hot—it's fucking delicious."

I laugh. "Since when do you eat scones?"

"I eat everything now." He winks at me. "Remember last night?"

It all comes back to me in a rush. I shriek with laughter and outrage. "Don't talk about that!"

He chuckles, grabbing me and pulling me close, not caring that I'm not quite dry yet, my damp body spotting the front of his shirt. He kisses me, his mouth pleasantly warm from the coffee.

"You're going to fucking kill it today," he says. "I can't wait to watch."

As always, Cole is right.

The entire experience passes by in flashes, like snapshots.

We're hustled through the studio at lightning speed, with barely enough time for me to goggle at the brightly lit stages and the bustling desks full of people before I'm in hair and makeup, a paper bib tucked into the neckline of my velvet jumpsuit to protect my clothes from the thick layer of powder being dusted over my face.

"Don't worry," the makeup artist tells me. "It looks like a lot, but under the floodlights, you won't see it at all."

The hosts pass by to introduce themselves. I don't watch much TV, but I've seen clips of Roger Roberts and Gail Mason, who have been running the DBS morning show for the better part of a decade. Like most celebrities, they're much shorter in person than you'd expect. Roger is barely taller than me, and Gale is so petite, you might mistake her for a fifth grader if you only saw her from behind and her helmet of highly teased hair didn't give her away.

Both are wearing even more makeup than I am, their microphones already clipped in place and a folder of prompts tucked under their arms.

"Where's your beret?" Roger ribs me in his broadcaster voice.

I wondered if that was something he turned on for the camera, but it sounds like he always speaks at top volume with careful enunciation.

"She's not a mime!" Gail laughs. Then, patting me on the arm, she says, "We'll see you out there in just a minute!"

The producer gives me a brief rundown of the show, including the point at which I'll be brought onstage and a few of the questions I'll be asked.

"We'll show slides of your paintings on the TV screen behind you," she explains.

"Right, yes." I nod like I understand, while glaring lights, bright colors, and ten different conversations scream at me from all sides.

Cole remains calm and steady, his tall dark figure so familiar to me that I look at him for comfort every time my anxiety threatens to explode.

I watch the show from offstage, marveling at the hosts' ability to talk and joke with each other while their producer barks orders into their earpieces.

"Twenty seconds till the next segment," she warns them.

With the speed of an auctioneer, Roger rattles off, "And that's why I don't cook turkey dinners anymore! Up next, we've got a little culture for you—an up-and-coming artist from San Francisco! She just had her first solo show at the Frankle Gallery, and she's here to explain painting to us! Let's give a warm welcome to Mara Eldritch!"

The producer shoves me forward. I feel myself striding across the stage, my body moving like a puppet on someone else's strings.

Even though I was warned, the overhead lights press down on me like heat lamps. I can already feel myself starting to sweat.

I forgot where the producer told me to sit. I take the chair closest to Gail, hoping I haven't made a mistake.

"Nice to meet you, Mara!" Roger booms, like we haven't already met before. His capped teeth and spray-on tan compete with Gail's glittering red holiday top and matching lipstick.

"Now, I can't draw a stick figure to save my life!" Gail trills. "How did you get your start in art?"

They're both staring at me, their eyes bright, their teeth gleaming.

Under the glaring lights, with the muffled motion of the camera crew all around us—everyone trying to be quiet but making the tiny shuffles and breathing sounds that humans can never entirely contain—I'm thrust back to the last time I sat on a stage, expected to perform, while my mind emptied like a sieve.

I can almost hear my mother snapping her fingers at me, ordering me to start.

I don't know what to reply. I've forgotten how to speak.

The silence drags on for several agonizing seconds.

Wildly, I cast my eyes around until they land on Cole.

He doesn't look nervous in the slightest. He stands next to the producer, his hands tucked in his pockets, smiling at me with perfect confidence. He mouths, "You got this."

I turn back to Gail.

The words flow out like I rehearsed them. "I'm mostly self-taught. I never went to art school. But I watched a lot of YouTube videos and took books out of the library."

"YouTube videos!" Roger laughs. "If that's all it takes, then how come I'm not an expert at golf yet?"

I give him a sly smile. "Well, I'm not three beers in when I paint."

Roger roars with laughter, and Gail shakes a finger at him. "She's got your number."

"Too true." Roger chortles. "The more I shank, the more I drink."

The rest of the interview passes in an instant. The questions are easy. I know exactly what to say.

The commercial break is my chance to escape. Roger and Gail give me brief handshakes, already preparing for the next segment. The producer hustles me off, saying, "Nice work! You'd never guess it was your first time."

"She's just being nice," I say to Cole as we pass through the greenroom once more on our way out of the studio. "I froze up at the beginning."

"It just looked like you were thinking," Cole says.

"I wasn't thinking. I was lost—till I looked at you."

Cole smiles. "You must be the only person in the world who finds me a calming presence."

"I certainly didn't at first."

"What did you think when you looked over at me?"

"I thought…even if I fuck this up, you won't be embarrassed by me. You'll still hold my hand on the way home."

"I knew you weren't going to fuck it up. You always find a way through."

As Cole and I gather our bags from the hotel and head back to the airport, I think to myself that humans don't actually learn things all on our own. Someone has to teach us.

And that's true with all kinds of things, not just learning French or the violin.

Someone has to teach us how to save money, set goals, date, be a good friend...

It might even be necessary for someone to believe in us before we can believe in ourselves.

Unloved children are held back because no one shows them the way.

Cole is so much more than a lover to me. He's the teacher I never had. In some ways, he's the father I never had.

I blush, remembering what I called him last night when I was blitzed out and half asleep. I've never called anybody that word before.

I don't want to be another fucked-up girl with daddy issues.

But, god, it's nice to have a daddy.

―――――――

Returning to Sea Cliff feels like coming home. I run ahead of Cole into the house, practically skipping up the steps. I throw open the doors and inhale that familiar scent, increasingly mingled with my own shampoo, my perfume, and the old books Cole let me put on a shelf in the living room, even though the battered paperbacks clash with his hardcovers and leather-bound books.

I cook dinner for us both, delighting in using Cole's heavy-bottomed copper pots and wooden spoons. Almost nothing in this house is made of plastic. Even the items Cole never uses are of the finest quality, as much for decoration as for the formerly unlikely chance that somebody would make real use of the kitchen.

Cole only cooks the simplest meals for himself. Still, he's a keen student and watches carefully while I mix four egg yolks, freshly grated Parmesan cheese, and Italian herbs in a small bowl.

"That's a lot of bacon," he comments.

"If it's not half bacon and peas, then it's not carbonara." I laugh.

"I think the Italians might disagree."

"I'll tell you a secret that will shock you…I don't always like the most authentic food."

"What do you mean?"

"I know this is sacrilege, but sometimes I like the American version better. We take these foods from all over the world, amp them up, and put them on flavor steroids. San Francisco has the best food of anywhere—I'm convinced of it."

"How would you know?" Cole laughs. "You've never been to Italy."

"That's true," I admit.

I must look forlorn because Cole quickly adds, "I'll take you."

"I wish," I say, trying to laugh it off.

"I mean it."

I hesitate, my throat tightening. I have a desperate desire to visit Europe and see some of the most stunning art and architecture of human creation.

But I shake my head. "You've done too much for me already."

"I've done exactly what I want to do." Cole's expression is stern. "Don't try to prevent me doing more of what I want. You should know by now it's impossible."

I never know how to deal with Cole. He really is relentless.

I change the subject, saying, "Look at this—you can use the hot pasta water to thaw the frozen peas."

"Genius," Cole says with a small smile.

When I've stirred the sauce into the hot noodles and divided the two portions onto our plates, Cole twirls the carbonara around his fork and takes an experimental bite.

"Well?" I bounce in my seat.

"I take back what I said. This is really fucking good."

"Better than Italy?"

"You tell me after you try the real thing. You're the one with the best palate."

I flush with pleasure, attacking my own plate of food.

I've never enjoyed any compliments as much as Cole's. Men have always told me I was pretty, but that's the blandest of tributes. It says nothing about me as a person.

Cole compliments my taste, my opinions, my talents. He notices things nobody ever bothered to notice about me before, like the fact I can taste and smell more acutely than most people, which really does make me a better cook.

It's the silver lining of my sensory issues. While I'm often distracted or stressed by light, sound, smell, and touch, I also take deep pleasure from music and food, rich colors and textures, and the right kind of touch on my skin. It's a blessing and a curse. When everything is wrong, it's pure torture. But when all goes right, it's a gift I'd never give up.

Cole is more considerate of my sensory issues than anyone I've ever known. While he occasionally uses them to manipulate me, he's never tormented me like Randall used to do. Instead, Cole calls me his pleasure kitten and puts me in a state of such comfortable bliss that I'd do anything to be his pet and live in this house forever.

When we're finished eating, and Cole has washed and dried the dishes in his meticulous way, and I've put them back exactly where they belong, he says, "I have something to show you."

"What is it?"

"Come with me."

He takes me into the dining room, where we never actually eat, preferring to sit at the high countertop in the kitchen.

My laptop still sits in the same place. I suppose I've made this my office, not that I spend much time on my computer.

Cole opens the laptop before flicking through windows so quickly that I can hardly follow what he's doing.

Watching Cole navigate technology is eerie, his brain and fingers operating more rapidly than the machine itself.

"Have a seat." Cole gestures toward the chair next to his.

I slip into it, feeling uneasy.

When Cole has an objective in mind, he becomes highly focused to the point where he doesn't blink and hardly seems to breathe. His face is smooth and unsmiling, his dark eyes fixed on my face. It's when he looks the least…human.

He holds up a small black cylinder in his elegantly shaped hand. "I have something for you to watch."

Silently, I take the flash drive, our fingers meeting with an electric spark. "What is it?"

Cole doesn't respond, pushing the laptop toward me, waiting while I insert the flash drive into its slot.

The drive contains only one file: a video, twenty-eight minutes long.

My mouth has gone dry. When I try to lick my lips, my tongue rubs across them like cardboard.

I hover my index finger over the cursor. I'm frightened. I don't want to see whatever Cole is trying to show me, I know it won't be good.

He stands from his chair before coming around the back of mine, watching over my shoulder.

There's no way out of this.

I click the video to make it play.

The image that flickers onto the screen is dimly lit and grainy. It appears to be the interior of some kind of small house—wooden floors and walls, only one room that includes a kitchenette, a single bed, and a door to the outside. It could be a cabin or a shack.

A man kneels directly in front of the door, shirtless, wearing only boxer shorts, and his large misshapen feet splayed below. His graying hair is scruffy, his back hairy and sagging.

I recognize him immediately. I'll never forget the shape of that blocky head with its roll of fat where the skull almost meets the shoulders.

The wave of revulsion that washes over me is physical, so

strong that I have to clamp my hand over my mouth to prevent the carbonara from making another appearance. I want to jump out of my chair, but my legs are rubber, bent under the table.

I thought the video was silent. Now I hear Randall let out a low moan.

His nose is pressed against the door. He appears to be kneeling on something—possibly marbles. He squirms with discomfort but doesn't dare take his nose away from the door.

"I can't…" he groans. "I can't do it anymore…you're gonna break my fuckin' kneecaps."

"You spoke." Cole's chilly voice cuts through the video, clear and unemotional. "That means another hour."

Randall lets out a strangled sound that's part sob, part snarl of rage.

I'm mesmerized, staring at the screen. Watching this man endure the same punishment he inflicted on me at seven years old. I know how his kneecaps feel. There were no marbles in my case, but the wooden floor became agonizing all on its own as the hours crawled by.

Once, after three hours of punishment, I passed out and hit my head on the floor. Randall made me finish my time the next day.

I stare at his nasty old back as his hands shake, bound at the wrists with zip ties.

A maelstrom of emotions whips through me: guilt, fear, disgust, anxiety…

A dreadful spitefulness whispers, *Serves you right, you motherfucker.*

I thought I'd moved past this.

Now I find that the rage was always there, deep inside me.

What I told Cole was true: I hate Randall. I fucking hate him.

He delighted in tormenting me.

When my mother would frustrate him, he'd take it out on me.

He loathed me but couldn't leave me alone.

And always, there was that skin-crawling edge to his attention:

His eyes roaming over my body. His barking orders to put on the plaid skirt so he could whip me in it.

Even at seven, I knew. He was my stepfather, but his interest was anything but fatherly.

Randall can't hold the position anymore. His legs collapse beneath him, and he rolls over on his side.

Cole appears in the camera frame, striding forward, dressed in an outfit unlike anything I've seen him wear before—a plaid shirt and jeans with a baseball cap. In his hand, a pair of bolt cutters.

The punishment is swift. He snips off Randall's thumb.

Randall howls and howls, animalistic screams of pain that buzz with distortion in the shitty speakers of my laptop.

I jerk in my seat, instantly breaking out in a sweat, my heart racing at a gallop. "*Jesus! Fuck!*" I cry.

I don't know what I expected to see, but I've never witnessed anything so graphic. Every cell in my body screams at me to turn away, but my eyes are locked on the screen with sick intensity, my hands clamped over my mouth.

Cold and pitiless, the Cole on the computer orders, "Kneel on those marbles. Your time isn't up."

I look up at the real Cole standing beside me.

He's watching the screen with exactly the same expression as before, calm and focused, his hands clasped loosely in front of him.

I can't believe those are the same hands that wielded those bolt cutters just…just how long ago, exactly?

"When did you do this?" I whisper.

"Last night. While you were asleep."

My mouth falls open. I understand now why he booked that morning show for me—it seemed to come out of nowhere, but I'm sure he pulled the strings behind the scenes. "Was Randall in Burbank?"

"Close by."

I'm pulled back to the screen by a fresh round of cursing and screaming from Randall. He was only able to hobble back into position for a moment before falling over again. This time he loses his left thumb.

"Fuck," I cry, covering my face with my hands. "How long does this go on?"

Cole checks the time ticking away on the video. "Looks like twenty-two more minutes."

"Oh my god."

I don't think I can watch this.

"Did you kill him?" I ask Cole.

"Of course I did."

My heart races, the underarms of my shirt soaked in cold sweat. I can't believe I'm watching this. I can't believe I'm participating.

I'd come to terms with the idea that Shaw had to die, but this is something else entirely. Randall wasn't a threat to me. This is nothing but revenge.

More screams. Another finger gone.

"Why did you do this?"

"I told you." Cole's black eyes fix on mine. "I need to prepare you. You think you know what it means to set yourself against another person. To lure them, hunt them, overpower them, and take their life. But you don't know. You don't know how they'll beg and plead. How they'll do anything to survive. How they'll stick a knife in your eye the moment you lose focus, the moment you even think about offering mercy."

Randall is begging and pleading. He alternates between cursing at Cole, thrashing, trying to escape his bonds, then sobbing and sniveling, offering money, secrets—anything and everything he can think of to save himself.

"What do you want?" he howls. "*What do you want?*"

The Cole on the screen looks down at Randall like an avenging angel, dark and pitiless.

"I want you to give Mara her childhood back."

"*Fuck* Mara!" Randall snarls. "Fuck that little bitch, and fuck her mother, and fuck *you*! She deserved everything she got. I hope she rots in hell!"

"Wrong answer," the Cole on the screen says.

What follows is a bloodbath.

I stare and stare, all feeling draining from my body. All emotion, too. I become strangely calm, my head floating above my shoulders, my body a block of ice below.

I watch Cole murder Randall slowly, brutally, with obvious pleasure.

I watch my vengeance unfold in front of me.

When it's finished, Randall is nothing but meat on the floor. Those heavy hands can't hurt anyone anymore.

I feel hollow inside, all the anger, all the pain, all the resentment scooped out of me.

It's over now. Truly over.

I close the laptop screen and turn to face Cole. I can't tell if he's a monster or my savior. He looks the same as always: stark, beautiful, serene.

I ask him, "Did it feel good to do that?"

"Yes. It was deeply satisfying."

"Why? I already won. I'm happy now. I moved on."

Cole raises one black slash of an eyebrow. "There is no *moving on*. I learned that with my father. If Randall had died of old age, the anger wouldn't have died with him. You have to kill it. I killed it for you."

I don't know how I feel.

Or perhaps I feel everything at once.

It's wrong, so incredibly wrong.

And yet…it also feels like justice.

I wanted Randall dead. Now he is. He made me suffer. And he suffered in return.

Cole plucks the flash drive out of the laptop and holds it out to me once more.

"You put your life in my hands once, the night you came to my studio. Now I'll bet mine. Here's the tape. You won't turn it in. You know this was right."

He pushes the flash drive into my hands, forcing me to close my fingers around it.

I could leave the house and carry this directly to Officer Hawks.

But just as I knew Cole wouldn't hurt me, he knows exactly what I'm going to do.

I walk into the kitchen and drop the drive down the garbage disposal.

The next morning, I wake up alone in the bed.

Cole is giving me space to process what happened.

I understand now that all this was planned out by him, probably weeks ago. All through dinner, he knew what he was about to show me. He probably knew how I'd react. Even what I'd say.

He once told me there are very few surprises for him. In social situations, he always has a quick reply at the ready because he plays out the entire conversation in a fraction of a second, already knowing what he'll say and what the other person will respond, back and forth a dozen times, before either of them ever opens their mouth.

Everything is chess to him, and he's eight moves ahead.

When his opponent plays by the rules, Cole doesn't lose.

I throw a spark of chaos into the game.

Perhaps so does Shaw.

Or Shaw becomes less predictable when I'm in the mix, distracting Cole, forcing him to make decisions against his best interests.

We're entering the endgame now. Am I a valuable asset—a queen to his king? Or am I only a pawn Cole can't bear to sacrifice?

I keep waiting for guilt to overwhelm me.

The people Cole killed before were faceless avatars to me. I never met any of them. Most seemed to deserve what they got.

Randall is different.

I knew him. We sat at the same table. Ate the same food. I knew his favorite sports teams, the names of his sons, which movies he liked, and even what he sounded like grunting and puffing as he fucked my mother.

I hated the intimacy between us, but it was there. I knew him as human, as a man.

And I watched him die.

Should I be sorry for him?

I felt some pity last night, in the moment. Seeing his graying hair and his wretched begging.

But because I know Randall, I'm well aware of how little goodness lived inside him. I can't remember a single instance of kindness to me. Not one, not even when I was very small. Whatever he gave, he gave grudgingly, angrily, always rubbing it in my face afterward, lording it over me.

He was a petty tyrant.

Does anyone care when the tyrant's head is put on a spike on the city gates?

Does anyone shed a tear?

I'm certainly not crying.

In fact, as I rise from the bed, I feel clean and whole. A little bit lighter, as if I shed a weight I didn't even know I was carrying.

I float out of the room and down the stairs, looking for Cole.

I find him in the kitchen readying his customary breakfast.

It's nice starting the day with the same meal every morning, knowing you have control over the day ahead.

He passes me my latte, fresh and flawlessly prepared. Cole would never slap milk and coffee into a cup. To him, whatever's worth doing is worth doing well. He perfects his art even when that art is only a latte.

I sip my drink, naked under my silk robe, feeling the fabric against my skin and the clear morning light streaming in through the windows.

Cole stands behind the counter, his sleeves rolled to his forearms, the damp waves of his hair neatly combed back.

He looks like a man ready to work.

I say, "If we're really going to do this, then you're right, I have to be prepared. Tell me everything. Tell me how you met Shaw."

16

COLE

I knew I had to explain all this to Mara, but I've been dreading it.

I don't often feel regret. In fact, one of the few times I've ever felt it is the night I fucked up with Mara and she left the party with someone else.

I didn't use to regret anything about Shaw.

Now...I wish I had done things differently.

I look out the kitchen window to the bright, sparkling waters of the bay, not watching the boats drifting past, instead visualizing the flat green lawns and low modern buildings of the California Institute of the Arts.

I say to Mara, "It was my first year of art school. My mother was dead. My father was dead. My uncle was dead. I was an orphan, alone in the world.

"It didn't feel strange to me because I'd always been alone. People crowded around me, drawn by looks and money, the charm I can turn off and on at will. To me, all those people seemed the same and not like myself. I was a wolf in a world of deer. Especially once Ruben was gone.

"You probably know CalArts is small, only about a thousand students. Some of them were hoping for a career in film. Tim Burton is a famous alumnus, as we were reminded practically every fucking day.

"I doubted he was popular when he actually attended. Art school was no different from anywhere else I'd been. People didn't suddenly become high-minded simply because we were studying art. The same rules applied there as everywhere else: money, connections, and strategy mattered just as much as the work itself.

"All the rules of subterfuge applied as well. Classmates like Valerie Whittaker were always going to get the most direct instruction from Professor Oswald because he loved bending over her canvas when she wore one of her low-cut sweaters.

"That irritated some of the male students in the class. I thought it was only natural. Valerie was using every weapon in her arsenal. She was talented, one of the best in the class, and I found it amusing how she had the professor wrapped around her little finger.

"All the professors at the school were working artists themselves. They spoke with reverence of the Damien Hirsts and Kara Walkers of the world but couldn't hide the edge of envy that they had failed to become one of the greats themselves, scratching a living teaching the spoiled children of families rich enough to afford the tuition.

"If you were really poor, you could get into CalArts on a scholarship. That was the case with Alastor Shaw."

Even though she's been waiting for his introduction, Mara grimaces at his name, unconsciously touching the raised scar running up her left wrist.

"I disliked him immediately. Not because he was poor but because he kept insisting he wasn't.

"It's impossible to pretend to be wealthier than you are. You might as well plop yourself in the center of Kenya and try to convince the Maasai that you're one of them.

"Alastor was a terrible liar. His incompetence irritated me more than the lies themselves. After the Christmas break, he came back to school wearing a Rolex that was obviously fake. He kept flashing it at everyone, not realizing that Rolex is the McDonald's of luxury watches. Even a real one wouldn't have impressed at our school.

"He hadn't yet learned to ingratiate himself. No one particularly liked him. Back then, Alastor was moonfaced, awkward. Always trying to suck up to the popular students, especially me."

"Was he really?" Mara says in amazement.

"Oh, yes. He got rid of his glasses after the first semester, but he still had terrible skin, the haircut of an incel, and he'd wear tent-sized T-shirts with hideous bright graphics all over them…"

I pause, chuckling to myself. "Actually, those T-shirts might have been the inspiration for his entire aesthetic, now that I think about it."

Mara frowns, the much deeper well of sympathy she possesses distracting her from the inevitable end of this tale. "It almost makes me feel sorry for him," she says.

"Don't. Don't feel sorry for either of us. At least not until you've heard everything.

"Alastor fixated on me from the beginning. He'd try to set up his easel next to mine. Make conversation with me between classes. Sit near me at lunch.

"It took a couple of cuts, me humiliating him in front of other students, before he backed off. Even then, he was always watching me. Always close by.

"You'll probably understand that Alastor recognized something familiar in me. Those who don't feel the normal range of emotions are better at noticing when a smile comes a second too late or when it doesn't quite consume the whole face. We learn to imitate sympathy, interest, humor…but like Alastor's Rolex, some counterfeits are better than others.

"He tried to insinuate we were like each other. That we might have interests in common. I shut him down hard. I didn't want to think I was like anyone. Especially not him.

"Alastor hadn't developed his own style yet. He imitated the professors and other students. The hierarchy of talent in our classes quickly became apparent: I was at the top, along with Valerie

Whittaker and a few others. Alastor bounced between the middle and the bottom, depending who he was cribbing from on any given week.

"I was consumed by art school. It was the first time I'd felt a sense of vocation. I couldn't wait to get the fuck off campus and start working full-time. I only stayed because I was aware of how important it was to develop connections with professors and visiting lecturers. People in the art world who could help me once I had pieces to show.

"Professor Oswald liked me almost as much as Valerie. He invited us to private shows and introduced us to everyone. Similar to what I did when you and I first met."

Mara nods, understanding perfectly as she just experienced the same mentorship.

"Oswald was no genius. He was competent, but he'd been making the same broken-mannequin-type sculptures for decades, and Robert Gober was already doing that better. It was clear he was burned out, frustrated, barely scraping by with his shitty Buick and sport coats with holes in the elbows.

"Still, I liked him, or at least I found him useful and interesting to talk to. He knew an immense amount about his subject, and his suggestions for my work were helpful. I brought him a whole folder of sketches I had made for potential sculptures. Some were complex and would need custom equipment before they could be built. He went through each sketch, seeming particularly taken with a drawing I'd made for a massive figure that would look male from one angle and female from another."

Mara leans forward on her elbows, her chin cradled by her palms, fascinated by this story. I knew she would enjoy getting a peek at the younger version of myself, closer in age and stage to where she is now.

I'm not enjoying it as much. I don't look back on that time with the same arrogance I used to.

I push ahead, wanting to get it all over with as quickly as possible. "Professor Oswald was the first person who took an interest in my art. It meant something to me. So, when he participated in a show shortly after Christmas, I wanted to attend. Even though he hadn't mentioned it to me and I hadn't technically been invited.

"It was Marcus York who put me on the guest list. He's an old friend of my father's. Did I tell you that?"

Mara nods.

"It was the first time I'd spoken to him since my father had died. He was glad to do me a favor—after all, I was the one who inherited the money and the business, though I had no interest in running it myself.

"I went to the show. As soon as I got there, I could see everyone buzzing around Oswald's sculpture. I didn't hear a word they said. I just stood there staring."

Mara's eyes go wide as she anticipates what I'm about to say.

"It was an exact replica of the sketch I'd shown him. Almost every detail was the same. The main difference was that it was smaller than I'd intended—probably because he didn't have the means to make it bigger."

Even though she knew what was coming, Mara lets out a groan of outrage. She understands how violating it feels to have an idea stolen before you've even had a chance to bring it to life. "What did you do?"

"I walked up to him, almost in a daze. I didn't know what I intended to say to him, which was unusual for me. I saw his surprise that I was there and his look of squirming discomfort. But then he pushed that away and greeted me with as much friendliness as usual, clapping me on the shoulder, saying how glad he was that I had come."

"Did you confront him?" Mara fidgets in her seat, unable to stand the suspense.

"Not then. It would have made a scene, and remember, barely

anyone knew me yet. Oswald was the one with the connections and the tenure. This was his show.

"I stayed after class on Monday. I was too upset to be strategic. I blurted it out like an idiot: 'You copied my sketch!'"

"What did he say?" Mara murmurs through her hands pressed to her mouth. She's squirming with agitation, like she's the one who stole the idea.

"He scoffed in my face. He said, 'Don't be ridiculous. First of all, there's hardly any similarity at all between your sketch of a concept and my actual piece. And second, I've been talking about gender perception in my classes for months. If anything, your sketch was inspired by the lectures I gave as I was sculpting the piece.'"

"Motherfucker!" Mara shrieks, jumping out of her chair and pacing around the kitchen island.

There's no better audience for a story than Mara. She feels it all as if it's happening to her.

It takes several moments for her to calm down enough to take a seat again. "What did you say back to him?"

"I just stared at him. Truly impressed with the absolute magnitude of his bullshit. He was lying so intensely that he actually believed it. He'd been telling himself fairy tales late at night while working on the sculpture. Pretending it represented this and that, while shaving away the bits of his memory that recalled the exact dimensions and proportions of my sketch."

"Did you pull it out of your folder? Shove it in his face?"

I shake my head. "You'll never convince someone who's already convinced themselves. And you damn sure can't reason with them. I left his office, wondering what I had hoped to get out of that encounter. Did I actually think he'd publicly admit he'd stolen it? That he'd credit me for the work? Did I forget how humans operate? There was never going to be resolution or any kind of justice. I suppose I wanted to see acknowledgment in his eyes—shame, apology. But he robbed me of even that. He was so deep in delusion that he would have fought my allegations with all the outraged fervor of a man who'd actually been wronged."

Mara lets out a sigh of frustration, understanding only too well what it feels like to be on the wrong side of a power dynamic.

"He was only a professor, but he was far more powerful than me in that particular space. I was an infant in the art world. He could crush me under his boot if I dared make an accusation. Blacken my name before I even got started.

"I was furious with myself. I'd failed to see Oswald for what he was, failed to see his real intentions for me. I was blinded by my desire to be nurtured in this endeavor that was personal and emotional to me. I felt humiliated—not only from the theft but because I didn't see it coming.

"I stormed out of his classroom, running right into Shaw. He was eavesdropping with his ear practically pressed against the door. I could have cheerfully ripped his head off his shoulders, but I just shoved past him and kept walking.

"I told myself I'd let it go. I ripped up the sketch—there was no way to build it anymore without being called a plagiarist myself—and threw my efforts into new projects.

"I was having success at school, getting the accolades I craved from professors and fellow students. Maybe I really could have gotten over it. Especially if Oswald made efforts to make it up to me.

"Instead, he did the opposite. This was me not fully understanding human psychology yet—we both knew there was a debt between us. I wanted it repaid. But if Oswald acknowledged the debt, he'd have to acknowledge what he'd done. And he couldn't stand that.

"The sculpture he'd stolen was the most acclaimed of any he'd ever made. It sparked a renaissance for him, renewing interest in all his previous work, buoying him to new heights in his career.

"The more success he gained from it, the more invested he became in believing it was all his. At first this manifested as him avoiding me in class, interacting less with my work. But soon that wasn't enough—he had to enforce his narrative that I was talentless, that he was the real artist. He started marking me lower and even criticizing me to other professors. Telling them I was lazy, that my ideas were unoriginal. Protecting himself in case I ever decided to pipe up. He didn't know I'd already torn up the sketch."

Mara rests her hand on my thigh, understanding two things at once: First, the pain of being slandered to the people you most want to impress. Second, the fucking rage when that slander is based off a lie, the exact reversal of the truth.

"It ate at me, day after day. This man stole from me, and he wouldn't even acknowledge it. He was punishing *me* for it.

"I began to notice all the other things about Professor Oswald that were loathsome. As his ego swelled, he became more and more arrogant in class. More inappropriate to Valerie. More careless of which days he was supposed to lecture. More boastful about his own work.

"I felt there was only one way to right the scales. I could hardly sleep or eat. The itch to remove him from existence became physical. It made my heart race every time we were in class together."

Mara lets out a soft sigh, understanding what I'm about to tell her: the real crossing of the line.

"I'd killed twice before. When I killed Ruben, I thought it would be the only time. I knew what he was. I knew that even if I handed him every dollar of my father's estate, he'd still cut my throat in the night because I'd once annoyed him. I had to do it—it was him or me.

"The mugger in Paris happened in an instant, in a burst of rage that left the man's brains dashed on the wall before I even realized the other two had run. He scared me. My fear overwhelmed my self-control, and I acted without planning.

"Now I was contemplating something very different: a murder I would plan ahead of time and execute without real need. The damage was already done—or most of it anyway. Oswald was slandering me, still impeding my career. But this was as much about revenge as protecting my future interests."

I pause, pondering my state of mind at the time. "I believed I was gaining more and more control of my emotions by the day. I thought that made me powerful and better than other people. I had my emotions locked down so deep that I hardly felt anything anymore. My anger at Oswald was one of the first encounters that had stirred me in a long time. And I *was* angry. I *was* emotional. Much more than I would have admitted."

Mara squeezes my thigh. She still fucking feels for me. No matter what I did—whether it was justified or not.

"I gave him one last chance. I asked him for a letter of recommendation for a study abroad in Venice. It was a competitive program—only two students would be selected from our school.

"Oswald fixed me with this look of pretend sympathy and said, with what I'm sure he thought was complete sincerity, 'I wish I could Cole, but I really don't think anything you've made this semester justifies that sort of recommendation. Maybe next year, if you really come into your own.'

"I had just made a sculpture that had the whole classroom buzzing with envy, every student in that room wishing they'd thought of it first, half the girls snapping photos on their phones. Oswald gave it a B plus. I could have killed him for that alone.

"From that moment forward, I started planning. That was when I created my method, which has served me flawlessly since. I found an abandoned mine shaft far from hiking trails. You'll know where that was because it's where we first met."

Mara's eyes widen as she finally realizes what I was doing that night. I wasn't in the woods to find her—I was there to lose someone else.

"I spent four weeks researching forensic evidence and four more planning the event. It all went off exactly as I planned. I entered his house via an unlocked window I'd scouted before. I wore a full containment suit. Knelt on his chest before he even woke up, already strangling him, pinning him down with my weight. He looked up into my eyes, and I saw the comprehension on his face. He knew why I was killing him. I wanted him to know. I finally got the acknowledgment of what he'd done. It passed silently between us as he died.

"I dumped his body down the shaft in two industrial bins I'd bought in cash from a hardware store with no cameras. I doused his remains in oxygen bleach and left nothing in the house—not a single hair off my head, no blood from him. Only a little urine in the bed from where his bladder let go.

"The key to getting away with it is this: no body, no murder. I left his car in the driveway, but I took his wallet. He had no wife, no children. Our professors were hardly the picture of reliability. I knew it might be weeks before he was properly reported missing. By then, I doubted a police dog could get a sniff of anything in his house.

"I had no fear of being caught. In fact, in the aftermath, I felt deeply peaceful. No itch tormented me anymore. I had righted the scales."

Mara gives a slow shake of her head, understanding that wasn't the end of it. Not even close.

"Shaw knew," she murmurs.

"That's exactly right. Alastor watched it all happen, from the moment Professor Oswald turned on me. The other students knew I'd fallen out of favor, but only Alastor knew why.

"Once the news of the professor's disappearance spread across the school, Alastor intercepted me on the way to the library. By this point I'd given him enough verbal slaps that he knew better than to speak to me, but he did it anyway, sidling up and saying in his overly familiar way, 'I suppose you're glad to see Oswald gone.'

"I played it off. I said, 'The professors miss more classes than the students do. He'll be back when he remembers he needs his paycheck.' Shaw licked his lips, giving me this grin like we both knew better. 'I don't think so,' he said."

"Was he threatening to tell someone?"

"No, no, no. The game with Shaw has never been about exposing each other. He wants to be in on the secret together. He never intended us to be rivals: he wants to collaborate."

Mara's face blanches. She was another of Shaw's attempts at "collaboration." He began the process of killing her, hoping I'd complete it.

I take a breath. This is the part I didn't want to tell her. The part I've tried not to think about since. The only other thing that's ever made me feel guilty.

"At that point, as far as I know, Shaw had never killed anyone. I'm sure he'd thought about it, fantasized. Watched movies, read books, looked at porn that scratched a certain type of itch for him. But it was all theoretical. All imagination.

"I had taken fantasy into the real world. And to Shaw, I was a hero. An icon. Everything he wanted to be but wasn't. Any boy at our school with talent or swagger wanted to be friends with me. All the girls wanted to date me—none more than Valerie.

"I liked her, but I wasn't interested in dating anyone. All I cared about was the trajectory of my career. Now that Oswald was out of the way, every door stood wide open.

"Shaw was obsessed with Valerie. She had a specific look that you've probably seen replicated in every girl he's killed: slim, beautiful, long dark hair, and at least one tattoo."

"Everyone except Erin," Mara murmurs.

"That's right. Everyone except Erin."

"Even me."

"Yes," I admit. "Though for me, that had nothing to do with Valerie. I noticed you because of what you did with that dress. But I'm sure Shaw loved that our tastes were finally aligning."

"He wanted Valerie because he thought *you* wanted her."

"Yes. He could never understand the difference between respect and desire."

Mara sighs. "I don't know if they *are* that different. It wasn't your looks that drew me at first—I admired you. So much that it overpowered everything else."

"You didn't want me for my looks?" I pretend to be hurt.

Mara laughs. "Not back then. But don't worry, I've become much shallower. Now I notice them every minute of the day."

"Thank you." I smooth my hair back with both hands.

Mara snorts and punches me playfully on the arm. Then she remembers what we were discussing, and her smile falls away. "I'm guessing there's a reason I've never heard of Valerie Whittaker."

"Yeah." I'm not smiling anymore either. "There's a reason. They found her body draped across the lap of the Lincoln sculpture on our campus lawn. Her naked flesh was covered in bruises and bite marks. The first appearance of the Beast of the Bay, though I've never seen the police make the connection."

Even though she knew it was coming, Mara's face falls into lines of misery. She feels for each of these girls as if she knew them.

In this case, I did know Valerie. Mara is right to mourn her loss.

"Shaw left her there for me, like a cat bringing a dead bird to your doorstep. I didn't have to see his smug smile the next morning in class to know who did it."

I swallow the disgust rising in my throat. "He thought I'd be impressed. Proud of him, even. I shut him down hard. Turned away if he even tried to speak to me. That was the real start of our enmity. He'd shaken off my snubs before. But failing to acknowledge his first kill…that he couldn't forgive."

"Did you consider telling the police?" Mara asks.

"No. Shaw would expose me in turn. There was no evidence of what I'd done to Professor Oswald—Shaw hadn't found my dumping ground yet—but he could draw attention where I didn't want it.

"I felt sorry for Valerie, to a degree. But you have to understand, Mara, I had no real attachment to her or to anyone. Not until I met you."

For Mara, who bonds with everyone she meets, this must seem incomprehensible. Still, she nods, understanding me even on our point of greatest difference.

"Valerie's death drew much more attention than the professor's disappearance. The arrival of TV cameras was exhilarating to Shaw. That was when he truly transformed: he arrived at school with his hair freshly cut, wearing an outfit that was almost stylish. He spoke confidently to the cameras, telling them how close he was to Valerie, how wonderful she was, what a loss her talent would be to the art world, how he hoped whoever had done it would be caught quickly.

"Her death energized him. He made his first painting that scored the top mark in the class—an abstract in brilliant color."

Mara grimaces, finally understanding what each of those garish, vibrant canvases means to Shaw. His Technicolor rainbows are the energy he feels when he brutalizes a girl, ripping her soul from her body in wild, erotic abandon.

"That's what the inside of his head looks like," I tell Mara. "And that's why you have to be very fucking careful around him. I've killed from anger or because I felt justified. Shaw delights in it. There's nothing more erotic to him than causing pain, hearing a woman's screams as he rips her apart. If he ever gets the chance, he will slaughter you without hesitation. He *wants* to kill you. More than anyone else. More than he wants to kill me. He wants me alive to see what he's done to you."

Mara sways in her chair, her skin dull as chalk.

I take her cold hands in mine. "But that's not fucking happening," I assure her. "We'll make our plan, and he'll never get closer to you than the length of a room. You won't fight him. You won't even touch him. I'll do what needs to be done. I just need your help to create the illusion. He's bigger than me—I need one moment of surprise. Just one single moment."

Mara swallows hard. "I can do it," she says. "I want to do it. For Erin, for Valerie, for everyone he's killed and everyone else he'll hurt."

She lays her right palm over the scar on her left wrist and the left palm over the scar on the right, clamping her hands tight like a

covenant, like an oath. "And I want to do I it for me. He tried to kill me, too. I'm only alive because of myself. Because I ran down that fucking mountain."

I feel another bolt of guilt. I could have carried her down. But I wasn't awake. Mara hadn't enlivened me yet.

"Shaw has to die for you to be safe. But also because I'm responsible. I didn't think so at the time. I thought whatever he did was his business, that it had nothing to do with me. Now I see it differently. I may not be Doctor Frankenstein, but I helped flip the switch on that particular monster."

"We're the only ones who can stop him," Mara says.

"We're the only ones who will."

17

MARA

COLE AND I HAVE MADE OUR PLAN.

We've run over it again and again in the safety of his living room.

Cole said he would prepare me for our confrontation with Shaw. At the time, I stupidly thought that meant he would train me, like a fighting montage in a movie.

Now I realize how foolish I was.

I have no hope in an actual fight with Shaw—I might as well try to wrestle a grizzly bear. No training Cole could give me in months or even years could ever compensate for the imbalance in reach and mass.

Cole has no intention of me ever touching Shaw. But he's intensely aware of the danger I'll be in all the same. He knows what a killer can do.

So he drills me again and again and again, even though my only role is to be the mouse running from the cat.

Cole needs that single moment of distraction to put a knife in the side of Shaw's neck.

I'll lure Shaw.

I'll be the bait.

The real preparation was watching the tape.

Cole made me watch Randall die because I'd never seen someone killed before. Especially not someone I knew personally.

Cole knew I'd have to desensitize myself to blood, to screams, to the impulses of pity that might cause me to deviate from the plan. Cole knows the terror of violence, the physical effect it has on a person. He knows how it breaks apart your mind, causing you to act on instinct in all the wrong ways.

He drills me over and over and over so that in the heat of the battle with Shaw, I'll stick to our agreement.

"If worse comes to worse," Cole says, fixing me with his dark stare, "if things are going wrong…you run, Mara. You don't try to help me. You don't try to stay. You fucking run. Because he'll be right behind you—and if I'm gone, there's no one left to save you."

"That's not going to happen. He'll be dead before he even knows what's happening."

"That's the plan," Cole agrees.

That would comfort me, except I remember the old quote *no plan survives contact with the enemy.*

Another complication is the continued surveillance of Officer Hawks.

Cole complained to the SFPD. He has enough connections in city government that Hawks has been told to back off. Hawks ignored that order, still trailing Cole on his own off-hours, showing up to every event where they'll let him in the door, and visiting Clay Street more than the artists who keep studio space in Cole's building.

Hawks takes his opportunity to intercept me when Cole is at Corona Heights Park overseeing the final stages of construction on his monumental sculpture. Probably freezing his ass off because a frigid wind is blowing in from the bay.

Officer Hawks steps in front of me before I can touch the heavy glass doors of the Alta Plaza building.

The wind whips our hair into our faces—his as well as mine because Hawks hasn't had it cut in a while. In fact, his entire person looks ill groomed. All these after-hours stakeouts are taking their toll on him. He's unshaven, his eyes bloodshot.

"Doesn't it bother you?" he demands. "Sleeping with the man who killed your roommate?"

I round on him, equally as indignant. "I told you who killed Erin," I hiss. "I have to see him at every fucking party I attend. Shaw is the Beast, not Cole. Why don't you do your fucking job and arrest him?"

Hawks lets out a bitter laugh. "He's really got you fooled, doesn't he?"

"Cole isn't trying to fool me, and I'm not trying to fool him. We've seen each other's scars. You think you're a good man? I bet there's something you're ashamed of. Something you've never told anyone. Cole's told it all to me. *All* of it. I'm not saying he's a saint. But he *is* honest."

"An honest killer?" Hawks sneers.

"You've never shot anyone?" I sneer right back at him.

"I'm a cop. It's my job to catch criminals."

"Yeah? I bet you only shot them when you had to, right? I bet every time you pulled your gun out, you absolutely had to do it; there was no other way. No part of you made a judgment on that person. No part of you thought they deserved to die."

Hawks stares at me through the smudged lenses of his glasses.

My time with Cole has taught me to look for signals: the motions on the face that the mind can't control. For Hawks, it's a twitch of his right eyelid, blinking over his iris like a camera shutter.

He doesn't even know he's doing it.

We both know he sees a killer in Cole because he recognizes something familiar: a man who crosses the line when he feels it's necessary, when he thinks he's justified.

"I'm going to put him in prison for a hundred years," Hawks hisses, his nose inches from mine. "Help me to do it, or I swear to god, I'll book you as an accomplice. I'll make sure you see prison time along with him. You'll be splashed across every fucking paper: the Karla Homolka to his Paul Bernardo."

Hawks has no idea how accurate that may soon become. But not in the way he thinks.

I try to push past him. Hawks seizes my upper arm, digging his fingers into my flesh.

"You live in his house now. You could let me inside. Let me search the place—I'll do it when he's not home. He doesn't even have to know."

Hawks is unaware that Cole has cameras all over the house. Either way, there's no evidence to be found. Cole's not that fucking stupid.

He's only left evidence out in the open one time: inside *Fragile Ego*. I've begged Cole to buy the sculpture back and destroy it, but he doesn't want to. He says it's too beautiful.

This is the one point on which he is utterly irrational. Cole loves his art. He'd no sooner destroy it than he'd destroy me.

I almost want to let Hawks search the house just to show him how fucking stupid he's being.

On the other hand, he's not completely wrong. Cole is a murderer, just not the one he's looking for.

The only way to deal with Hawks is to keep him at bay until we can deliver Shaw gift wrapped. Just in time for Christmas.

Calmly, I remove Hawks's fingers from my arm, grabbing his pinky and bending it back until he lets go.

"You're wrong," I tell him flatly. "You'll see it for yourself soon enough."

"What's that supposed to mean?"

"The Beast of the Bay kills three times. Have you noticed that?"

Hawks goes still, his eyes glinting behind his glasses. "Last time was four."

My stomach lurches. *Can't think about that. Picturing Erin drowned on my bed doesn't fucking help her.*

"The point is he started a new cycle. Why don't you try tailing Shaw on your off-hours? Either you'll catch him in the act…or you'll save some poor girl from becoming his next victim."

To his credit, Hawks actually considers this idea. But then his eyes narrow, and he hisses, "Sounds like you want to clear the way for your boyfriend's nocturnal activities."

I'm losing my patience. "If that's what you think, there's no point continuing this conversation. I would *never* help a man hurt another woman. I'm a ladies' lady."

Shaking off Hawks, I storm into the building.

Sonia is already hurrying over, having seen the whole thing through the window. She looks ready to have ripped Hawks a new asshole if he hadn't let go of me.

Sonia is also a ladies' lady.

When she sees I'm fucking fuming, she puts her arm around my shoulders. "You want me to call his boss? Or better yet—I'll call Cole."

"No need. I told him off myself."

"I'll bet you did." Sonia grins approvingly. "You're turning into quite the little hellcat."

I let out a laugh, thinking that Cole calls me a pleasure kitty and Sonia calls me a hellcat. I really don't mind either of those descriptors. In fact, they suit me perfectly.

"I don't want to claw his eyes out. But I will if I have to."

Sonia snorts. "Now you sound like Cole. Must be a hazard of working here. We all become a little more...utilitarian."

Sonia and I part ways at the stairs, her attending to the monumental labor of running Cole's empire, and me heading upstairs to work on my newest series.

Sonia is right. Cole is rubbing off on me, and so is she. We always become like the people who surround us. No human is an island. We're more like rocks in a tumbler, knocking against one another's rough edges, polishing and refining one another as we pass.

These days I have no problem with the company I keep.

18

COLE

Shaw dies on Christmas Eve.

That's the plan.

I've gone over it with Mara a thousand times, but I still hate that I have to involve her. She's the bait, and the bait is never entirely safe from being swallowed whole.

We're attending the East Bay Artists' Christmas party. In the art world, this is the biggest rager of the year—bigger than Halloween or New Year's. Holding it on Christmas Eve probably means something, that artists lack the traditional family ties that would usually consume this night of the year. That used to be true for me.

Tonight I wish I were home with Mara, far from anyone else.

At least she looks fucking stunning. I love showing her off. Wish I didn't have to ruin it all in a few hours' time.

Mara wears a glittering gown, the halter top cut almost down to the navel, the long skirt hiding the fact she's wearing her favorite boots beneath. No high heels tonight—that would be very stupid.

Her makeup is full of sparkles, too, her hair tumbling down her back in dark waves, diamond stars and moons pinned all over it. She looks like the night sky come to life.

Her arms are bare, the long scars running up both wrists still dark and raised. They'll probably never fade.

Tonight they're meant as an invitation to Shaw: *Come finish what you started.*

I know he'll be here, though I haven't seen him yet. He wouldn't miss the biggest event of the year.

The party is in the Castro, on Market Street. The old baroque theater is currently being renovated, so all the seats have been removed, leaving plenty of space for socializing and dancing. The movie screen remains, playing a loop of psychedelic images: Time-lapse videos of flowers blooming, withering, dying. Raindrops falling upward in reverse. Spiraling mandalas that break apart and reform like beads in a kaleidoscope.

The music pumping from the speakers is dark and insistent, perfect for my current mood.

♫ *"On My Knees"—RÜFÜS DU SOL*

Right before we left the house, I tucked a knife in the pocket of Mara's long black evening coat.

"I'm not going to need that," she said.

"I don't care," I snapped. "You're taking it anyway."

The knife is freshly sharpened, the blade finer than a razor's edge. I have its twin in the pocket of my tux.

Shaw won't use a gun, and neither will I. A knife is far more personal—and far more effective, once we're in close range.

I'll keep my promise to Shaw: the next time we're alone, only one of us will leave alive.

We circulate through the crowd, Mara staying close by my side as we both search for Shaw. It's easy for me to make conversation with anyone we pass because I'm used to scheming and chatting at the same time. It's harder for Mara. Her smile is strained, her eyes darting around the party.

I keep my hand on the small of her back to calm her.

She makes a sharp sound, drawing in a breath.

"Do you see him?" I mutter.

"Not Shaw—Hawks is here."

Fuck.

I turn to look, spotting him over by the open bar. He's dressed in a rented tux to blend in, but his best disguise is his scruffy face and uncombed hair. That's what really makes him look like one of us.

Hawks has been demoted again. He was in charge of the investigation of the Beast of the Bay for two short weeks—then Alastor made another kill, and Hawks was booted back down the ladder.

Mara was devastated when she heard the news of another body on the shore. She said we waited too long to attack Shaw.

"The Christmas party is our best chance," I told her. "If we don't play this off flawlessly, if we tip him off in any way, it won't work. He'll bolt, and we'll be right back where we started."

In a way, it benefits us. That was the second girl in the cycle. Shaw will be aching to complete the triad.

And Mara is the perfect prize.

If I know anything, it's that Shaw is salivating to take her from me. He wants it more than he wants money or success. Killing Mara would be the ultimate act of domination over me, Shaw ascending to his final form.

Too bad I'm gonna put him in the ground instead.

I want to get this over with. Where the fuck is he?

Mara frets. "We can't do anything if Hawks is here."

"Don't worry about that—he's not on the guest list, and there's no way in hell somebody brought him as a date."

I take a short detour to whisper in Sonia's ear. Ten minutes later Hawks is hustled out of the party, arguing with security all the way out the door.

Sanity is a fragile thing—a few taps with a hammer, and the whole psyche can crack. I think Hawks has had more than a few taps.

As Hawks leaves, Shaw arrives. He's dressed in a midnight-blue tux, a stunning redhead on his arm. The girl looks suspiciously like Erin Wahlstrom. I doubt that's a coincidence—we knew Shaw would come, and he knew we'd be here, too. He can't resist turning the knife one last time on Mara.

She watches Shaw twirl the redhead around the dance floor, her shoulders stiff with fury.

"Just a few more hours," I promise her. "Then he'll pay."

"Bleed every fucking drop out of him," she replies, never taking her eyes off Shaw.

We wait for him to get comfortable. We wait for the night to progress. This is an important part of the hunt: the false sense of security. Let the prey come into the clearing. Let them approach the water. Let them lower their head to drink. Only then does the crocodile lunge up out of the water.

Shaw drinks his champagne. He flirts with the redhead and with anyone else who passes within his view. Occasionally, he throws glances in my direction or in Mara's. I ignore him as I have at other events where we've been forced to share space. I'm never the one who approaches Shaw; it's always the other way around.

Mara and I dance together.

She's already beginning her part of the charade. She pretends to drink too much champagne, leaning heavily on my arm. And I pretend to become annoyed with her, snapping at her once or twice, before she spills her drink on my trousers, and I stalk off, annoyed, abandoning her on the dance floor.

This is phase one.

Mara goes to the ladies' room to collect herself. She'll splash water on her face, pretend to attempt to sober up.

Meanwhile, I search for Sonia.

I find her engrossed in conversation with a broker named Allen Wren, pitching him on Mara's newest series.

"She's in high demand these days. Each painting sells for more than the last. If you've got potential buyers, you'd better put the wheels in motion—even a few weeks could cost them thousands."

"You're not going to railroad me, Sonia," Wren says, wagging his finger in her face. "I've been burned on these so-called rising stars before."

"Not this one," Sonia promises, sipping her drink. "Have you seen her work in person? Photographs don't do it justice. The paintings glow, Allen. They fucking glow!"

"I'll come take a look this week." Wren finishes his own drink in a gulp and leans forward to run his fingertips down the back of Sonia's arm. "But why don't you ever come visit my gallery, Sonia? It's been months since I had you alone in one of my back rooms…"

Sonia arches an eyebrow at him, not shaking off his hand. "I'll consider it… I liked what I saw last time…"

They both jolt upright when they see me standing only a few inches away. Sonia blushes and gives an embarrassed laugh, while Wren doesn't even try to hide what he was up to.

"Your fidus Achates is very persuasive, Cole. I think I'd do anything she asked…"

"Come dance with me," I say to Sonia, ignoring Wren.

This is such a strange request that Sonia accompanies me without question, following me onto the dance floor and slipping into a formal position better suited to a waltz than the music actually playing.

She looks up at me quizzically. "Where did Mara go?"

"The bathroom."

This is the part of the plan that neither Mara nor I particularly like. She wanted to explain everything to Sonia, but I told her that would be a mistake. Most people are terrible actors. If Sonia knows she's playing a part, Alastor will see it. I need her discomfort to sell the story.

Alastor must see everything exactly as I've arranged, exactly as follows:

Mara returns from the bathroom.

Sonia tries to cede her position on the dance floor, but I won't let her. I'm rude to Mara, deliberately dismissive. Mara answers sharply, carrying a fresh glass of champagne that sloshes onto the ground as she gestures angrily.

Sonia pulls away from me, trying to apologize to Mara. We're already ignoring Sonia, locked in an argument that escalates because I intend it to. I'm cruel and cutting until real tears sparkle in Mara's eyes, until she's red-faced and shouting back at me.

We're drawing the attention of our fellow partygoers, but I don't make the mistake of seeing if Shaw is watching, too. I pretend to be entirely engrossed in the argument, trying to quiet Mara, grabbing her by the wrist.

Mara pulls her hand away. When I won't let go, she slaps me across the face. The slap is sharp, cutting through the music.

I release her wrist, saying, "Fuck off, then, you fucking lush."

I don't enjoy saying these things. In fact, I hate it. But it has the desired effect. Mara storms away from me, off toward the coat check to retrieve her purse and coat.

I don't watch her leave. Instead, I snatch a glass of champagne off the nearest tray, toss the liquid in my mouth, and ask Betsy Voss to dance.

Betsy is glad to take me up on the offer, slipping her hand into mine and saying, with ill-concealed curiosity, "Trouble in paradise? Don't let her get away, Cole—you're such a gorgeous couple."

"She's more trouble than she's worth," I mutter.

I haven't lied in a while. I'm out of practice. The words feel clumsy on my lips.

"You don't mean that," Betsy says.

I don't bother to answer. All that's required now is for me to keep dancing, looking as miserable as I feel.

This is the trickiest part. Will Shaw take the bait?

He has to slip out of the party without me seeing—or at least with me pretending not to notice.

He might not leave at all.

The seconds tick past. I can see him in my peripheral, still dancing with the redhead. Twirling her, laughing loudly, pretending to have the time of his life, his smile as phony as my fight with Mara.

Mara gathers her bag and coat, then storms out of the party.

Even then, Shaw lingers. I begin to believe he's not going to follow at all.

Then, at the very edges of my hearing, through a break in the song, I catch his booming voice saying, "Let me get you another drink."

Shaw parts ways from the redhead, first heading toward the bar, then altering course to slip around the corner of the ornate plaster pillars leading into the theater.

Got you, motherfucker.

The trout is chasing after the bait, his mouth wide open. I can't wait for him to swallow the lure before I slip in the hook.

Shaw follows Mara out the double doors.

I leave the opposite way, heading toward the glowing movie screen, pushing my way through the emergency exit into the alley behind the theater.

I don't have to follow Mara because I already know where she's going.

I'm so intent on sprinting ahead of her that I don't realize I'm not alone in the alleyway. Close behind me, I hear the click of a safety coming off. Then comes the voice of Officer Hawks ordering, "Don't fucking move."

I turn slowly, already knowing I'll be staring down the barrel of a gun.

Hawks is still dressed in his rented tux, though he's lost the bow tie and unbuttoned the top two buttons. His glasses are slightly askew, the eyes behind them bloodshot with lack of sleep and at least one or two glasses of EBA champagne.

"What do you think you're doing?" I say, trying for boredom in my tone but unable to hide the edge of tension running underneath. I don't have time for this—I don't have time for any delay at all.

Hawks doesn't give a fuck about my plans.

He's here to ruin them.

"Turn around and put your hands behind your back," he barks. "I'm arresting you."

Fuck, fuck, FUCK!

"You can't arrest me," I sneer. "You have no warrant and no probable cause."

"Turn around," Hawks hisses through his teeth, "or I'll put a bullet between your eyes."

Fuck!

I turn slowly, trying to buy time as my mind races.

My options are few.

"Mara just left the party," I tell him. "Shaw is following her. He's going to kill her."

"Shut the fuck up." Hawks comes up behind me. I hear the clink of metal as he pulls out his cuffs.

The urge to yank my hands away, to fight him, is overwhelming. He closes the manacle around my wrist one-handed while keeping his gun shoved against my side.

He frisks me roughly, finding the knife in my pocket.

"What's this?" he crows. "Looks like probable cause to me. Can't wait to run that through analysis."

I want to slam the crown of my head against the bridge of his nose. I'm dying to do it.

Does he really think I'm stupid enough to carry a murder weapon around in my pocket?

I mean…one I've already used.

"We have to get to Mara!" I try one more time. "I can show you where they're going."

"Shut *up*," Hawks hisses, jamming the barrel between my ribs. "I want to shoot you. I'm fucking itching to do it. Just give me a reason."

I keep my mouth shut as he hustles me to the end of the alleyway, to the cruiser parked a block down the street.

God *damn* it! I was hoping he brought his own car.

He shoves me in the back, where the doors have no interior handles and I'm trapped behind the thick metal mesh separating the driver from the back seat.

Hawks drops my knife into an evidence bag and stows it in the trunk before climbing into the front.

"This is pointless," I tell him. "I'll have a team of lawyers down at the station in an hour. I'll run this all the way up the chain—you'll be writing parking tickets in Excelsior by the time I'm finished with you."

"Yeah?" Hawks scoffs. "Well, at least I get to ruin your night first."

He's right about that. With the speed the SFPD moves, I won't even get my phone call within an hour. By then, Mara will be long gone.

Hawks turns right on Eighteenth Street, driving away from Corona Heights Park.

In the moment his head is turned, watching for cross traffic, I slip my bound wrists under my legs, bringing them around in front of me. Hawks glances at the rearview mirror. I sit still, pretending I haven't moved at all.

I wait, the seconds whipping past, the car traveling several agonizing blocks in the wrong direction.

Then Hawks turns onto Sanchez and speeds up. He's distracted, changing lanes to merge into traffic.

Leaning back against the seat, I lift my feet and drive both heels into the metal mesh as hard as I can. I kick it once, twice; Hawks shouts and swerves the wheel, scrabbling for his gun. My heels break through on the third kick, knocking Hawks in the jaw and shoulder, sending the car careening in the opposite direction.

Hawks pulls his gun free, but now there's no mesh between us. I drop my wrists over his head and pull the chain back against his throat, yanking it so tight that he has to let go of the wheel entirely, and the gun, too, grabbing for the chain with both hands as he strangles.

The cruiser barrels into the cars lined along the street, hitting the

bed of a Tacoma and flipping over. Hawks and I are both unbuckled. We're flung out of our seats, still grappling and twisting in the air before landing in a crumpled heap on the car's inside roof.

I keep throttling him with all my strength as he claws and punches backward. He hits me in the eye and the ear. I hang on doggedly, choking him until I feel him losing strength. His blows weaken. Finally, he slumps forward, both of us covered in broken glass, bleeding from a dozen cuts.

I ease the pressure off his throat.

There's no covering this up—I just assaulted a police officer. I'm in deep shit. I don't need Hawks dead on top of everything else.

I steal the keys off his belt, unlock the cuffs, then leave him there with a livid chain mark across his throat and his pulse still beating.

I crawl out the shattered windshield of the cruiser.

A half dozen people have already gathered around, pulling out their phones, calling the police and an ambulance.

They stare at me as I slither out of the cop car, cut to ribbons by the glass, blood pattering on the cement from the side of my face, my knees, and my hands.

"Are you okay?" a girl asks me.

A bald man in glasses takes a step back, understanding what it means that I was in the back of the cop car when it crashed.

"You better wait here for the ambulance…" he says hesitantly.

I'm not waiting for shit.

Ignoring the bystanders, I turn and start running back in the direction of the park.

I'm not returning exactly the way we came—I'm cutting through cross streets, sprinting down sidewalks and through alleyways, taking the most direct route to Mara.

I'm running faster and harder than I've ever run in my life. My shoes pound the pavement, my chest flaming like a furnace stuffed full of coal. My head throbs where it slammed against the car door as the cruiser flipped over.

I can't pay attention to any of that—all I can do is sprint and sprint until I taste blood in my throat.

I've been delayed too long.

Mara might already be dead.

19

MARA

THE WIND HITS ME LIKE A SLAP AS I RUN DOWN THE STEPS OF THE theater.

For once, it actually feels like Christmas Eve.

The air is so cold that my breath comes out in silvery plumes and my sweat freezes on my skin in an instant. Thick clouds blanket the night sky, blocking out every star.

I'm hurrying up Castro Street, trying to find the right pace where I can stay ahead of Shaw without losing him.

I have to look distraught, which isn't hard to do. Fighting with Cole was awful. I know we were both playing a part, but it made me feel like shit hearing him speak to me that way, seeing the ugly look on his face. I hated putting Sonia in the middle. I'll have to apologize to her for that—assuming I'm still alive come morning.

Alone in the dark, I think this plan seems like madness.

I know Cole is close behind me. In fact, he should be running ahead by now, taking the direct route so he can beat me to the park. I fight the urge to glance back over my shoulder, to check if Shaw is following as well.

I turn left on Sixteenth, slowing my pace just a little, behaving as if I stormed off in a rage but am cooling down now.

It's almost midnight. I've never seen the streets so empty. I pass several houses with parties in full swing: Christmas lights strung up in the windows, music thudding and people laughing. The sound of merriment from a distance always makes me feel lonely.

No one's out on the sidewalk with me. Barely any cars drive past. Everybody already got where they're going.

I've almost reached Corona Heights Park.

As I cross Flint Street, I feel the unmistakable sensation of eyes on my back. Every sound becomes painfully acute: the rattle of dry leaves blowing up the street and the scrape of my boots mounting the curb.

Shaw is behind me. I fucking know it.

I know it because I feel it.

My flesh prickles, the sparkling gown scraping across my skin. The air goes still, the pressure dropping.

I've reached the park entrance.

I pause for a moment at the head of the winding pathway leading into the trees.

If Shaw is watching me, I want him to think I passed this way by chance and that I've only just thought of Cole's sculpture on the flat top of the park, almost completed.

I hesitate, shifting my weight back and forth on my feet, as if I know I should continue along my way but am drawn by curiosity, wanting to see the sculpture in the moonlight.

I take one step along the sidewalk, then turn abruptly, heading into the park instead, striding with purpose.

The path is narrow, bordered on both sides by cypresses and eucalypti. As I round the first bend, I'm sure I hear the grit of heavy footsteps following me. I stop, standing still in the middle of the path. The sound stops, too. When I resume walking, I hear him following again.

My heart rate doubles.

This is what I wanted. I wanted him to follow. But now that I know he's right behind me, I can hardly breathe. I want to get up to the sculpture as quickly as possible because that's where Cole will be waiting.

I hurry up the long, winding path to the flat top.

Twice I stop and look behind me. The second time, I catch the edge of a dark figure stepping back behind a tree, only a dozen yards behind me.

"Cole?" I call out, as if I think it might be him.

Only silence answers.

I can imagine Shaw standing behind that oak, grinning to himself, his white teeth gleaming in the dark like a Cheshire cat's.

He's waiting. Watching me. Making sure we're truly alone.

I continue up the path, adrenaline coursing through my veins.

Each creak of a branch, every rustle in the bushes makes me want to scream. It doesn't matter if Shaw can see the tension in my body, if he can see my footsteps quickening. He knows I'm frightened, and that's just fine—it will only excite him.

He'll think I came here stupidly in the heat of the fight, only now realizing that someone might have followed.

The air feels thick and expectant, as if even the wind is holding its breath to see what will happen next.

I step out of the trees, finally arriving on the high flat vista where Cole built his sculpture.

It towers over me, the glossy black walls of the labyrinth over twenty feet tall.

The entrance yawns like a mouth. I know the route through because Cole showed me his diagram dozens of times. But I'm also aware of how disorienting it will be inside, with no proper lights and several false paths designed to trick me.

I step out into the clearing, slowly approaching the entrance. My boots crunch over the frosty grass, the sparkling train of my dress whispering behind me.

Something soft touches my cheek.

I look upward.

Puffy flakes of snow drift down from the thick bank of clouds.

I stare in astonishment: I've never seen snow in San Francisco in all my life. It feels surreal, as if this is only happening to me. As if I truly stepped into another world.

I turn to look back the way I came, at the tangled tunnel of branches and the dark path beneath.

A figure steps into view: Tall, broad, and dressed in a midnight-blue tuxedo. Fists clenched at his sides. Chin lowered like a bull as he stares at me.

We both stand fixed in place. Frozen like ice sculptures. Waiting for the other to move.

Shaw's lips split apart in a grin.

He lowers his head and charges.

♫ *"Survivor"—2WEI*

He barrels toward me, his arms pumping, his legs churning, his head down like he's a linebacker, crossing the space between us with horrifying speed.

I don't have time to think or even to scream.

I turn and sprint into the labyrinth.

The black glass envelops me, cutting off the outside world. The walls appear sleek and featureless, but I know there are hidden doorways in the glass, impossible to find unless you stand at just the right angle or run your fingers down their length until you find the openings.

I don't have to do that because I already know the way.

I hurtle down the dark alleyway, taking a hard right, then a left. I head to the next intersection and run down the middle branch, hoping I'm losing Shaw with all these turns.

Cole should already be inside the labyrinth, hiding up ahead.

My chest burns, my legs shaking beneath me. I underestimated how frightened I'd be and how heavily it would affect me: my legs are rubber, and my feet are stone lumps inside my boots.

I'm starting to worry that I misremembered the turns and I

should have gone right instead of left at this last turn. The reflective glass disorients me. Ghostly versions of myself chase along my left and right side, splitting off at dizzying angles every time I turn. These bits of motion in my peripheral make me jump and spin, thinking Shaw is right behind me. Now I'm not even certain if I'm going the right way. I might have turned all the way around.

If I followed the route, then I should meet Cole soon. He should be waiting in the center of the maze.

I run to the next intersection, expecting to see him, expecting him to give me the nod that means, *Keep running. Head to the exit. I'll get Shaw as he passes.*

I burst into the middle of the labyrinth, which is a perfect circle with eight pathways leading off like the spokes of a wheel. A black glass obelisk marks the exact center point, jutting upward into the cloudy sky.

The snow thickens, whirling downward in a spiral.

I see the obelisk, I see the snow, but I don't see Cole.

He isn't here. I'm all alone.

Where the fuck is he?

I spin in a circle, searching for him.

We agreed he'd be here.

We agreed he'd give me the sign that it was safe to run through.

Cole was supposed to slip into the wall up ahead. I'd wait for Shaw, make sure he followed. The moment I saw him, I'd sprint down the aisle. As Shaw chased me, Cole would jump out and bury his knife in Shaw's neck.

That was the plan.

But I'm standing here all alone.

Shaw will be here any second.

What do I do? What do I do?

Shaw's heavy footsteps pound toward me.

Without waiting for him to reach the middle, I sprint down one of the spokes. This isn't the way I was supposed to go, but it doesn't fucking matter. If Cole isn't here, I only have two options: run all the way out and flee from the maze, or hide in the walls.

Shaw is chasing after me way too fucking fast. He's probably visited the maze himself, late at night while it was being built. He knows the way through. He's faster than me. If I run, he'll catch me.

If I hide, it might give Cole enough time to find us both.

Where is he?

I thought he'd be here. I was so sure of it. Not for a second did I believe he'd let me down.

He won't let me down.

He'll be here.

I just have to stay alive a little longer.

I dart into a tiny alcove hidden in the glossy black wall. There are a dozen of these niches scattered through the maze. I try to make myself as small as a mouse, stifling my panting breath, covering my mouth with both hands while gasps leak out in a frosty mist, harsh and ragged.

I can hear Shaw's breath, even heavier. He's puffing like a buffalo, winded from chasing me.

I hate that sound. I really fucking hate it.

His thudding steps pause as he reaches the center of the maze. I can hear him turning this way and that, staring down each spoke, searching for me.

His voice cuts through the night: "I know you're in here."

I press both palms over my mouth.

His tone is low and flat, devoid of emotion. Just like the night we met.

I know you're awake.

He cut me open. Left me to bleed out on the ground.

We'll see who bleeds tonight.

Slipping my hand into the pocket of my coat, I find Cole's knife and close my fingers around the handle.

Cole said to stick to the plan no matter what.

Well, the plan is fucked.

I'm the one hiding in the walls. I'm the one with the knife.

Slowly, carefully, I flick it open.

The blade snaps into place with a minute *click*.

I can feel Shaw stiffening, his head jerking up, his ears straining to find the direction of the sound.

"There's no point hiding, Mara. Come on out and we'll talk. Face-to-face. Woman to man..."

He gives a nasty chuckle.

He's coming closer, his heavy steps slow and measured. He knows I'm hiding close by.

"Are you afraid I'm going to hurt you? Don't worry...I just want a little taste..."

I think he turned down the path next to mine. I hear his voice moving off at an angle. But just as quickly, he turns and strides back.

"You might even like it. Some girls do...at least to start... Your roommate Erin certainly enjoyed herself..."

He's walking down my aisle now, I'm sure of it. Drawing closer and closer...

"The first time we fucked, she was bouncing and squealing so loud, it echoed up the staircase... Half the party must have heard her. The second time...well, the second time I wasn't as nice..."

He's walking right past me. The opening in the wall sits at an angle. I've wedged myself into the farthest corner, out of view.

I see a slice of Shaw's broad back as he passes. I see the carefully combed waves of his sandy-colored hair and the high collar of his tuxedo jacket. In between is the nape of his neck...thick and muscular but unprotected...

I clench tight to the knife, slipping out of my hiding place, stepping behind him, smooth and silent as his own shadow...

"I bit her nipple off and swallowed it whole." Shaw chuckles.

I stab the blade toward the base of his neck, planning to bury it in his spine.

Maybe it's the motion that gives me away, or some whispering sound…

Shaw whirls around. The knife embeds in the back of his shoulder, wrenching out of my hand. Shaw's bearlike arm swings around, clouting me in the side of the head, sending me flying into the glass wall.

"You fuckin' *bitch*!" he howls, clamping his hand over his shoulder. He's trying to reach behind him, trying to grip the knife. His arms are too thick—his fingertips graze the handle, but he can't pull it out.

He rounds on me, his face flushed with fury, genuinely outraged that I dared to fight back.

I'm already leaping to my feet again, sprinting away from him, back into the center of the maze.

My feet slip on the freshly fallen snow, and I almost eat shit rounding the corner. I can hear Shaw barreling after me, grunting through his teeth, utterly enraged.

I'm running in a mad panic, all memory of the labyrinth wiped from my mind. I'm back in the center, but I don't remember where I came in, so I don't know the way out.

I pick a spoke at random and sprint down it, taking turn after turn, praying I'm not about to run down a blind alley into a dead end.

I find another alcove and jump into it, planning to hide again, but when I look back the way I came, I realize something awful: I've been leaving footprints in the snow. I can see exactly which way I came, and so will Shaw. He can follow me as easily as if I left a trail of bread crumbs for him.

I drop out of the niche and sprint once more, my legs wobbling, my chest burning, and my eyes watering so badly, I can hardly see in front of me. Snowflakes whirl into my face, sticking in my eyelashes, blinding me. The black glass walls seem to go on and on in every direction. A dozen ghostly Maras stare back at me every way I turn, their faces pale, their eyes black holes of terror.

I cross over my own footprints. I can see Shaw's right on top of them, twice the size, his weight churning up the dirt. I can't hear him, but I know he's close, following my prints, hunting me.

Picking up the skirt of my dress so it won't drag, I run backward down the aisle. When I reach the next intersection, I run forward again, then backward once more.

I still can't hear him. Where the fuck did he go?

Is he hiding in the walls now?

Is he about to jump out at me?

I'm staring around on all sides, wild-eyed, fighting the waves of panic threatening to overwhelm me.

Where is he? How do I get out?

Dazed and distracted, I see my own reflection running right toward me.

I slam into the smooth black glass before falling backward onto my ass. Scrambling up again, I hear a low laugh.

Shaw stands at the other end of the aisle.

I'm trapped.

There's nowhere to run.

He's cornered me in the dead end.

Shaw isn't running anymore. He approaches calmly, casually. He's smiling like he did as he walked through the Technicolor spiderweb, knowing he has every advantage, and I have none.

He only pauses to reach behind his shoulder once more, finally catching the handle of the knife and wrenching it out of his back with a grimace. He examines his own blood on the blade, as dark and glossy as the labyrinth walls.

"Got me good, didn't you, you little cunt?" He holds the knife upright, the tip as wickedly sharp as the point of a fang. "I ought to peel your fucking face off with this. See how pretty Cole finds you then."

He opens his fingers, letting the knife drop to the ground, the impact causing a spatter of scarlet to flick across the snow.

"I don't use a knife," he says, giving me that blindingly white smile, bracketed on both sides by boyish dimples. "Why would I need one when I've got fingernails and teeth? I'm gonna rip you apart with my bare hands. That's what I like, Mara—I like the taste of your throat tearing against my tongue. I like the feel of your eyeballs giving way under my thumbs. I want you breaking, cracking, ripping. I want your warm blood pumping down my arms."

I'm so afraid that I've passed right through to the other side.

A deathly clarity settles over me.

This is it. This is the end.

Whatever happens, I won't give in. If he kills me, I'm going to take some pieces of Shaw along with me.

I slip out of my heavy coat, letting it fall behind me. Allowing the soft flakes of snow to settle in my hair and on my bare shoulders. Feeling their cool kiss one last time.

"You tried to murder me before," I tell Shaw. "As a killer and an artist…you're mediocre."

Shaw's upper lip twists from a grin into a snarl. His teeth clench so hard, I can almost hear them cracking. With a howl, he charges down the alley.

He's running right at me, getting bigger and bigger until his shoulders almost touch both walls.

He's a wrecking ball swinging right at me. There's nowhere to run.

Out of a passageway in the dark glass, Cole barrels into Shaw, diving at his legs, sending them both tumbling end over end until they slam into the opposite wall.

There's no strategy. No plan.

Cole is already gasping and sweating and bleeding everywhere before the fight has even begun. He grapples with Shaw, no element of surprise on his side. From the second they make contact, it's a brutal, bloody melee.

They fight and claw, biting, punching, and kicking, rolling over and over in the snow. The ground becomes a morass of churned-up mud and bloody slush.

This is like no fight I've seen: desperate, hectic, vicious. I can hardly tell one man from the other as they punch each other's throats and gouge each other's eyes. This is how predators fight: not to win, but to kill.

Shaw is bigger, stronger. Cole is faster, but that's of limited use now that they're already on the ground. Cole gave up all the advantage when he tackled Shaw, taking him down before he could plough into me.

Cole turns, wild-eyed, bloody-mouthed. "*Mara, run!*"

I've never seen him scared.

He thinks he's going to lose.

He thinks we're both going to die.

I've been trapped in the dead end, pressed against the cold glass, unable to move because the fight is too wild—I don't know to help.

But now I know what to do.

I dart forward, leaping over the men's churning legs, running away from them down the narrow passageway.

Shaw gives a strangled yell of rage, thinking I'm escaping. Cole is silent, his arms locked around Shaw, keeping him right where he is.

So much snow has fallen that, for a moment, I can't find it. Then I see the glint of steel. I dive my frozen fingers down into the ice, closing around the handle. I pull out the knife, already stained with Shaw's blood.

My fingers are so cold that I can hardly feel them. I grip the handle tight all the same.

"*Cole!*" I shout.

He gives me one swift look, and in that moment, the terrifying computer in his head runs a thousand calculations.

He rolls onto his back, letting Shaw take the advantage straddling him, throttling him. Cole puts himself in the vulnerable position, Shaw's hands around his throat.

Cole grips a fistful of Shaw's hair and jerks it back, shoving the heel of his palm against Shaw's jaw, wrenching his head to the side, exposing his throat.

Our eyes meet.

I'm holding the knife, sharp as a fang, dark on its point like venom.

Shaw is the spider, but I'm the snake.

I've never seen a spider kill a snake.

Sprinting forward, I slash the knife across Shaw's throat in one long swinging arc.

Blood scythes across the snow, a parabola of crimson on the white canvas.

Shaw sinks to his knees, parting his lips in stunned surprise.

He can't even raise his hand to stem the flow.

Blood pumps from his throat, a fresh spurt with every heartbeat, each more vivid than the last.

I've never seen anything so beautiful.

I watch him die, the snow drifting down, his last breath hanging like smoke in the air before dissolving into nothingness.

He slumps and falls. His body hits the ground, heavy and dull. Not a man anymore or even a monster—just a sack of meat.

Cole rises from the ground.

He's covered in Shaw's blood and his own, his skin wetly gleaming in the moonlight.

I look at my hands drenched in blood. Droplets patter on the pristine snow.

Then I look at Cole again, and his face breaks into a grin of relief.

♫ *"Always Forever"*—*Cults*

We run to each other, Cole sweeping me up in his arms. He spins me around as snow spirals around us. He kisses me, his mouth warm in the cold, sweet and salty with the taste of copper on his tongue.

Our breath mixes silver between us. His wet hands slide over my skin, leaving red streaks vivid as paint.

He kisses and kisses me, both of us warm and alive, Shaw cooling on the ground.

Distantly, I hear sirens.

I don't care who it is or how long we have until they find us. I don't care what happens when they do.

All I care about is Cole, his arms wrapped tight around me.

He saved me and I saved him. Not just from Shaw but from everything else in this world that wants to destroy us—the demons outside and the ones within.

I don't need anyone else.

I just need one person to make me the center of their universe. I want us to be two stars locked in orbit, burning bright in the blackness of space.

The snow reflects on the glossy black walls, swirling all around us.

Cole whirls me around and around, his mouth locked on mine.

He presses me against a cold black wall, then lifts the sparkling skirt of my gown around my waist. I'm yanking at the waistband of his trousers, ripping off the button, pulling them open.

He thrusts inside me, his cock blazing hot, our gasps puffing into the air, steam rising off our skin. The cold can't touch me. I'm pure fire, burning and burning but never consumed.

I'm floating outside my own body, watching from a distance. I see us entwined, my legs around his waist, my arms around his neck, his tongue in my mouth, and his hands gripping me tight.

We're wrapped together, twisted up. Not one snake but two, the black and the white.

We're the same.

And I like what we are.

20
COLE

I FUCK MARA IN THE SNOW, IN THE COLD, LIKE SHE'S THE ONLY warmth in the universe, and I have to stay inside her or freeze.

The scent of her skin fills my lungs, rich and alive.

The pleasure I feel is so much more than physical.

I finally realize what happiness feels like. There's no malice in it. No greed. It's not something you seek for yourself.

It flows between two people, around and around, back and forth, given and received in the same breath.

Her happiness makes me happy. And even if it didn't, I'd want it for her anyway.

That's what loving her means—I want her safe, protected, flourishing, whether it benefits me or not.

The feeling hits me so hard that I let out a groan. Mara touches my face, tilting it so I look right in her eyes.

"I love you," I tell her.

"I know," she says.

That's what makes me come. Not the physical act of fucking— the emotion of it. Finally being known. Finally being understood.

I explode into her. It rips through me, pleasure and pain, exactly how I need it—the only way that satisfies.

She clings to me, biting down hard on my shoulder, tasting my blood in her mouth.

When I set her down, the sirens are closer.

"Listen." I hold tight to her hand. "I need you to do something for me. Can you do it quickly before it's too late?"

"Yes," Mara says at once.

I retrieve her coat and wrap it around her shoulders, explaining exactly what I need.

When I'm done, Mara nods and kisses me once more.

Then she runs away through the maze, leaving me alone with Shaw's body to wait for the cops.

21

MARA

THREE MONTHS LATER

IT TAKES SEVERAL MONTHS, A TEAM OF LAWYERS, AND SOME HEFTY "donations" to the right people before Cole is entirely in the clear.

In the end, the chief of police pins a medal on Officer Hawks's chest for closing the case on the Beast of the Bay.

Hawks scowls through the entire press conference, not at all pleased with the deal Cole struck with the SFPD: Hawks gets the credit, and Cole gets fifty hours of community service for flipping a police cruiser in the middle of Sanchez Street. He's been serving his time at the Bay Area Youth Center, teaching delinquents how to draw.

He comes home from his sessions in a surprisingly good mood.

"Some of these kids show real talent."

"What kind of talent?" I tease him.

Cole grins. "All kinds—that's why I like them."

Cole's lawyers argued that he was wrongfully arrested, that he had no choice but to escape after he witnessed Shaw abducting me off the street and dragging me into the labyrinth.

I supported this story, including the part where it was Cole who cut Shaw's throat while I fled back to Cole's mansion. I pretended to be disoriented and in shock, freshly showered and hiding in bed in my pajamas when the police finally found me.

They couldn't question me too hard since I'd been telling them all along that Shaw was the Beast. I was the girl who'd had to escape him *twice* because they wouldn't listen to me.

It helped that the cops uncovered a mountain of evidence in Shaw's apartment.

Most damning was Shaw's collage of stolen driver's licenses. He'd spray-painted them gold, hiding them within one of his Technicolor paintings. When the cops scraped off the paint, they found the IDs of Maddie Walker and twenty other victims, including Erin.

They also found the wallets of two missing men: art critic Carl Danvers and Professor Oswald. The papers noted that Danvers attended a party with Shaw shortly before his disappearance and that Shaw was one of the professor's students at CalArts when he likewise went missing. The professor's wallet finally allowed the death of Valerie Whittaker to be linked to the Beast.

Cole was extremely pleased that I managed to break into Shaw's apartment before the cops showed up.

"And you didn't leave a single print!" he said admiringly.

"I learned from the best." I grinned back at him.

I've come a long way on my journey, to the point where planting evidence is exhilarating rather than horrifying. I'm beginning to understand how even the most reckless acts can feel like a game, the high stakes only enhancing the fun.

Still, I'm glad it's over.

Or I suppose I should say *almost* over.

I have one piece of unfinished business to resolve.

I'm standing on the front step of a dingy single-level house in Bakersfield. The grass is unwatered and uncut, the garden beds nothing but bare dirt.

I ring the bell several times before I hear someone shuffling inside.

At last the door cracks open. An eye presses against the space, peering out suspiciously.

For a second, she doesn't recognize me.

Then she pulls the door wide, straightening, blinking in the garish spring sunshine.

I almost wouldn't recognize her either.

She's chopped her hair to shoulder length, frizzy and uneven. Threads of gray are poorly covered by an at-home dye job. She's gained weight, enough that she fills out the baggy oversize sweatshirt that once belonged to me. As faded as it's become, I still remember that retro Disney logo on the front. I never actually went to Disneyland—I bought the hoodie at a thrift shop, hoping other kids would think I'd been.

Makeup from the night before cakes around her eyes, settling in the wrinkles beneath. The lines are deep, etched in place from every ugly expression she's carried, hour after hour, day after day, all these years.

Her face bears record of every scowl, every sneer. There are no smile lines at the corners of her eyes—only trenches on her forehead, between her eyebrows, and in marionette lines running from her nose to the edges of her mouth.

She's become a witch from a fairy tale. Transformed by misery. The darkness inside finally reflected on her face.

Those gray-blue eyes still glitter with malice. They're the same color as mine—cold as San Francisco fog blowing in off the bay.

A part of her will always be in me.

But I choose which part.

"Hello, Mom."

I see her struggle.

She prefers to be the one showing up unannounced on people's doorsteps. She hates that I'm trespassing in her space, catching her unawares.

On the other hand, she's been trying to find me for years. She can't possibly slam the door in my face when she's finally getting what she wants.

"What are you doing here?" she croaks.

I must have woken her, even though it's ten o'clock in the morning. The sour scent of unwashed clothing, spilled wine, and stale cigarettes wafts out of the house. A familiar smell for me—one that recalls my earliest days.

"I brought you a gift." I hold up a bottle of merlot, her favorite.

Her eyes flick to the label and back to my face, narrowing. I've never bought her alcohol in all my life.

"A peace offering," I say. "I have something to discuss with you."

I already know she won't be able to resist. The wine is only half as tempting as what she really wants: the chance to dig information out of me.

"Fine," she grunts, holding the door wider and retreating into the house.

That's as good as an invitation.

I cross the threshold before closing the door behind me.

It takes a moment for my eyes to adjust to the interior gloom. I stand still until they do so I don't trip over the piles of pizza boxes, empty beer cans, overflowing ashtrays, discarded clothing, scattered shoes, stacks of old magazines, junk mail, and moldering paper plates marked with the remains of meals long past.

"Sit anywhere," my mother says, flopping on a pile of blankets on the ratty sofa—clearly the same place she was sleeping moments before.

I have to move a pile of old newspapers off the closest chair before I can likewise sit down. I recognize the paper on top: it's the same one Arthur showed me during my last shift at Sweet Maple. The one that contains a picture of me in the arts section.

A tiny smirk plays over my mother's lips as I set the papers aside.

She sparks up a cigarette, holding it in her usual way: pinched between thumb and index finger like it's a joint.

I know her habits so well. Their familiarity repulses me, like an old journal entry that makes you cringe.

"Do you have a bottle opener?" I ask.

Of course, she has a bottle opener. I might as well ask if she has toilet paper. It's probably even *more* of a necessity in her eyes.

"In the kitchen," she says, making no move to stand and retrieve it.

This is a power play—making me fetch the corkscrew and the glasses, waiting on her like I used to.

I anticipated this, and it suits me just fine.

I carry the wine into the kitchen, which is even filthier than the living room. The stove top is piled with so much clutter that I doubt she's ever laid eyes on the burners, let alone used them to cook. When I snap on the overhead light, several roaches dive under the pile of dirty dishes in the sink.

The cabinets are empty. I find the glasses in the dishwasher, among a pile of plates speckled with green mold. Swallowing bile, and avoiding the roaches the best I can, I wash the cups in the sink. I have to swish a little water in the Dawn bottle to get the dregs of soap out.

My mother doesn't call out to see what's taking so long. I hear the faint crackle as she sucks on her cigarette, followed by an exhale and a wracking cough that rattles in her chest.

The glasses are wet, with no paper towel to dry them. I shake them off, then search for the bottle opener. Unsurprisingly, it's out in the open on the kitchen counter, next to my mother's keys, an open tube of lipstick, and a handful of loose change.

Next to that, a dozen prescription bottles, some with her name on them, some bought or stolen. Most are already empty. Especially the Adderall.

It took me six months to get off that drug. Six months of stomach cramps, diarrhea, nightmares, trembling. Then two years more to stop craving it.

All so my mother could steal a prescription I never needed in the first place.

I bring the glasses out filled to the brim.

My mother takes hers, saying, "Where's the bottle?"

I retrieve it from the kitchen before setting it on the coffee table between us, atop a stack of old *Vogue* magazines. I'm not the first person to do this—Anne Hathaway's face is already distorted by several wet rings.

♫ *"Girl With One Eye"—Florence + The Machine*

My mother takes three swallows of the wine, gulping it like cool water after a long race. Sighing in satisfaction, she leans back against the threadbare cushions of the sofa. Now she's smiling, smoke drifting up from her cigarette, hanging over her head like her own personal storm cloud.

"Come back to brag?" she says.

"Not exactly."

"What, then?" she snaps. "What do you want?"

She can't imagine anyone visiting her on purpose, for the pleasure of her company.

In this case, she's right.

"I saw you gave another interview about me."

She lets out a snort of air, the closest thing she has to a laugh. "Don't like me spilling all your secrets?"

My mother still has the mannerisms of a beautiful woman—she arches her eyebrow in the same haughty way, holding her cigarette with theatrical flair.

Men used to fall at her feet. She had this dark confidence that sucked them in, until they realized everything about her is an act. She's allergic to the truth; she won't tell it even when it would benefit her to do so.

It will be difficult to get what I want from her.

"I don't care what you say to reporters," I tell her. "It doesn't matter. Nothing you do can tear me down now."

"'Cause you're fucking some artist?" She scoffs. "You're nothing without him. When he's tired of you, he'll toss you aside, and you'll be right back where you started."

She takes another gulp of wine, the glass more than half-gone.

She really believes what she's saying. The world is so ugly to her, people's motivations so cruel.

I could almost feel sorry for her.

Almost.

I say, "You're telling your story, not mine."

She sets her glass down hard, a little wine sloshing over the rim. "You think you're better than me because you stroll in here in your fancy new clothes? *'Cause you got your name in the paper?* I know who you really are. I fucking birthed you. You're weak, you're stupid, you're lazy, and you're nothing but a filthy little whore. You can paint a billion paintings, and not one of them will change what you are inside."

Triumphantly, she picks the glass up again, downing whatever remains inside.

I watch her swallow it all, my own wine sitting untouched.

"Good," I say softly. "Now that you've finished, we can address what I actually came here to discuss."

She frowns, furrowing her forehead. "What the fuck's that supposed to mean?"

I reach in the pocket of my suede jacket before pulling out a bottle of liquid pseudoephedrine. "I put this in your drink. You might have noticed a little bitterness, but it obviously didn't stop you from chugging it down."

"You spiked my drink?"

Color rises up her neck from the collar of my stolen sweatshirt.

"Poisoned it, actually."

She makes a move to get up from the couch, but she's already unsteady. Her elbow buckles under her.

"I wouldn't do that if I were you. You'll be dead before the ambulance arrives."

"You sneaky little *bitch*! You filthy, nasty—"

"I wouldn't do that either," I snap.

She stops talking, closing her mouth like a trap. Her eyes water until the pupils swim. Her chest hitches. Some of this is fear. The rest is the drug taking effect.

"That's better," I say, as she sinks back down.

"What the *fuck* do you want?" she hisses, panting fast.

"I have the antidote. I'll give it you. I just want to know one thing."

"*What?*" She's writhing against the cushions, the pseudoephedrine taking hold.

I stare at her, my face still as stone, not showing a hint of sympathy. "I want to know my father's name."

She's grunting, squirming on the cushions. Her face is deeply flushed now, her skin sweating. Her breath grows more and more shallow. "*Fuck you*," she snarls.

"Suit yourself." I stand from my chair.

"Wait!" Tears run down both sides of her cheeks, mixing with the sweat. She clutches the front of the hoodie, pulling it away from her chest as if that will ease the pressure.

"Tell me his name," I say quietly, relentlessly.

She's groaning and writhing, pulling at the shirt.

"Tell me. You don't have much time."

"*Arghhhh!*" she groans, rolling on her side and then on her back again, thrashing around in the blankets, trying to ease the pressure any way she can.

I feel nothing but the relentless drive to squeeze this secret out of her. The one thing of value she could tell me but always refused.

"Tell me," I order, my eyes fixed on her face while she twists in agony.

She makes a mumbling sound, drooling at the strained edges of her mouth.

"Tell me!"

She shakes her head like a toddler holding their breath, her eyes slitted, hatefully obstinate all the way to the end.

"TELL ME!" I roar, and I slap her hard across the face.

The pain jolts her. Fear replaces stubbornness as she finally realizes I'm not fucking around.

"I DON'T KNOW!" she howls, her voice ripping in her throat. "I NEVER KNEW! Are you happy, you fucking cunt? I never knew who he was! I don't even remember it happening."

She rolls off the couch, shoving the coffee table with her hip as she falls, toppling the bottle of wine so it tumbles on its side and pours the liquor onto the floor with a steady *glug, glug, glug*.

I make no move to right the bottle.

I don't touch my mother either.

I watch her squirm and buck, her face the color of brick, her hands twisting into claws as she grasps at her chest.

Her mouth moves silently, her lips trying to form the word *antidote*.

I look down at her, pitiless. "There is no antidote. There never was. Nothing can save you. Just like nothing can change you. You are what you are…dead to me."

I leave her lying there, twisting and croaking out her last breaths. I won't even give her the comfort of my company. She can die alone, like she was always going to.

Instead, I carry both glasses of wine back to the kitchen and dump them down the sink. I wash the glasses and return them to the dishwasher before wiping my fingerprints off every surface I touched: the Dawn bottle, the faucet, the handle of the dishwasher, the interior of the front door…

By the time I'm finished, my mother has stopped moving.

I don't bother to clean up the wine, but I remove my prints from the bottle before laying it back on its side.

I doubt they'll autopsy her body. The effects of pseudoephedrine are similar to a heart attack. Even if they run a full-panel blood test, the cornucopia of drugs in the house will muddy the waters. She was trying to kill herself long before I helped her along.

Leaving the house feels much better than entering.

The warm sun bathes my face, the fresh breeze reviving my lungs.

A handful of cherry blossoms float across the lawn, blown from the trees in the neighbor's yard. A single petal lands on my palm before fluttering away again.

I feel as light as those petals, alive on the air.

I meet Cole in Yerba Buena, where the party is already in full swing.

♫ *"INDUSTRY BABY"—Lil Nas X & Jack Harlow*

I'm showing my new series, the Other Gender. This one isn't drawn from my past. It's an examination of female empowerment through the iconography of the ages.

I've painted gender-swapped versions of Attila the Hun, Alexander the Great, Suleiman the Magnificent. I'm showing the history of the world if women were the only members of our species. Marilyn Monroe sings "Happy Birthday" in her see-through dress, dancing on the lap of a female JFK who smokes her cigar with all the same lust in her eyes but a sense of playfulness, too, of mutual enjoyment.

The music blasting from the speakers is nothing like my last show: it's boisterous, confident, triumphant.

Because that's how I feel.

I'm on top of the fucking world right now. I don't need to hear what everyone thinks of my show. I fucking love these paintings. I loved every minute of making them. I put them out with overflowing pride, with confidence that everyone who saw them would feel something new.

The women walking the gallery are laughing and pointing out their favorite images to their friends.

I've deliberately invited every woman in this city whom I admire. I want them all here, celebrating who we are and what we can accomplish.

It's not about wishing we were JFK. It's about planning how we *will* be, in the not-too-distant future. The next person who stands behind the presidential pulpit and gives a speech that enlivens the heart of the nation won't be an old white man.

I put Sonia in charge of the whole thing, from the guest list to lighting to marketing materials. This is Sonia's gallery, a new space she's renting on a twelve-month lease, primo real estate in the heart of the east end. The palatial galleries are already filling with her favorite female artists, some local, some international.

This is her debut as much as mine. She's holding court in a stunning black gown, closing deals faster than her newly trained assistant can keep up.

I raise my glass to her across the room in a silent toast to her future success. She grins back at me, letting Allen Wren believe he's getting some kind of deal on the hottest new artist out of Mumbai as he signs the purchase agreement.

Cole is just as busy, arguing with Marcus York at top volume. Marcus is trying to rope him into another sculpture, this time for Golden Gate Park.

"No fucking way! The last one almost killed me."

"What, from a little snow? Come now, we'll build this one in the summer!"

"We won't build it at all 'cause I ain't doin' it."

"You need time to think."

"I need time to drink," Cole says, seizing another glass of champagne off a passing tray. "I don't know if I'm going to work at all this year."

"You don't mean that." I slip between him and Marcus York to steal a quick kiss. "You love working."

"I used to love working," he says, grabbing a handful of my ass, not giving a fuck if York is still watching. "Now I'm distracted by more interesting things…"

"Well, I'm sorry to hear you say that." I pretend to pout. "Because I heard about an opportunity opening up in Venice…"

I pull the plane tickets out of my purse, fanning them open dramatically in front of him. "I need a hot young artist to accompany me… I could write you a letter of recommendation if you're interested?"

"What's gotten into you?" Cole pulls me into the adjoining gallery so he can kiss me deeper and harder. "Whatever it is, I like it…"

I tilt my head up, running my tongue along the side of his neck, all the way to his ear. Then I murmur, "I took a little drive this morning. Stopped in Bakersfield."

Cole goes still, resting his hand on my lower back.

There's no hint of play in his voice now. "Did it satisfy?"

I hesitate, examining how I feel.

"It feels right," I say at last. "It feels good."

I feel him smiling, his face pressed close to mine.

"Because it is," he growls.

EPILOGUE
COLE

**VENICE
ONE WEEK LATER**

♬ *"Bust Your Knee Caps"—Pomplamoose*

MARA AND I STROLL ALONG SALIZADA SAN MOISE IN THE HEART of Venice. It's the middle of *Carnevale*. Everyone around us wears full costume.

A grinning *arlecchino* in a colorful diamond-print suit dances in the doorway of a glassworks shop, while a white-coated *pulcinella* serenades us from the balcony of the Bauer Hotel. Even the gondoliers punting the famous canal boats have dressed as characters from the *commedia dell'arte*.

Mara wears a black velvet jacket and breeches. A magnificent scarlet ostrich feather adorns her tricorn hat, her pale white mask stopping above her crimson lips.

She looks like a pirate queen.

Carnevale is the perfect environment for my pleasure kitten. She's soaking in the wild sea breeze, the scent of fresh fried *moleche*, and the chaotic color and music of the street fairs bursting out of the narrow alleyways between the opulent old buildings.

Had I come here alone in my twenties, I never could have appreciated the beauty of this place. Great cities are living things, and people are as much a part of their architecture as the buildings themselves. If I'm not here to laugh, and drink, and dance, and fuck on my gorgeous balcony overlooking the canals, then why am I here at all?

I needed to feel that I was alike to *one* person to realize I'm not so unlike the others.

Mara is my other half. Not my twin but the parts of me that were missing.

I always thought the emptiness that plagued me was the reality of the human condition. I never imagined the hole inside me could be filled by someone else.

In all my arrogance, I missed a basic truth other people already understood: Everything is better when you share it with someone else. Nothing feels insurmountable when you aren't alone.

It's so optimistic that I'd be embarrassed to say it out loud. And yet it's how I feel. I'm vibrating with the joy of it, every brilliant scent, color, and sound a manifestation of what I'm experiencing inside.

I've never felt so much a part of the world around me. I'm the happiness of the day, and the day exists to buoy me up.

Right as I'm thinking that, some drunken oaf stumbles into my path, dumping his spritz down the front of my trousers, drenching my brand-new Italian leather loafers.

"*Scansarsi!*" he shouts. "*Brutto figlio di puttano bastardo Americano!*"

Since I speak Italian flawlessly, I catch every word of that insult.

I turn to Mara, that old anger blazing in my eyes.

The drunk stumbles alone toward a dark alleyway. I could easily follow him. In the chaos, no one would remember another *rugantino* in a black mask.

Mara follows my gaze, her eyes flicking ahead to the alleyway, vibrant and alive beneath the smooth white porcelain of her mask.

Before I can move, she dashes ahead of me, seizing the drunk by the shoulder. She plucks the plume from her hat and draws it across his throat in one sharp motion, the scarlet feathers liquid bright against his neck.

The drunk—insensible to manners but fully alive to horseplay—pretends to stiffen and fall over dead in the gutter, clutching his throat dramatically and making gurgling sounds.

"There." Mara rejoins me, her feather tucked back into her pirate hat. "I got him for you."

"Thanks," I say. "Saves me the trouble."

Read on for a sneak peek of Sophie Lark's wildly addictive

BRUTAL PRINCE,

the first book in the Brutal Birthright series

1

AIDA GALLO

FIREWORKS BURST INTO BLOOM ABOVE THE LAKE, HANGING suspended in the clear night air, then drifting down in glittering clouds that settle on the water.

My father flinches at the first explosion. He doesn't like things that are loud or unexpected. Which is why I get on his nerves sometimes—I can be both those things, even when I'm trying to behave myself.

I see his scowl illuminated by the blue and gold lights. Yup, definitely the same expression he gets when he looks at me.

"Do you want to eat inside?" Dante asks him.

Because it's a warm night, we're all sitting on the deck. Chicago isn't Sicily—you have to take the opportunity to eat outdoors whenever you can get it. Still, if it weren't for the sound of traffic below, you might think you were in an Italian vineyard. The table's set with stoneware brought from the old country three generations ago, the pergola overhead thickly blanketed by the fox grapes Papa planted for shade. You can't make wine out of fox grapes, but they're good for jam at least.

My father shakes his head. "It's fine here," he says shortly.

Dante grunts and goes back to shoveling chicken in his mouth. He's so big that his fork looks comically small in his hand. He eats like he's starving, hunched over his plate.

Dante's the oldest, so he sits on my father's right-hand side.

Nero's on the left, with Sebastian next to him. I'm at the foot of the table, where my mother would sit if she were still alive.

"What's the holiday?" Sebastian says as another round of fireworks rocket up into the sky.

I tell him, "It's not a holiday. It's Nessa Griffin's birthday."

The Griffins' palatial estate sits right on the edge of the lake, in the heart of the Gold Coast. They're setting off fireworks to make sure absolutely everybody in the city knows their little princess is having a party—as if it weren't already promoted like the Olympics and the Oscars combined.

Sebastian doesn't know because he doesn't pay attention to anything that isn't basketball. He's the youngest of my brothers and the tallest. He got a full ride at Chicago State, and he's good enough that when I visit him on campus, I notice girls stare and giggle everywhere he goes. Sometimes they pluck up the courage to ask him to sign their T-shirts.

"How come we weren't invited?" Nero says, soaked in sarcasm.

We weren't invited because we fucking hate the Griffins and vice versa.

The guest list will be carefully curated, stuffed with socialites and politicians and anybody else chosen for their usefulness or their cache. I doubt Nessa will know any of them.

Not that I'm crying any tears for her. I heard her father hired Selena Gomez to perform. It ain't Halsey, but it's still pretty good.

"What's the update on the Oak Street Tower?" Papa says to Dante while meticulously cutting up his chicken parm.

He already knows damn well how the Oak Street Tower is doing because he tracks absolutely everything done by Gallo Construction. He's changing the subject because the thought of the Griffins sipping champagne and brokering deals with the haut monde of Chicago is irritating to him.

I don't give a shit what the Griffins are doing. Except that I don't like anybody having fun without me.

So, while my father and Dante are droning on about the tower, I mutter to Sebastian, "We should go over there."

"Where?" he says, gulping down an entire glass of milk. The rest of us are drinking wine. Sebastian's trying to stay in tip-top shape for dribbling and sit-ups or whatever the fuck his team of gangly ogres does for training.

"We should go to the party." I keep my voice low.

Nero perks up. He's always interested in getting into trouble. "When?"

"Right after dinner."

"We're not on the list," Sebastian protests.

"Jesus." I roll my eyes. "Sometimes I wonder if you're even a Gallo. You scared of jaywalking too?"

My two oldest brothers are proper gangsters. They handle the messier parts of the family business. Sebastian thinks he's going to the NBA. He's living in a whole other reality than the rest of us. Trying to be a good boy, a law-abiding citizen.

Still, he's the closest to me in age and probably my best friend, though I love all my brothers. He grins back at me. "I'm coming, aren't I?"

Dante shoots us a stern look. He's still talking to our father, but he knows we're plotting something.

Since we've all finished our chicken, Greta brings out the panna cotta. She's been our housekeeper for about a hundred years. She's my second-favorite person, after Sebastian. She's stout and pretty, with more gray in her hair than red.

She made my panna cotta without raspberries because she knows I don't like the seeds and doesn't mind if I'm a spoiled brat. I grab her head and give her a kiss on the cheek as she sets it down in front of me.

"You're going to make me drop my tray!" She tries to shake me loose.

"You've never dropped a tray in your life."

My father takes fucking forever to eat his dessert. He's sipping his wine and going on and on about the electrical workers union. I swear Dante is drawing him out on purpose to infuriate the rest of us. When we have these formal sit-down dinners, Papa expects us all to stay till the bitter end. No phones allowed at the table either, which is basically torture because I can feel my cell buzzing again and again in my pocket, with messages from who knows who. Hopefully not Oliver.

I broke up with Oliver Castle three months ago, but he isn't taking the hint. He may need to take a mallet to the head instead if he doesn't stop annoying me.

Finally, Papa finishes eating. We all gather as many plates and dishes as we can carry to stack in the sink for Greta.

Then Papa goes into his office to have his second nightcap, while Sebastian, Nero, and I all sneak downstairs.

We're allowed to go out on a Saturday night. We're all adults, after all—just barely, in my case. Still, we don't want Papa to ask us *where* we're going.

We pile into Nero's car because it's a boss '57 Chevy Bel Air that will be the most fun to cruise around in with the top down.

Nero starts the ignition. The flare of the headlights reveals Dante's hulking silhouette, arms crossed, looking like Michael Meyers about to murder us.

Sebastian jumps. I let out a shriek.

"You're blocking the car," Nero says drily.

Dante says, "This is a bad idea."

"Why?" Nero can make his voice innocent even when not a single person on this earth believes he's innocent. Of anything. "We're just going for a drive."

"Yeah?" Dante says, not moving. "Right down Lake Shore Drive."

Nero switches tactics. "So what if we are? It's just some Sweet Sixteen party."

"Nessa's nineteen," I correct him.

"Nineteen?" Nero shakes his head in disgust. "Why are they even—Never mind. Probably some stupid Irish thing. Any excuse to show off."

"Can we get going?" Sebastian says. "I don't wanna be out too late."

"Get in, or get out of the way!" I shout at Dante.

He stares a minute longer, then shrugs. "Fine. But I'm riding shotgun."

I climb over the seat without argument, letting Dante have the front. A small price to pay to get my big brother on team Party Crashers.

We cruise down LaSalle Street, enjoying the early summer air streaming into the car. Nero has a black heart and a vicious temperament, but you'd never know it from the way he drives. In the car, he's as smooth as a baby's ass—calm and careful.

Maybe it's because he loves the Chevy and has put about a thousand hours of work into it. Or maybe driving is the only thing that relaxes him. Either way, I always like seeing him with his arm stretched out on the wheel, the wind blowing back his sleek hair, his eyes half-closed like a cat.

It's not far to the Gold Coast. Actually, we're practically neighbors—we live in Old Town, which is directly north. Still, the two neighborhoods aren't much alike. They're both fancy in their own ways—our house looks right over Lincoln Park, while theirs fronts onto the lake. But Old Town is, well, just what the name implies: pretty fucking old. Our house was built in the Victorian era. Our street is quiet, full of massive old oak trees. We're close to St. Michael's Church, which my father genuinely believes was spared the Chicago Fire by a direct act of god.

The Gold Coast is the new hotness. It's all pish-posh shopping and dining and the mansions of the richest motherfuckers in Chicago. I feel like I sprang forward thirty years just driving over here.

Sebastian, Nero, and I thought we might sneak in around the

back of the Griffin property—maybe steal some caterers' uniforms. Dante, of course, isn't participating in any of that nonsense. He just slips the security guard five Benjamins to "find" our name on the list, and the guy waves us on in.

I know what the Griffins' house looks like before I see it because it was big news when they bought it a few years back. At the time, it was the most expensive piece of residential real estate in Chicago. Fifteen thousand square feet for a cool twenty-eight million dollars.

My father scoffed and said it was just like the Irish to flash their money. *An Irishman will wear a twelve-hundred-dollar suit without the money in his pocket to buy a pint.*

The Griffins can buy plenty of pints. They've got money to burn, and they're literally burning it right now, in the form of the fireworks show still trying to put Disney World to shame.

I don't care about colored sparks—I want the bougie champagne ferried around by the waiters, followed by whatever's being stacked into a tower on the buffet table. I'm gonna bankrupt these snooty fucks by eating my weight in crab legs and caviar.

The party is outdoors on the sprawling green lawn. It's the perfect night for it—more evidence of the luck of the Irish. Everybody's laughing and talking, stuffing their faces, and even dancing a little, though there's no Demi Lovato performing yet, just a normal DJ.

I guess I probably should have changed clothes. I don't see a single girl without a glittery party dress and heels. But that would have been annoying as hell on the soft grass, so I'm glad I'm just wearing sandals and shorts.

I do see Nessa Griffin, surrounded by people congratulating her on the monumental achievement of staying alive for nineteen years. She's wearing a pretty cream-colored sundress—simple and bohemian. Her light-brown hair is loose around her shoulders, and she's got a bit of a tan and a few extra freckles across her nose like she was out on the lake all morning. She's blushing from all the attention, sweetly happy.

Honestly, out of all the Griffins, Nessa's the best one. We went to the same high school. We weren't exactly friends since she was a year behind me and a bit of a Goody Two-Shoes. But she seemed nice enough.

Her sister, on the other hand…

I can see Riona right now, chewing out some waitress until the poor girl is in tears. Riona Griffin is wearing one of those stiff, fitted sheath dresses that looks like it belongs in a boardroom, not at an outdoor party. Her hair is pulled back even tighter than her dress. Never did anybody less suit flaming-red hair—it's like genetics tried to make her fun, and Riona was like, *I'm never having one goddamned moment of fun in my life, thank you very much.*

She's scanning the guests like she wants to bag and tag the important ones. I spin around to refill my plate before she catches sight of me.

My brothers split off the moment we arrived. I can see Nero flirting with some pretty blond over on the dance floor. Dante made his way over to the bar 'cause he's not gonna drink froufrou champagne. Sebastian disappeared entirely—not easy to do when you're six six. I'm guessing he saw some people he knows; everybody likes Sebastian, he's got friends everywhere.

As for me, I've got to pee.

The Griffins brought in some outdoor toilets, discretely set back on the far side of the property, screened by a gauzy canopy. I'm not peeing in a porta potty even if it's a fancy one. I'm gonna pee in a proper Griffin bathroom, right where they sit their lily-white bottoms down. Plus, it'll give me a chance to snoop around their house.

This takes a little maneuvering. They've got a lot more security around the entrance to the house, and I'm skint of cash for bribes. Once I throw a cloth napkin over my shoulder and steal the tray abandoned by the sobbing waitress, all I have to do is load up a few empty glasses, and I sneak right into the service kitchen.

I drop the dishes off at the sink like a good little employee, then duck inside the house itself.

Jiminy Crickets, it's a nice fucking house. I mean, I know we're supposed to be mortal rivals and all, but I can appreciate a place decked out better than anything I've ever seen on *House Hunters*. *House Hunters International*, even.

It's simpler than I would have expected—all creamy, smooth walls and natural wood, low modern furniture, and light fixtures that look like industrial art.

There's a lot of actual art around, too—paintings that look like blocks of color and sculptures made of piles of shapes. I'm not a total philistine—I know that painting is either a Rothko or supposed to look like one. But I also know I couldn't make a house look this pretty if I had a hundred years and an unlimited budget to do it.

Now I'm definitely glad I snuck in here to pee.

I find the closest bathroom down the hall. Sure enough, it's a study in luxury—lovely lavender soap, soft, fluffy towels, and water that comes out of the tap at the perfect temperature, not too cool and not too hot. Who knows—in a place this big, I may be the first person to even step foot in here. The Griffins probably each have their own private bathroom. In fact, they probably get tipsy and get lost in this labyrinth.

Once I finish, I know I should head back outside. I had my little adventure; there's no point pushing my luck.

Instead, I find myself sneaking up the wide curved staircase to the upper level.

The main level was too formal and antiseptic, like a show home. I want to see where these people actually live.

To the left of the staircase, I find a bedroom that must belong to Nessa. It's soft and feminine, full of books and stuffed animals and art supplies. There's a ukulele on the nightstand, and several pairs of sneakers were kicked hastily under the bed. The only things not clean and new are the ballet slippers slung over her doorknob by their ribbons. Those are beat to hell and back, with holes in the satin toes.

Across from Nessa's room is one that probably belongs to Riona. It's larger and spotlessly tidy. I don't see any evidence of hobbies in here, just some beautiful Asian watercolors hanging on the walls. I'm disappointed Riona hasn't kept shelves of old trophies and medals. She definitely seems the type.

Beyond the girls' rooms is the master suite. I won't be going in there. It seems wrong on a different level. There has to be some kind of line I won't cross when I'm sneaking around somebody's house.

I turn in the opposite direction and find myself in a large library. Now this is the kind of mysterious shit I came here for.

What do the Griffins read? Is it all leather-bound classics, or are they secret Anne Rice fans? Only one way to find out…

Looks like they favor biographies, architectural tomes, and yes, all the classics. They've even got a section dedicated to the famous Irish writers of yesteryear, like James Joyce, Jonathan Swift, William Butler Yeats, and George Bernard Shaw. No Anne Rice, but they've got Bram Stoker at least.

Oh, look, they've even got a signed copy of *Dubliners*. I don't care what anybody says—no one understands that fucking book. The Irish are all in on it, pretending it's a masterwork of literature when I'm pretty sure it's pure gibberish.

Besides the floor-to-ceiling shelves of books, the library is full of overstuffed leather armchairs, three of which have been arranged around a large stone fireplace. Despite the warm weather, there's a fire going in the grate—just a small one. Actual birch logs are burning, which smells nice. Above the fireplace hangs a painting of a pretty woman, with a carriage clock and an hourglass beneath it. Between those, an old pocket watch.

I pick it up off the mantel. It's surprisingly heavy in my hand, the metal warm to the touch instead of cool. I can't tell if it's brass or gold. Part of the chain is still attached, though it looks like it broke off at about half its original length. The case is carved, so worn that I can't tell what the image used to be. I don't know how to open it either.

I'm fiddling with the mechanism when I hear a noise in the hallway—a faint clinking sound. I slip the watch into my pocket and dive behind one of the armchairs, the one closest to the fire.

A man comes into the library—tall, dark-haired, about thirty years old. He's wearing a perfectly tailored suit, and he's extremely well-groomed. Handsome but in a stark sort of way—like he'd push you off a lifeboat if there weren't enough seats. Or maybe even if you forgot to brush your teeth.

I haven't actually met this dude before, but I'm fairly certain it's Callum Griffin, eldest of the Griffin siblings. Which means he's just about the worst person to catch me in the library.

Unfortunately, it seems like he plans to stick around a while. He sits in an armchair almost directly across from me and starts reading emails on his phone. He's got a glass of whiskey in his hand, and he's sipping from it. That's the sound I heard—the ice cubes clinking together.

It's extremely cramped behind the armchair. The rug over the hardwood floor is none too cushy, and I have to hunch in a ball so my head and feet don't poke out on either side. Plus, it's hot as balls this close to the fire.

How in the hell am I going to get out of here?

Callum is still sipping and reading. Sip. Read. Sip. Read. The only other sound is the popping of the birch logs.

How long is he going to sit here?

I can't stay forever. My brothers are going to start looking for me in a minute.

I don't like being stuck. I'm sweating from the heat and the stress.

The ice in Callum's glass sounds so cool and refreshing. God, I want a drink, and I want to leave.

How many fucking emails does he have?

Flustered and annoyed, I hatch a plan. Possibly the stupidest plan I've ever concocted.

I reach behind me and grab the tassel hanging from the curtains. It's a thick gold tassel attached to green velvet curtains.

By pulling it to its farthest length, I can just poke it in around the edge of the grate, directly into the embers.

My plan is to set it smoking, which will distract Callum, allowing me to sneak around the opposite side of the chair and out the door. That's the genius scheme.

But because this isn't a fucking Nancy Drew novel, this is what happens instead:

The flames rip up the cord like it was dipped in gasoline, singing my hand. I drop the cord, which swings back to the curtain. The curtain ignites. Liquid fire roars up to the ceiling in an instant.

This actually does achieve its purpose of distracting Callum Griffin. He shouts and jumps to his feet, knocking over his chair. However, my distraction comes at the cost of all subtlety because I also have to abandon my hiding spot and sprint out of the room. I don't know if Callum saw me or not, and I don't care.

I'm thinking I should look for a fire extinguisher or water or something. I'm also thinking I should get the fuck out of here immediately.

The second idea wins—I go sprinting down the stairs at top speed.

At the bottom of the staircase, I plow into somebody else. It's Nero with the pretty blond right behind him. Her hair is all messed up, and he's got lipstick on his neck.

"Jesus, is that a new record?" I'm pretty sure he only met her about eight seconds ago.

Nero shrugs, a hint of a grin on his devil-handsome face. "Probably."

Smoke drifts down over the banister. Callum Griffin is shouting in the library. Nero gazes up the staircase.

"What's that about—"

"Never mind." I seize his arm. "We've gotta get out of here."

While dragging him in the direction of the service kitchen, I can't quite take my own advice. I cast one look back over my shoulder. Callum Griffin stands at the head of the stairs, glaring after us with murder on his face.

We sprint through the kitchen, knocking over a tray of canapés, and then we're out the door, back on the lawn.

"You find Sebastian; I'll get Dante," Nero says. He abandons the blond without a word, jogging off across the yard.

"What the hell?" she says.

I run in the opposite direction, looking for the lanky shape of my youngest brother.

Inside the mansion, a fire alarm starts to wail.

ABOUT THE AUTHOR

Sophie Lark writes intelligent and powerful characters who are allowed to be flawed. She lives in the mountain west with her husband and three children.

The Love Lark Letter: geni.us/lark-letter
The Love Lark Reader Group: geni.us/love-larks
Website: sophielark.com
Instagram: @Sophie_Lark_Author
TikTok: @sophielarkauthor
Exclusive Content: patreon.com/sophielark
Complete Works: geni.us/lark-amazon
Book Playlists: geni.us/lark-spotify